COWBOYS
DON'T CRY

COWBOYS
DON'T CRY

Charles Berry

UNIVERSITY OF NEW MEXICO PRESS

Albuquerque

© 2011 by Charles Berry
All rights reserved. Published 2011
Printed in the United States of America
15 14 13 12 11   1 2 3 4 5

LIBRARY OF CONGRESS CATALOGING-IN-PUBLICATION DATA

Berry, Charles, 1933–
Cowboys don't cry / Charles Berry.
        p. cm.
ISBN 978-0-8263-4989-7 (paper : alk. paper)
1. Cowboys—Fiction.
2. Southwestern States—History—20th century—Fiction.
I. Title.

PS3602.E76363C69 2011
813'.6—dc22
                                        2010023090

PROLOGUE

"Vernon is dying," the voice on the other end of the line says.

"I know," I say.

"How did you know?"

I bite my tongue to keep from saying I've known for over two weeks. People never understand how, from time to time, I know things before they happen. I want to say he's really not dying, that he's just making a change of direction, but Willy Frazier wouldn't understand that either, so I ignore the question. "Where is he?" I ask.

"He's still at the old ranch headquarters. I tried to get him to let me take him to a hospital or a nursing home in El Paso. Hell, it ain't safe for that old man to be out there all by hisself. He don't even have a telephone. Just has that old Meskin to look after him. But you know Vernon; he told me to go to hell."

"Sounds like him," I say, smiling.

"Ol' Pablo came over here 'while-ago and asked me to call you. Says it looks like the old man don't have much longer."

I do a mental check to calculate my driving time and figure out things I'll need to do around my law office so I can be gone a few days. I know Pablo wouldn't have asked him to call if the end wasn't near. "Listen, Willy," I say, "I'll be there as soon as I can, and I'll take care of everything. I'd appreciate it if you'd just leave the old man be. If I need any help, I'll call you. Tell Pablo I'll be there by daylight."

By pushing the old Mercury hard, I reach El Paso by 3 a.m., hit Interstate 10, and head east. I haven't driven down this way in years, and this is the first time I've been here since they finished the Interstate. It misses all the small towns along old Highway 80 that snakes down the Rio Grande Valley, and I don't see any familiar landmarks. It all looks so different that after a while I begin to wonder if I'm going the right direction, until I see a highway sign telling the mileage to Fabens. Then, in the clear desert air, I see scattered lights along the valley, and I can tell I'm traveling across the flat mesa parallel to the valley below.

Nothing looks the same. What happened to the little towns— Tornillo, Acala, McNary? I've heard they are only ghost towns now, but somehow I never believed it. I wonder if anything of the old farmhouse up at Acala remains, or the house in Fort Hancock behind Franklin's store, or the old depot at McNary. I wonder if anything remains of my past. In spite of all that old Vernon taught me, I find myself wanting to rebel against the change—to turn the clock back somehow.

Looking at my watch, I speed up. I'm going to have to hurry to get to the ranch by daylight.

I see a sign. "Horseshoe Bend." I know that's not the name of a town, but I remember a sharp curve in the railroad track as it makes its way down the steep terrain from the foot of Blanco Mountain into the valley. I turn off, circle under the freeway, and head north. Soon I'm on familiar ground, following what used to be a dirt road leading to the Delaney Ranch headquarters. The road is paved now, and soon I pass a large ranch house with white painted fences and a larger sheet metal barn. This will be Willy Frazier's place. I understand he's been very successful since he bought the ranch from Vernon Delaney. Willy built a modern headquarters and agreed to let Vernon live at the old headquarters as long as he wanted. It had also been agreed that Vernon could be buried in the cemetery where his wife and only son were buried long before I remember.

The pavement ends right past the new Frazier place and quickly turns into the rough, narrow washboard road I remember. After about two miles of bouncing, I turn into the old headquarters just as the first light of dawn appears in the east.

I see Pablo standing on the porch of the old adobe house looking for me. A broad toothless smile breaks the ancient weathered face, and he steps off the porch, walking stiffly to embrace me as I step out of the car.

I push the bedroom door open as quietly as I can, but a hinge squeaks. A kerosene lamp is still burning on the night stand by the old brass bed. The first thing I notice is that familiar old pipe laying next to the lamp.

"That you, Speck?" Vernon Delaney asks in that familiar deep, raspy voice that seems surprisingly strong for a dying man.

I can't help wincing even after all these years at the sound of that name I've always hated. I take a wrinkled old hand in mine and feel its weakness.

"How you feeling, Vernon?"

As my eyes adjust to the dim light, I'm shocked at first at how thin he is, but his eyes are surprisingly bright, and he still has most of his teeth, even if the front ones are worn almost to the gums from holding that old pipe in his mouth. In spite of his thinness, he looks good for a man of ninety-one years. I begin to doubt for a minute that he's dying.

"There's some verses I picked out for you to read over me in the book over there," he says, gesturing toward an open Bible on the bureau. "I want you and Pablo to bury me out there by Mary and Little Vernon. I don't want nobody else there, you understand?" I can feel him weakly squeezing my hand for emphasis. "One more thing. I need you to be sure Willy Frazier takes care of Pablo like he promised. Will you do that?"

"Don't worry, I'll take care of everything just like you want me to."

"Good, then sit down and tell me what you been doin' for the past few years. How's your family? How's your law practice?"

Just like that. The business is out of the way and he wants to visit. Pablo shoves a straight-backed wooden chair behind me, and I sit down. I have a thousand things I want to say to him, a thousand questions to ask him, but I figure it's best to go along with what he wants for a while.

"Well, the wife and I have an eight-year-old daughter who's pretty as a picture. We live in a small adobe house in Albuquerque, and I'm now a partner in the firm I've been with since we moved up there."

I can see the old face relax, and I go on talking for several minutes before I notice the hand I'm holding is getting cold, and that his eyes are closed, and I can't see him breathing.

"Vernon," I say. There's a note of panic in my voice. I shake him gently, but there is no response. I try in vain to find a pulse. I yell for Pablo, but then I see the peaceful look on his face. There is no distress, no sign of a struggle to stay alive, and I realize he had waited for me to arrive, and as soon as he was satisfied I would take care of everything, he quietly took his leave. I might have expected something like this from him.

I find Pablo in the tool shed calmly putting the finishing touches on a wooden coffin. "Vernon is dead," I tell him.

Pablo looks up and nods then turns back to his work. "I built it out of the lumber from the old barn door. It's what Mr. Delaney told me to do. Willy will never miss it anyway. He's probably gonna tear all these old buildings down."

As the sun is sinking low on the western mountains, Pablo and I finish digging the grave and lay Vernon to his final rest where his body can disintegrate, become a part of the desert sands he loved so much. I cry, unashamed, as I read the verses, add a prayer of my own, and we cover the grave.

Then while Pablo sets the grave marker he has carved to match the other two, I walk up above the small hill, following a narrow trail on top of the large rock outcropping that stands as a protective watch over the little cemetery below the ranch house. From my perch I survey the old headquarters and the hazy desert that spreads below me. I watch the sun disappear behind the distant mountains on the other side of the Rio Grande.

I spent only one summer here on this ranch, but this is where I grew up.

Looking east in the evening dusk, I can make out the big cliff above Dead Horse Canyon. At the bottom of the cliff I can see a rock monument that marks another grave where I laid to rest someone else I loved a long, long time ago. I begin to remember how it was then, how I thought it would never be like it is now, with all of us gone from the valley.

CHAPTER 1

I blink. Now I see him. He's a little over an arm's length from my face, looking me straight in the eye with those dark beady eyes. I see the black forked tongue lashing out at me like a small black bolt of lightning, and over the top of his head, I see the blur of movement waving back and forth making that heart-stopping racket. This is the first time in all my six years that I've seen a live rattlesnake up this close.

I stay frozen like Dad always told me, but I can't keep from blinking. I'm surprised by the smell of fear coming from the snake because the burning glare in those dark beady eyes threatens attack. I begin to ache from the tension of remaining rigid.

Slowly the glare in his eyes softens. He says, "I don't want to hurt you, but I will if I have to."

I say, "I'm more scared than you are, for sure."

I don't think anything is unusual about how we communicate like that—without words. I talk to lots of animals the same way. When I tell Mom and Dad about talking to animals, they act like they don't believe me, so I don't usually tell anyone about it anymore.

The flag behind the snake's head stops waving and the sudden quiet surprises me, almost hurting my ears. He turns his head slightly; the black lightning disappears. He looks back, straight in my face. The eyes are full of sadness. I want to reach out and touch him but the black lightning reappears, so I stay frozen.

He turns his head to the side again and then quickly swings his head to look back the other direction. I don't realize that by this action he has checked out the situation all the way around us.

He looks to the side again and moves a little, then looks back at me. The black lightning reappears. I don't move. He moves further off to the side, slowly; then he looks back. I don't move. He slithers off leaving a wavy track in the warm desert sand. I watch as he moves up a nearby sandhill into a mesquite bush. Just before he moves out of sight, he looks back again. His eyes are sad. I feel sad too, sad he has to run away and hide, sad we can't be friends. I want to call him back, to talk to him, tell him how I like to ride ol' Paint in the desert sandhills and chase imaginary outlaws pretending to be Roy Rogers or Gene Autry. I'd like to tell him that's what we were doing when we came upon him, and he scared ol' Paint so bad she jumped out from under me, and I fell face first in the sand in front of him. I want to tell him we didn't mean to hurt him or scare him. I want to tell him we can be friends, and ol' Paint and I will come visit him.

I want to talk to him, but I know it's not safe. He might think I'm trying to hurt him, and he might bite me. So I turn away too.

I'm walking along the edge of the sandhills where the plowed ground stops when I see Dad running toward me. I can tell he knows something is wrong because he left the tractor, the Poppin' Johnny he had been driving, standing in the middle of the field, slowly popping out smoke rings. I can hear the strong engine of the bright green tractor chugging as each smoke ring shoots into the air.

"What happened, Son? Are you hurt? I saw Paint runnin' toward the corral with her tail in the air, and I knew she musta bucked you off."

"Naw, I'm okay. A snake scared ol' Paint, and she jumped out from under me." I can hear my voice quivering and feel my heart pounding in my throat.

"You sure you aren't hurt? It sure scared me when I saw Paint without you."

"I got sand in my face, and I couldn't see at first. But when I heard him, I stayed froze like you always told me. Finally, he went off in the bushes." For the first time I think about hurting. It seems I hurt all over, and I've begun to tremble.

"Let me look." His big calloused hands tenderly push my shaggy red hair back as he looks me over. "I guess you're okay, just a little scratch. Did you see the snake? What kind was it?"

"It was a rattler."

"Let me get the hoe off the tractor," he says, starting toward the Poppin' Johnny, "and we'll go kill him."

"Dad—don't. He didn't hurt me." I've managed to stop shaking now.

"Son, we have to kill him if we can find him. Besides, we'll hang him on the fence and maybe that'll make it rain, like the Meskins say. You can go on to the barn if you want to."

Ol' Paint is standing at the gate waiting to be let in the corral, trying to act as if nothing has happened. I can tell she's worried, though. The last time she bucked me off, Dad gave her a severe switching. I go over and talk to her and tell her it wasn't her fault. Her eyes brighten and she walks over to the haystack and starts to munch some alfalfa. She never does say she's sorry. I tell Paint that Dad is going to try to find and kill the snake, but I hope he hides real good so Dad can't find him.

Paint looks at me sharply. She hopes Dad will find and kill that vermin.

"If I hadn't seen him in time, he would've bit me," she warns. We're talking without words, just like we always do.

It isn't long before Dad comes walking up with the big rattlesnake hanging over the handle of his hoe. He swings it over the barbed wire fence just east of the wooden corral.

"Boy! He's a big one!" Dad says. "And look at those rattlers. He's got seventeen! I'll get Jack Beatty to skin him out and tan his hide, and we'll hang it on the wall. Just look at them big fangs. That's what they bite you with."

I walk close and see the crushed head with surprisingly few skinned places. The eyes are glazed over, dead now.

"Sorry, ol' Snake," I say. I look at ol' Paint still munching at the hay stack. She looks back at me but doesn't say anything. I want to cry, but I don't. Dad says cowboys don't cry.

About an hour later it rains.

"Where's that big snake hunter?" With his dark eyes twinkling, Uncle Jack comes into the kitchen, picks me up over his head, and swings me around. His small lanky frame is surprisingly strong. "Why, I'd never even seen a rattlesnake by the time I was your age, and here you are only six years old and already found and killed one over six feet long!"

"I didn't kill him!" I yell as I grab a handful of his straight black hair.

"Well, no matter," he says, setting me back on my feet. "You found him."

I know he's only humoring me. Making over me like I was a baby, and I hate it.

"Your dad used the hoe handle to kill him. Didn't slice him up with the blade, so he'll look good hanging on the wall. It sure proved what the Meskins say when it rained after he was hung on the fence, didn't it?"

Junior breaks in, "Aw, hangin' a snake on the fence don't make it rain."

"It sure as hell rained here at the house and in the sandhills, didn't it?" Uncle Jack says.

Junior's eyes flash back as dark as Uncle Jack's. "Yeah, but it only rained for about fifteen minutes. That didn't do no good."

Junior is skinny like me, but there the resemblance ends. He is a lot taller and, in spite of the blond hair, he has an olive complexion. Sometimes people don't believe we are brothers. In the summer time, he gets so dark people accuse him of being part Mexican. All I ever get in the summer is more freckles and sunburn.

"Well, listen to mister know-it-all ten-year-old big brother." Uncle Jack isn't ready to give up the argument. "It's the first time it's rained any for about a month and a half. What do you think made it rain?"

Dad interrupts the argument as he comes in the back door, stopping to stomp his feet and wipe the mud off his shoes on a gunnysack Uncle Jack had laid by the door. "Let's get some supper going." He walks over to the table and strikes a match to light the kerosene lamp, adjusts the wick, and sets the globe over the flame. The warm glow reflects off the white-washed adobe walls and overcomes the duskiness that has set in.

"When's Mom comin' home?" Junior asks.

"I don't think she'll make it till next week. She had to go all the way up to Dell City. There's about twenty people up there she has to count for the census."

"Where's Sis?" Junior asks. There's a kind of whine to his voice, and I know he doesn't really care where our sister is. He just wants a better cook to fix his supper.

"Sis is spending the night over at Harmon's," Dad says, pulling a skillet out of a cabinet. "I guess with your mom gone she gets tired of being the only woman around us men."

"How far is Dell City?" Junior asks, kind of wistful.

"It's way up in the northern part of the county. 'Bout sixty miles of dirt road. I sure hope that ol' Ford holds together."

Uncle Jack breaks in, "Oh, I forgot to tell you, the guy from the Census Bureau left off a box of forms for her. He didn't know if she would need them with her up there."

"Well, it's too late now if she does," Dad says. "Here Junior, you open these two cans of beans. Scout, you go get some kerosene for the stove. Uncle Jack, it's your turn to wash. I'll cut potatoes to fry, and I think there's some of that ham left in the icebox. Y'all want anything else?"

"Yeah," Junior says. "Anything but beans and leftovers."

I take the gallon jug from its bracket on the cookstove and go out the back door, leaving Junior to complain. It has already gotten dark, but there's no moon yet. The cool desert air makes me shiver. The rain was just enough to cool it off and make it smell clean and fresh, and the blooms on the tornillo tree by the back door add a sharp sweetness to the smell. A cricket chirps by the corner of the house, and at the same time a bullbat flitters silently by diving at bugs. The stars are so bright I have no trouble finding my way to the kerosene barrel that sits on a rack just east of the house. The beauty of the night has wrapped itself around me like a magic spell, and I sense a comforting presence I can't explain. But the spell is broken when I remember the dead snake hanging on the barbed-wire fence down at the corrals. Mingled with all this beauty, death is in the air too. It's always there. Even in six short years, I've learned that. I want to know why.

I hang the jug on the spigot and open it full force, listening to the kerosene gush out and the change in sound as the jug fills. I step back to keep from breathing the fumes, and that's when I sense some movement off to the side. I look into the dark shadow of the adobe wall but see nothing. When the jug is full, and I turn off the faucet, I can hear movement among the lumber stacked next to the wall. I look into the dark, straining to see. I hear a whimper.

It's Queenie and something is wrong! I can make out her head in the darkness in a large hollow among the lumber where I had seen her sleeping before.

I reach in and pet her. She whimpers again, and I feel her straining as though she's in pain. I reach in with my other hand and run it along her back and side. My hand falls on a wet, slimy lump by her hind leg. It wiggles under my hand, and I jump back. Then I know what it is.

"Dad! Junior! Queenie's having her puppies," I yell, running to the back door.

"Well, leave her alone," Dad says, "and bring that kerosene in here."

"But, Dad, she's in pain. She's in the lumber pile. You need to check her."

"Oh, she's all right. Animals always have some pain when they give birth," Dad says as he takes a lantern off the shelf. He flips up the globe, strikes a match on his pant leg, and lights the wick. "How many pups does she have?"

"I only found one."

"Well, the best thing to do is just leave her alone," he says as he comes out the back door with the lantern held high so he can see ahead. Junior and Uncle Jack follow close behind.

"I already put some gunnysacks and an old blanket in that hole in the lumber pile where she sleeps. They'll be warm and comfortable in there," Dad explains as we march single file to the wood pile.

Queenie's yellow-brown coat shines in the light of the lantern. She looks up with those friendly Labrador eyes and flops her tail against the blanket. One roly-poly that looks like a little mouse with its eyes closed, the same color as his mother, is struggling at her milk. She's licking a second one clean. Off to the side of the enclosure, a third is trying to wiggle off in the wrong direction. He's coal black with a white collar. Dad reaches in and picks him up to place him against his mother's breast. He squeals and yips like he's being killed. When he finds the milk, he slurps like a hog.

"Ha, he's a toughy," Dad says. "I thought that black collie of John Haskel's got to her. No question about that now."

Queenie shivers and strains.

"She's got a couple more in her," Dad says.

In spite of his objection that Junior has to go to school tomorrow, we're able to talk Dad into letting us get some blankets and stay up and watch Queenie have her other pups. Amid my flurry of questions about why puppies are born with their eyes closed and how they know how to nurse as soon as they're placed close to their mothers tits, Dad patiently gets us fed and settled in the blankets with the lantern up where we can see Queenie and her pups. At the same time, he explains that their eyes are closed because the puppies are born before the eyes develop enough for them to be open and that God gives all animals an instinct to know how to nurse when they're hungry.

"It's one of the wonders of nature," he says.

As we sit huddled, watching the puppies nursing at Queenie's breast, I keep seeing visions of the sad eyes of that old snake. Maybe it had little ones that are left out there all alone tonight. I'm all mixed up. Here's new life right here in front of me, but I keep thinking of that dead snake.

"Wake up, Scout, Queenie's trying to have another pup!" Junior is shaking my shoulder. "Look, she's having trouble. Go get Dad."

Cursing softly under his breath about being awakened at three o'clock in the morning, Dad comes out to the lumber pile and reaches in and rubs Queenie's tummy. "Hold her head down so she can't bite me, Junior." Junior is almost standing on his head to reach in over the lumber to get both hands on her head. Queenie whimpers but doesn't try to fight as Dad uses his fingers to reach inside her rear. He reaches in further and then pushes hard. Queenie groans. Dad quickly removes his hand and the pup slides out on the blanket.

Instead of leaving the new arrival for Queenie to clean, Dad picks it up and wraps a rag around it.

"The runt of the litter. Had his head turned around backward. He's only about half as big as the others."

"Let me see, Dad," I plead.

"No. I'm going to get rid of him now. He's too scrawny. He'll never survive."

"Dad . . . Don't!"

"No, Scout, it's the best way. He's too weak to fight with the others for the milk. It's best to put him out of his misery now. I think that's the last one. Y'all go on in the house now and go to bed. I'll be there in a minute. Queenie and her pups need to be left alone for a while."

It all happens so fast it doesn't look as if Queenie even notices the latest arrival is taken away. She seems very happy with her puppies.

As I climb into bed and close my eyes, I see visions of three little golden puppies and a black one with a white collar nursing at their mother's breast, but then the pleasant vision is interrupted by the ghost of that old rattlesnake hanging dead on the barbed wire fence, and then I can hear the whining of the little runt pup that never even got to know what it's like to nurse. They're all there together, the live ones and the dead ones. They all look at me at once.

"Can't you see?" says the old snake. "Don't you understand?"

But I don't understand. I lay there scared, goose bumps on my legs and arms with my spine tingling. I shiver, trying to shake off the vision, but I can't. Finally, I go get in bed with Dad and snuggle up close beside the big man. Feeling warm and safe now, I lie there wondering what the old snake wanted me to see.

By Easter all the pups are gone except the black-and-white one. Junior calls him Tuffy. Dad has given the others away. Says we can't afford to keep them. Queenie doesn't seem to mind. No one does, except me. I want to cry because I feel like they're all dead now. But I don't shed a single tear. I know a real cowboy wouldn't cry about something like that.

By early summer Mom is home again, and our kitchen is filled with the smell of coffee and frying bacon. Everyone is closely watching Mom cook pancakes and home-cured bacon for breakfast on the griddle over the kerosene stove. Dad and Uncle Jack are sitting at the round oak table drinking coffee. Junior and I are drinking Ovaltine, and Sis is setting the table with plates, knives, forks, and a big bowl of butter. In the middle of the table is a big bucket of hot molasses.

This is the first Saturday after school let out for the summer, and it's our first breakfast since Mom got home from taking the census. She's almost finished that job except for a few loose ends and will be staying at home most of the time now, so we'll be like a family again.

"Mom, do you think Queenie misses her puppies?" I say in Spanish.

"Yes, honey, I'm sure she does," Mom says in English. She pushes back a loose strand of long black hair and walks over and runs her hand through my hair, shaking my head lovingly. I sense there is a kind of sadness about her, and I wonder if it's because she knows how I feel about things dying. She finds an excuse to adjust something on the table and in the process pats Junior on the shoulder. She lets her hand drag across Sis's waist and stops to adjust the bow of the small apron Sis is wearing before she returns to the stove. Then she continues, "but it's the nature of all animals to wean their babies and make them learn to take care of themselves. So, while she misses them, I'm sure she is also proud they have grown up big and strong enough to go live someplace else." I get the feeling she's talking about something besides the pups, but I don't know what it is.

"Now she won't feel like she has to spend all her time hunting rabbits to feed them," she says. There's a faraway sound to her voice, like she's forgotten who she's talking to. She falls silent as she spreads pancake batter on the smoking griddle. Everyone is watching her closely, already tasting the pancakes.

Dad breaks the tense silence as we all wait for the first stack of pancakes to be set on the table. "I saw Sonny Walsh yesterday in Acala, and he told me he bought a Shetland pony for Georgie, but he's so mean and wild, Georgie can't ride 'im. He said he'd give you boys a dollar a piece if you can break and gentle 'im so Georgie can handle 'im."

"Wahoo!" Junior yells as he jumps up, knocking over my cup of Ovaltine. "Hear that, Scout? We can ride over there and get him this morning and start breakin' him this afternoon."

Sis throws a wet dishrag in my face. "Clean up the mess you made or you can't have any pancakes."

Junior doesn't miss a beat, jabbering about what fun we're going to have with that Shetland, as he grabs the rag off my face and wipes up the spilled milk. Luckily, my cup was almost empty.

Slowly it sinks in why he's so excited. We've heard Dad say before that Shetland ponies are mean and not good for young kids to ride. They'll bite and kick like a wild mule, he had said. But if he thinks we can ride him and gentle him, then he must think we're not just kids anymore. We're real cowboys.

Mom slowly pours the last of the bacon grease into a coffee can, walks over to the table, and slams the large skillet on the table in front of Dad. I about jump out of my skin. Her eyes are dark and burning.

"Boots McBride, how can you even think of saying something like that and letting these little boys think they may be allowed to try to break a horse! I'll not have them breaking a neck or a leg or arm over some stupid Shetland pony."

"Now, Laura . . ."

"Don't you now Laura me! You tell Sonny Walsh to forget it. He should have known better than to buy an unbroken horse for a five-year-old boy. Let him do the horse-breaking himself."

I'm moving my head back and forth from one to the other as they argue, hoping against hope that I'm going to get a chance to be a real cowboy. It doesn't look good. Mom never gives in easy.

"Aw, Laura, don't get all het up," Uncle Jack says. "Both these boys can ride about anything. They can ride as good as most men and a lot better than any sixteen- or seventeen-year-old kid you can find in school these days."

"I don't care. There's a lot more to breaking a horse than riding him. Suppose one of them gets kicked or run over or that stupid horse falls on them. Suppose they get tangled in a rope and get dragged to death."

I feel an emptiness in my stomach that doesn't have anything to do with being hungry. It looks like our horse-breaking days are already over. But in the next instant, Dad comes to the rescue.

"Well, I really hadn't figured on just turning 'em loose with him," he says a little sternly, as if he resents having to defend his idea. "I figured they could go get him, and then I can help 'em with the breaking to be sure nobody gets hurt."

Mom really lights into him. "How are you going to watch them every minute? How are you going to save them when they get kicked in the head or one of them gets a rope tangled around his foot? Are you going to watch over them all the time?"

Behind Mom I can see the pancakes still cooking on the stove but Mom seems to have forgotten them as she glares at Dad. I'm surprised when Dad talks back.

"No," he says, "I cain't live their lives for 'em and neither can you. We have to let 'em try things if they are gonna learn how to live without us lookin' after 'em all the time. Seems to me you'd wanna let 'em take a few chances and suffer a little pain now and then rather than have 'em grow up to be milk toast. I'll watch over 'em as close as I can, but I think we ought to let 'em learn how to do it."

I've never heard Dad talk back to Mom like that before.

Mom doesn't say anything, and I see her shoulders slump just a little, but her eyes are still burning. She and Dad look at each other intently. Finally, Dad smiles and says, "You gonna let the pancakes burn?"

Mom is awful quiet all through breakfast, but Dad winks at me. I think that wink means I'm going to get to break that pony. I'm so excited I can't eat at first, but after I take my first bite, the pancakes are so good, I can't seem to stop.

A little while later, I'm so full I really don't feel like riding, but I don't dare admit it and miss my chance. We saddle ol' Paint, and I climb up behind Junior with my arms around his waist to hold on. With Queenie and Tuffy barking and running ahead, we strike out in a lope down the barrow ditch beside the highway, underneath the big cottonwood trees, and then along the canal until we reach a mesquite and catclaw thicket of uncleared land. Then we follow a narrow path until we come out on a good dirt road and take a short cut across a plowed field to the Walsh farm house.

Mr. Walsh is just finishing the milking as we ride up. "You boys here for that pony already? I figured you'd be scared of him. He already kicked Georgie in the stomach."

With my arms around Junior's waist, I can feel him bristle. "We'll try 'em," he says between his teeth.

I'm beginning to think I would rather go back home without more, but then I see him in the corral behind the barn. I can't believe it! He's beautiful. Black-and-white paint, just like ol' Paint. In fact, you'd think he was her colt except one side of his face is white all the way up to his ear, and the eye on that side is as white as his skin.

"Georgie named him Champ after Gene Autry's horse. But that was before he got kicked. He may call him something else now," Mr. Walsh chuckles as we walk into the corral with the midget horse.

I can't get over how small he is. He could walk under ol' Paint without touching if she'd just draw up her belly a little. He walks up to me, and I reach out to pet him, but Mr. Walsh grabs him by the halter and pulls him away. "Be careful. He might bite."

It's hard for me to believe this beautiful little animal can be half as bad as they say.

A few minutes later, we are trotting along the narrow path through the thicket of mesquite and catclaw. I'm riding behind Junior, holding on with one arm around his waist and holding the lead rope with the other. Champ is following close behind. A low-hanging mesquite limb catches onto Junior's stirrup, then, as it comes loose, it swings back hard hitting Champ in the flank. Champ lunges forward into ol' Paint's rear. Paint starts kicking, Champ swirls, and the kicking match is on.

I pull on the lead rope, but the action is too much for me, and I feel myself turning a somersault over backward as I fall down between the rear ends of the two horses, their hind legs lashing out at each other. Everything is a blur as I wait to be beaten to death by those flying hooves, but I can hear Junior yelling as he kicks ol' Paint in the side with his heels to make her dart forward away from the fray.

With both eyes closed tightly, I'm lying on the ground in the middle of the trail with my hands covering my head. I taste the dust in my mouth and nostrils, and I feel grit on my face. After a while, I realize the fight is over and everything is quiet. Miraculously, I haven't been touched by either horse.

I slowly look up. I still have the lead rope in my hand. Champ is standing with his head down facing the other direction, watching me out of the side of his white eye.

I stand up slowly. "Come on, Champ." I gently pull on the lead rope.

WHAM! The lights go out.

I can hear Junior crying and cussing. "I'll kill that son-of-a-bitch. Scout! Are you okay? Speak to me!" He keeps shaking my shoulder.

My head is spinning. I feel sick at my stomach. I roll over and lose my breakfast, retching until my toes curl up. Junior holds my head up out of the mess and, when I stop heaving, rolls me over on my back and wipes my mouth with his bandanna. "You'll be okay. Take it easy. Where'd he kick you?"

The mixture of dust and vomit are strong in my mouth and nose. "I don't know." Tears are running down my cheeks, stinging under my chin. With my hand I feel a lump under my chin, and my shoulder hurts.

Junior looks me over, "Yeah, I can see. He clipped your chin and shoulder."

Queenie comes up and licks me on the face. Tuffy smells my puke.

"Get away from there!" Junior swats him on the nose. Both dogs are panting like they've been running hard.

Ol' Paint is standing close by with her head down, watching me carefully. "I knew you couldn't trust that runt," she says.

"Aw, he was just scared," I tell her. Then to Junior I ask in Spanish, "Where's Champ?"

Junior reaches over and pets Queenie. "When he kicked you, Queenie was on him like flies on cow plop, and he took off back down the trail. I don't know how far they chased him. Soon's you feel like riding, we better go catch him. He might get out on the highway and get run over."

Just around the bend in the trail, we find Champ standing with his head down, looking very miserable. The lead rope got tangled in a catclaw bush, and he hadn't been able to pull loose. Both hind legs show spots of red where Queenie's teeth made their mark.

This time Junior wraps the lead rope around the saddle horn and keeps Champ's head up beside us to avoid another kicking match.

At home, Dad comes out to tell us how to do it. With him are Uncle Jack and Pedro, the Mexican boy whose family works for us. Dad calls them "wetbacks" because, he says, they crossed the Rio Grande to get here illegally. We go right to work. We tie Champ to a post in the corral, put my saddle on him, and tie an old dried cowhide to the saddle horn so it drags right under his hind legs as he walks. When we turn him loose, the kicking starts all over again, but this time Champ is doing it all by himself, and the cowhide won't go away.

"Stop! Don't keep hurting yourself, Champ," I keep saying under my breath, but he won't listen. Finally, after what seems like forever, he stands in a corner heaving and sweating, his hocks raw and bleeding. We leave him wearing the saddle and cowhide the rest of the day.

I wake up to the sound of the old red rooster crowing. A couple of other young cocks join in the morning serenade. I lay there enjoying the cool morning breeze on the screened-in porch. It's still dark, and the stars are shining, but a few clouds hanging over the mountain begin to show the first signs of redness to signal the coming day.

Champ! I wonder how he's doing. I bet he learned not to kick yesterday. I slip out of bed quietly so as not to wake Junior, pull on my pants, and ease out the front screen door. Tuffy finds me quickly and licks my bare feet as I stop to scratch his black shiny coat. Champ is standing with his head down in the corner of the old chicken coop where we put him for the night. Dad had been afraid that, if we put him in with ol' Paint, they might get into a fight, and if we put him with ol' Blackie, he might chase her and get her so upset she wouldn't give any milk.

The bucket of water Junior had set in for him to drink is dry, so I go to refill it. At the water pump, I hang the bucket on the spout and pump away. "Ker-chunk, ker-chunk." The water flows in spurts each time I raise the handle and push it down.

Blackie says, "Good morning," sticks her head over the fence, burps up a cud, and stands there chewing and watching me. She is real close, and I can smell her sweet breath mingling with the desert air along with the odor of fresh water, the nearby alfalfa stack, and manure in the corrals. The life all around me in the early morning twilight makes me feel giddy and light as a feather. A red-winged blackbird trills out his greeting to the world from the nearby maize field. I can feel that strange presence like a magic spell again, and this time there is nothing to break it.

I set the full bucket in front of Champ's nose and he takes a drink. "Poor Champ," I say, rubbing his neck. He doesn't answer. All his hair is matted together from sweat. I get an old curry comb off a fence post and start to comb him over. He still doesn't say anything, but I can tell he enjoys the scratching because he leans toward me. Ol' Paint hangs her head over the fence and tells me I better not trust "that runt." I give her a dirty look and tell her to mind her own business.

As I work toward the shoulder, Junior appears at the fence, watching. "You better hold on to his halter as you move back so he can't turn away from you and kick you."

I can't imagine him wanting to kick me while I'm scratching him, but after what happened yesterday, I take hold of the halter in one hand and comb with the other, pulling his head toward me as I work back from his withers.

Tuffy walks up to smell his hind leg. Junior yells, "Look out!" But it's too late. Champ's quick kick sends Tuffy sailing across the pen. I pull on the halter but there is no resistance, for Champ takes the opportunity to grab my unprotected side in his teeth and then sling me to the ground. Crying out and expecting a further attack, I try to roll away and get out of the pen, but there's no need. Champ stands there calmly looking first at me and then at Tuffy, both of us moaning in pain.

I grit my teeth to keep from crying, and Junior helps me back to the house. "We'll have to tell Dad about him kicking you too."

"No! Dad'll kill him!" I have to grit my teeth to keep from crying again.

"Maybe the bastard should be killed. Anyway, I'm telling Dad, but we won't tell Mom if we can keep from it."

There's only a small piece of skin missing, but the welt raised by the teeth marks feels as big as Dad's fist. Dad gently soothes the wound with Dr. Watkins Salve that Mom had just bought from the Watkins peddler, covers it with a piece of white cloth dug out of the rag drawer, and tapes it in place. The pain begins to ease. "You feel better now?"

"Yeah, it still hurts, but I'll be okay."

"Junior, go get my whet rock. It's out in the shed with my butcher knives," Dad says as he pulls his long pocket knife out and feels the sharpness of the blades.

"Dad . . ." I cry.

"Son, if he's ever gonna be worth a damn, he has to learn just like you do. I told Sonny we'd probably have to cut him. The sign is right, so we may as well get it done right now before he hurts somebody else."

I feel a moment of relief. At least the pony isn't going to be killed, but I'm not sure what Dad has in mind is much better.

As we walk back down to the corrals with Tuffy limping slowly behind, I tell Dad I still don't understand why the little pony has to be cut. I'd seen bull calves and hogs castrated before, but I couldn't understand why.

"Well, there's reasons for different animals, but stud horses, bulls, and even boars tend to be very mean and unruly as long as they ain't had their nuts cut out," Dad tells me. "Once that's done, their attitude changes completely. Horses get to be good ridin' or workin' horses, bulls get gentle so we can fatten 'em as steers, and the same thing happens to hogs.

"Now, in Champ's case, we got a choice. We can send him back home and li'l Georgie won't have a horse he can ride or even pet. We can take him out in the mountains and turn him loose to live in the wilds, but he's so little he'll either starve to death or the coyotes'll kill him. Or, we can change his attitude and make him a good riding horse that'll have a long life and help Georgie grow up to be a man. Which would you rather do?"

Without waiting for an answer, Dad waves for Uncle Jack, who is on a tractor out in the cotton fields, to join us at the corral. At the barn, Dad gets a water bucket and pours a small amount of Lysol in the bottom, puts a white rag in, and hands the bucket to me. "Go pump the bucket about half full of water and stir it up with the rag. Here, hold on to this catgut too," he says, as he hands me a small bottle with what looks like a spool of thread and some kind of liquid in it.

As I come back with the water in the bucket, Dad says, "Junior get that big soft rope hangin' by the stall." He holds up his knife to examine the blade as it sparkles in the sun and then runs his thumb over the edge. "I think that's sharp enough. Scout, I want you to hold this knife real careful. Wash it in the Lysol and then don't let it get dirty. You have it ready to hand to me along with the catgut when I tell you."

With Junior holding Champ's head, Dad ties a big noose in the middle of the big soft rope, slips it over the pony's head so that it fits like a collar around his shoulders. Then he and Uncle Jack, one on each side, slip a loop of the rope around each hind leg and back through the big noose.

"Now when he goes down, Junior, you get on his head and hold him down." With that, Dad nods to Uncle Jack, and they each pull their end. In a flash, the ropes are made secure, and the pony is lying flat on his back with his hind legs pulled close to his chest where he is unable to kick.

"Hand me the rag," says Dad, moving fast now. He quickly washes the exposed penis and testicles and instructs me to hand him the knife. With a thumb and forefinger, he pulls the skin tight over one testicle, the knife glints in the sun as it marks a white slice the length of the lump. A second slice and the testicle pops out. "Hand me the catgut." Without looking up, he holds his big hand toward me. Still moving quickly, Dad ties a piece of the catgut tightly around the cord, then with a scraping motion of the knife the testicle is cut free. Automatically, Dad hands the testicle toward me, but when I hesitate to take it from his hand, he looks up at me, grins, and then tosses the white mass of flesh over the fence and outside the corral. "Here, Tuffy!" Dad yells.

The second nut is removed the same way in short order. The wounds are painted with black pine tar and the ropes are untied. "Make him get up, Junior," Dad orders when the pony seems reluctant. "We want to be sure he stands up and drains good."

As Champ struggles to his feet, and I watch the surprisingly small amount of blood trickle down each hind leg, Dad turns to me. "You okay?" He looks me closely in the eye.

I'm determined not to show how queasy my stomach feels. "Sure, why wouldn't I be?" I hurry to clean the knife, empty the bucket, and wash it out with clear water from the hand pump.

Three days later, Dad comes in from the fields early. "Junior, get ol' Paint saddled. Scout, get your saddle. This is a perfect time for that wild mustang to learn to be a gentleman."

"But, Dad, he's still so sore he can hardly walk."

"That's what I said, this is a perfect time."

With my saddle on Champ, Dad slips off the halter and replaces it with the neatest little hackamore he had made just to fit the little horse. It has leather reins and a lead rope that ties into the back of the little nose band.

"Okay, Junior, you get on ol' Paint and snub this lead rope up as close as you can around your saddle horn. Hold his head high so he can't buck.

"Scout, I'll hold him close, and you climb aboard."

With a knot in my stomach and a lump in my throat, I put my foot in the stirrup and swing up on the little horse, and, small as he is, it seems like I'm sitting on top of a tower. Champ tries to jump, but Dad, ol' Paint, and Junior hold him snug.

Dad looks at my old brogan shoes in the stirrups. "If you keep this up, I'm going to have to get you boys some real cowboy boots," he says. "Now, Junior, I'll let go, and you just start off slow and ride around the corral. Scout, you hold one rein in each hand. Real cowboys don't hold on to the saddle horn."

Champ tries again to jump, and again Junior holds him snug. Before long, I begin to imagine myself on the back of a mean black bronc, and I can hear a rodeo announcer calling my name to be crowned World Champion Bronc Rider. Then in the next second, everything changes. Champ pulls free of Junior's grip and swings his head one direction while his rear end goes another. It feels like all four of his feet are off the ground, and I'm holding on with my knees, doing my best not to grab the saddle horn. I'm vaguely aware of everybody yelling at me.

"Ride 'em, cowboy!" I hear Uncle Jack yell. Then suddenly, Champ's head goes down and his back is bowed. His feet hit the ground for a second, and I feel myself sliding out of the saddle. There's more yelling. I don't know what they're saying. I don't have time to right myself before he does it again. I grab for the saddle horn, but it's too late. Before I know it I'm flat on the ground.

My back hurts and my shoulder and my head. I hear a big sob coming out of my chest, and I know there are tears in my eyes. I don't know if I'm crying because I'm hurt or because I'm scared or just mad.

Dad is looking down at me. "Get up, Scout," he says. "Stop that bawlin' and git back on 'im."

I can hear his disappointment in me, and that makes me want to cry even more.

Through the tears in my eyes, I watch them catch Champ and snub him up to Junior's saddle horn again. Then they look at me and wait silently for me to mount again. If I have any doubts about getting back on, they vanish when I look at the glare in Dad's eyes.

This time Junior holds him tight, and we circle the corral three times.

"Give him a little more slack now, Junior," Dad says, and Champ again begins jumping against Paint, trying to get his head down, and I feel myself slipping to the side. I grab the saddle horn and pull myself back upright. The security of the horn is so strong I can't turn loose, and I keep a death grip on it as we circle the corral at a fast trot.

"That's enough," Dad yells at last. I'm swelling with pride, feeling my confidence again as Dad holds Champ for me to dismount, but he slips the saddle off and stands looking at me. I can see disappointment in his eyes.

"I don't know," he says. "Maybe I was wrong about you. I never figured you'd grab the saddle horn like a sissy."

CHAPTER 2

The windows are all steamed up. The big water kettle on the kerosene stove is whistling like a train coming round the bend. I'm standing naked in the middle of the kitchen. I've already poured three buckets of water I pumped from the hand pump in the kitchen corner into the tub. Mom pours hot water out of the kettle into the big Number 3 galvanized tub. "See if that's warm enough," she says.

I stick my toes in and stir the water around. I say in Spanish, "It's okay." With all the steam and heat from the kerosene stove, I'm starting to sweat, so even though the water is a little cool, it feels good. I sit down and start to get myself wet all over. I keep my knees drawn up to my chest, otherwise I'd have to put my feet on the concrete floor outside the tub. Mom comes over, stoops beside the tub, dips in a wash rag, soaps it up, and starts to scrub my face and ears. She holds up my long red hair as she scrubs the back of my neck and then drops it.

"You'll have to wash your hair too. Since it's Saturday, your Dad has to go into town this afternoon anyway. Maybe he can take you and Junior with him, and you can get a haircut while he's taking care of business. Then you'll both be ready for school to start next week."

Still in Spanish, "Mom, will Pedro ever come back?"

Pedro and his family have left, and I'm not sure why, except that there was some kind of trouble. I miss Pedro. He is just a little older than I am, and since he couldn't go to school either, we had played together a lot. Neither he nor his family spoke English, so they had taught me Spanish.

Still in English, Mom answers, "I don't know, honey. His family had to go back to Old Mexico. The Immigration took them away. They may not ever get to come back. You really miss them, don't you?"

I'd heard Dad say the Immigration took them away before, but I still don't understand why. They didn't do anything wrong. Remembering the empty feeling in my stomach when Dad told me they were gone, I feel the anger at the Immigration rising in my chest. Still speaking in Spanish, I say, "He's the only friend I have I can speak Spanish to. Even ol' Paint doesn't speak Spanish. And nobody makes tamales and tortillas and beans like Tomasita." Mom is the only one I can talk to about my talks with ol' Paint. Even if she doesn't believe me and thinks it's only a game, at least she doesn't tease me about it the way Junior and Dad do.

Still in English, "I know. I don't know what I would have done without them here to look after you while I was away taking the census this past year. When they wouldn't let you start school last year, I thought I was going to have to take you with me everywhere I went."

Switching to English, "Aw, I had ol' Paint to look after me during the daytime and Dad's not such a bad cook."

"Yes, but Dad and ol' Paint wouldn't have taught you to speak Spanish. You've gotten so good at it now, you don't seem to realize whether you're speaking Spanish or English," Mom says with a laugh. "Anyway, you'll be starting to school next week, and you'll be so busy you won't have much time to worry about it."

Still in English, "Mom, what's it like when you go to school?"

"You'll see next week. You'll have lots of fun."

As I lean forward so Mom can scrub my back, I try to imagine all the fun.

Mr. Hillsboro finishes cutting Junior's hair first, and Junior goes across the highway to Levine's Hardware Store to visit with Mike

Levine. I'm left alone with a bunch of strangers in the barber shop, but I'm not scared since Mr. Hillsboro has given me a haircut before. He puts the raised seat in his barber chair and tells me to climb up. As he pins the sheet around me and starts clipping, a large old cowboy ambles in and sits down in the one empty seat. His old run-over boots go almost up to his knees, and he has his pants legs tucked inside. His faded Levi's barely hang on his hips, and his stomach hangs over so far I can't see his belt in front. His scraggly gray beard is almost an inch long, and his mustache is stained brown from tobacco smoke. The wide-brimmed Stetson he wears is greasy and caked with dirt all the way around where the crown meets the brim. He throws it on the hat rack next to him, and his unruly gray hair falls down in his eyes.

Pushing the hair back with one hand, he pulls a pipe out of his black leather vest pocket with the other. Then he searches his shirt pocket and pulls out a can of Prince Albert. He fills the pipe, packs the tobacco with a calloused, stubby finger, and lights it with a match he strikes on his pant leg.

I'm so fascinated with the pipe, which is carved in the shape of a bull's head with ivory horns, that I don't realize he is sizing me up carefully with his narrowed pale blue eyes. The pipe curves down from his teeth and rests on his chin. As the blue smoke rises from the pipe and his mouth between puffs, he points at me with the match still burning between his fingers and says, "Aren't you Boots McBride's youngest kid?"

His voice is so deep and gruff, I'm dumbstruck. Mr. Hillsboro laughs, "He sure is."

He shakes the match out and throws it in the corner. "My God! Last time I saw you, you was in wet diapers. What do they call you? Speck? On accounta all them freckles?" Then without giving me a chance to answer, "They tell me you can't even ride a Shetland pony."

I feel my face flush. Does the whole world know about Champ bucking me off? Does everybody know about the tears too? Before I can help myself, though, I blurt out, "I can too! Me and my brother broke Georgie Walsh's Shetland this summer." I'm telling the truth. By the end of the summer, Champ had gotten real gentle.

"Ha! I bet you never rode him."

"I did too! He only bucked me off twice all summer." Why do I feel I have to prove anything to this old buzzard? Why am I saying things I don't mean to say?

"Really? Well, I don't know. I bet you had to hold on to the saddle horn, and if he bucked you off twice, I bet you were scared to get back on him." Everybody in the barbershop laughs.

"I did not! I wasn't . . . I . . . I . . . I'm no coward!" I'm fuming. I want to tell him that, even if I did grab the saddle horn that first day, I never did again, but I'm so mad I can't say any more. He gets up and walks over to the barber chair and pulls my arm out from under the sheet. I double my fist up and resist.

"Open your hand. What have you got in there? Let me see."

Even though I don't have anything in my hand, I refuse to open it and try to pull it back under the sheet.

"I bet you got a handful of freckles in there, don't you?"

"No. I don't!"

"I bet you do. You got so many on your face, if you got any more, you have to carry them in your hand." Everybody in the barber shop laughs again.

He lets go my arm, and I stuff it back under the sheet. I can feel my face burning and a lump in my throat. I wish I could get out of here.

As he walks back to his chair he says, "I bet you even slumber in the bed, don't you?"

I don't know what that means, but I'm not admitting anything. I don't like the way the barbershop crowd is enjoying my bout with the old man, but the old man can't seem to get enough of it.

He sits back down and puffs on his pipe. "If you're such a good cowboy, why don't you come out to my place. I got a bunch of broncs for you to break."

I'm so mad now, I defiantly refuse to answer even if the lump in my throat is so big I probably wouldn't be able to say anything if I wanted to. I just glare back at those intense pale blue eyes. My face is still burning.

Finally, he nods and points the mouthpiece of the pipe at me. I can see it's partly chewed away. "Yeah, you're Boots's boy all right.

True to the bone." He hooks the pipe over his teeth and rests it on his chin again. The puffs of smoke come easier now. Slowly, his eyes drift away as though he is remembering something someplace else, some other time.

At last, Mr. Hillsboro peels off the sheet and shakes the bright red hair on the floor. I slip out of the chair and dart for the door, but before I can make it, the old cowboy says, "I mean what I say, Speck. You want to ride some horses, get your old man to bring you out to the ranch."

I can hear them laughing as the screen door slams behind me, and I make my way across the highway to the hardware store. As I walk up to the sidewalk, I can see my reflection in the plate-glass window. I look close to examine the freckles on my face. The light isn't very good so I can't see them very well, but I know they're there. I rub my hand on my cheek, wishing I could rub them away.

I find Junior and Mike Levine talking and laughing in back of the hardware store. I want to stay and listen to the big guys talk, but I can tell they don't want me around, so I hang around the front of the store a while until Junior and Mike finally come out of the back, still laughing and looking like they've been saying things they shouldn't say.

Dad pulls up in front and toots the horn. I walk out to meet him, but Junior is still talking and laughing with Mike. Dad yells at Junior at least four times before he comes running and jumps in the pickup beside me. Junior slams the door just as Dad starts the pickup and puts it in gear.

"Well, it looks like you boys are all sheared and ready for school to start."

"Look," says Junior. "There's Mr. Delaney coming out of the barbershop."

The old gray-haired cowboy, minus his shaggy beard, steps off the stoop and lets the screen door slam behind him as he strikes a match on the barber pole, covers it with his hands to protect it from the breeze, and sucks the flame down over the tobacco in the bull's-head pipe.

He turns his back to us and walks across the caliche parking area, apparently heading toward a dusty old truck. I can see daylight between his bowed legs as he ambles along in his run-over boots.

Dad speeds up heading right for the old man. I cringe close to Dad as he pushes in the clutch and lets the Chevy pickup coast along quietly. I can't decide whether to be scared or glad. Does Dad know how mean that old man is? Does he know about me being picked on in the barbershop? Is he going to run over the old man?

The pickup swerves silently alongside the old man, and just as we pull even, Dad leans out the window, slapping the pickup door with his fist and yells, "Watch out, you old warhorse."

The old man jumps to the side, obviously startled, then breaks into a broad tobacco-stained grin. His teeth are worn down where he hangs his pipe. "God damn you, Boots McBride! Git outta that pickup, and I'll whup your ass!"

They're going to fight!

"Well, I would," Dad drawls leaning out the window to shake the old man's hand, "but it's getting late, and if I don't get these kids home for supper, I'll really get an ass kickin'."

"When you and them boys comin' out to see me?" He sounds almost wishful.

"Soon's I can. We'll start pickin' cotton pretty soon, so it'll be after that."

"Aw, you damn dirt farmers are always workin'. You'll never come. Bring them boys out, and I'll teach 'em how to rope a steer."

"We'll be out. You'll see. It's about time to breed that paint filly, so you know we'll be out."

"Ol' Jim and I'll be waitin'. Tell Laura I said, 'Hidey.'"

Dad waves as he shifts the gear stick between my feet, slowly lets out the clutch, and starts off.

I turn and look out the back window and see the old man lighting his pipe again. I can see daylight between his legs from this direction too.

Then, as the pickup hums past the fields and irrigation ditches, I get up my nerve and ask, "Dad, who was that man back there?"

Dad reaches down from the steering wheel and pats my leg beside his on the pickup seat. "Why, Scout, don't you know Vernon Delaney?"

Junior breaks in, "He's who we got ol' Paint from when she was a colt."

I suddenly remember one day a long, long time ago—it must have been at least two years—Dad drove up and called us out to see what he had in the car trunk. As he raised the trunk lid, a spindly-legged little horse fell out on the ground. She'd been orphaned, and we had to feed her on a bottle. It's hard for me to realize that same spotted little horse was the same ol' Paint around which my life is centered today.

What's even harder for me to believe is that Dad appears to be friends with that mean old cowboy. Junior even seems to like him. I don't care. I don't like him, even if he did give us ol' Paint. And I'm not going to let him teach me to rope. I can learn to rope without him.

"Where did you know him?" I ask Dad.

"Oh, I've known him a long time. He's an interestin' old cuss. His folks crossed the Pecos River in a covered wagon and homesteaded the country over by Sierra Blanca when he was a kid. They sent him back east to some big college, but he came back here to run the ranch after his folks died. Your mom and I used to go out and visit him and his wife before you were born. His wife has died since then. He had a son too, that got killed when a horse fell on him."

"Who's Jim?"

"Jim is his prize stud horse. He's probably the best stud in the county. Soon's the time's right, we'll take ol' Paint out for him to breed."

I don't want to think about ol' Paint going anywhere near old Vernon Delaney and his damned old stud.

Her gray-streaked hair is pulled back in a bun as big as a beefsteak tomato on the back of her head. She stands there, tall, with her hands on her hips, eyes blazing. When she speaks, her voice is like lightning crackling in a thunderstorm.

"Now students, you have to learn the playground rules before you can go out to recess. I'm going through them once before we go out, and if you have any questions, you tell me.

"First, you march in line out to the playground and stand in line until I tell you it's okay to play.

"Second, no standing in the swings.

"Third, no rock throwing.

"Fourth, no speaking Spanish on the playground.

"Fifth, when the bell rings, you re-form in line, and I will tell you when to march to the water fountain. After everyone has had a drink, we will march back to the classroom."

Boy, I don't know if I'll ever learn all these rules. Every time we do something, she has a long list of rules we have to follow.

She marches us out to the playground and tells us to play. Suddenly, it dawns on me she never told us how to play, and I don't know how, so I stand there watching the other kids. They're all just standing around too.

Finally, one little blond-headed girl says, "Miz Harbour, can we go swing in the swings?"

"Yes, you may."

Willy Frazier asks, "Can we slide on the slide?" I'm not sure I like Willy Frazier. He was one of the kids who came to take one of Queenie's pups.

"Yes, you may."

Willy turns to a skinny kid standing by him and says, "Come on, Bubba, let's go slide." They run over to the slide and climb up to the top and Willy slides down, turns and yells for Bubba to follow him. Other kids go over to the swings and slide.

I never have slid on a slide or swung in a swing, so I just stand and watch. Apparently, I'm not the only one. Two other boys are still standing near me watching the others. Finally, one of them says to the other in Spanish, "Have you ever done that before?"

"No, I don't want to," says the other also in Spanish.

"Have you ever done it," I ask the first also speaking Spanish.

"Once at a church in El Paso, my brother made me go down a slide, but it scared me."

"It sure looks high," I observe. "I wish Junior was here. He'd show me how."

"Who's Junior?"

"He's my big brother. He's in the fifth grade."

"Miz Harbour! These boys are speaking Spanish on the schoolground!" None of us had seen the little girl with the long black hair standing behind us.

"All right, Scout, Manuel, and Armando, you know it's against the rules to speak Spanish on the schoolground." Miss Harbour is suddenly towering over us. "Didn't you boys hear me explain that before we came out here?"

"No, Señora," I say.

"What did you say?"

I can feel the lightning is about to strike. What did I say wrong? I fight the lump building in my throat and manage to mumble something, not realizing it's in Spanish. "I didn't know you're not supposed to speak Spanish on the schoolground."

"Are you sassing me? Speak English."

I don't know what that means. I want to say I didn't even know we were speaking Spanish, but the words stick in my throat. I look at Manuel and Armando. They're as scared as I am.

"I can see I'm going to have to make an example of you boys right now. You stand right here until recess is over. You're going to get a paddling when we get inside."

I can tell Manuel and Armando are as bewildered and scared as I am, but neither of them starts to cry or beg.

It seems like we have to wait forever. I don't know what's going to happen, but the waiting sure doesn't make it any easier. This school business isn't at all what I thought it would be. I'll be glad when I start having fun like Mom said I would.

When the bell rings, Miss Harbour makes us walk at the front of the line and march to the water fountain. "Drink some water," she commands. My mouth is as dry as a bone, but with the large lump in my throat, I can't swallow. It does feel good to let the water run in my mouth and out again. It looks like Manuel and Armando are having the same problem.

"You three boys just stand right there by my desk." As we march into the classroom, I can feel my face burning with all those kids sitting there looking at me.

She speaks again, and this time her voice is like low, angry thunder. "Now, before we went out to play I carefully explained all the rules. I have three boys here who don't believe they have to follow the rules, so we have to teach them a lesson."

With ruler in hand, she takes Armando by the arm. He tries to pull away, but her grip is like a coyote trap. "Now, you Meskin boys should certainly know better. You live here in America and the language is English. The best way to teach you the language is to prevent you from speaking anything else. Your parents should have told you this before you came to school."

With that, she proceeds to give him three hard whacks on the butt with her ruler. Armando whimpers, but he doesn't cry. "Now go take your seat." Shoving him toward his desk, she turns to Manuel and applies the same. He glares at her without a whimper. Turning to me, she says, "It may not be wrong for an Anglo like you to speak Spanish on the playground, but it is certainly wrong for you to encourage them, and you'd better not ever sass me again." I get five whacks. It hurts like hell, but there's no way I'm going to cry. She shoves me toward my desk, and as I stumble down the aisle between desks, I wonder what an "Anglo" is and what she means by "sass."

As I slide into my desk, the black-headed tattletale is sitting in the desk behind mine. "Your face is red as a beet," she jeers.

"Nah na nah na nana, you got a spanking second day of school." The cotton-headed boy is pointing his finger at Armando.

"You leave him alone. He didn't do nothin'," I say.

"Well, Meskin lover, what you gonna do about it?" I get shoved from behind by Bubba Hillis. He's the biggest boy in class. I turn and grab his shirt as I go down. He falls on top of me, and the wrestling match is on.

"Here, here. You boys stop that." I feel myself being picked up by my shirt. It's a teacher I've never seen before. "You two boys march right into your classroom and stay there. I'm reporting you to Miss Harbour."

Bubba doesn't look at me as we walk into the schoolroom and sit down at our desks. The waiting starts all over again. During the eternity until the bell rings, I imagine every possible horrible wrath of Miss Harbour being released upon me. A lump swells in my throat, and the pit of my stomach feels empty and sick. Across the room I hear Bubba whimper.

I'm not going to cry, I say to myself as I bite my lip. I'm not going to cry like that sissy no matter what. By the time the bell rings, I'm so tense it seems a relief to see the class return to the room, even though I know it means certain death is coming with them.

Miss Harbour orders Bubba and me up front. This time she is holding a paddle. It's a lot bigger than the ruler she used yesterday.

Bubba starts bawling as he walks up to the teacher's desk. "Please don't spank me. Please don't spank me," he pleads.

Miss Harbour grabs him by the arm, turns him around, and with two spats on his butt, tells him to go sit down and stop bawling. Turning to me, lightning strikes out of those eyes, and the thunder feels like it will knock me down. "This is the second time in two days, young man. I'll see if I can't teach you to behave yourself. Bend over and grab your knees."

It seems like she is going to beat on me forever, and every whack seems harder. My butt is stinging like it has turned raw. I count seven whacks. I feel the lump in my throat and sickness in my stomach melt into anger and hatred.

Finally, she stops beating on me, takes a step back, glaring. "Now, do you think you can behave yourself?" she says.

As I straighten up, I resist the urge to rub my butt. I look her directly in the eye. "That didn't hurt," I say between my teeth.

She grabs me by the arm and the paddle is swinging again. Each whack feels like it lifts me off the floor. This time I lose count. But I still glare at her, refusing to cry.

I'm an eagle perched on a high canyon wall. I can see the little people dragging their cotton sacks way down in the canyon below. I spread my wings and jump, sailing, free of any contact with the world. I don't try to flap my wings. I'll just let myself sink through that cloud below and . . . WHUMP!

"Scout! Quit jumpin' off the trailer. You keep shakin' the scales."

I turn over on my back and just lie there. It feels as if I'm still floating in the white soft fluff with the smell of dry smashed wooden-like cotton burrs all around me.

WHUMP! Another cotton sack is thrown into the trailer beside me, followed by Uncle Jack, who begins to shake the cotton out. As the hand-picked cotton falls out of the long canvas bag, he deliberately covers me with the white fluff. I just lie there holding my breath. Finally, he kicks me gently in the side.

"Come on, Scout. You'll smother under there."

I stick my head out and breathe. "It'll be all your fault if I do."

Uncle Jack throws the empty cotton sack over the side to the wetback waiting on the ground. "Come on, git outta here and quit jumpin' around. I can't weigh the cotton sacks with you jumpin' around shakin' the trailer." He climbs over the side and down the ladder leaning against the tall sideboards of the trailer.

I love to play in the fresh picked cotton. I don't get to do this very often now that I go to school. But there's no school today. School is out for Thanksgiving vacation. Yesterday, everybody including the farm hands took the day off. A lot of people came over to the house, and we had a big turkey dinner with dressing. Everyone ate until they complained about being too full. But Dad was anxious to get started picking cotton again this morning. "We'll finish in about three more weeks," he'd said.

I slowly climb up the sideboards, sticking my toes between the slats for support as I pull myself up. As I get my hands on the top slat, I walk up with my feet in the cracks as high as I can, sticking my butt in the air. Then, I stand up straight, balancing on my toes on the narrow slats.

WHAM! WHACK! An outlaw is trying to knock me off the canyon wall. I duck his swinging fist, but I lose my balance and fall over backward. Down, down, I fall, into the bottom of the canyon.

WHUMP! I land on my back and bounce, then settle into the soft white fluff again.

"Scout, God damn it, I mean it! Why don't you go get a cotton sack and help like Junior does?"

"Hey, Scout, come down here. I want to show you something." It's Juan, one of the wetbacks, speaking in Spanish.

I answer him in English, "You better not speak Spanish or I'll tell Miz Harbour, and she'll give you a whippin'." Two or three other cotton pickers standing waiting to be weighed in laugh, but I hear someone ask in Spanish what I'd said.

"What did you say?" Juan asks in Spanish. "Tell me in Spanish." A lot of the wetbacks try to get me to speak Spanish because they know I can understand it, but something inside me won't let me. I start to try, and the memory of that whipping comes searing into my mind. It's fear, I think. I'm a coward, I think, but still, the words won't come.

"What you want to show me?" in English.

"Come on down here and see," in Spanish.

Ol' Paint is standing tied to the corner of the trailer. "Come on, Scout," she says. "Let's get outta here. I'm tired of standing around." She paws the dirt.

"Aw, you're just mad because you can't jump in the cotton."

As I step off the ladder on the ground, Juan grabs me with the help of Uncle Jack and I don't know who else. They stuff me in an empty cotton sack. I try to kick and tear out of the heavy canvas bag, but it's hopeless. "Let me out of here!" I scream. "I'll smother."

"I have a live cotton sack," says Juan. "How much do you pay for live cotton sacks?" he asks Uncle Jack.

"I don't know, let's weigh it and see. I don't think it's worth more than half a cent a pound."

They peel back the sack enough so my head is sticking out and use the shoulder strap to tie it securely around my neck so I can't get out.

"Lay it over there with the other sacks, and we'll weigh it after the others."

"Come on, Uncle Jack. Get me outta here," I beg.

"Can't right now. Got all this other cotton to weigh in first."

It's no use, so I just lie there watching as they lift the long round stuffed cotton sacks up to the scale which is hanging from a timber bolted to the sideboards of the trailer.

"One-hundred-twenty pounds," Uncle Jack says, as he makes a note in the notebook. The sack is lifted up and the strap unhooked so the sack can fall free.

Juan catches the sack over his shoulder and climbs up the ladder, dumps the sack inside the trailer, jumps in behind it, and proceeds to shake out the cotton.

"At this rate, this trailer will be ready to go to the gin tomorrow," Uncle Jack observes.

Ol' Paint looks at me lying among the cotton sacks waiting to be weighed. "I hope you're happy. Now you'll know what it's like to be left tied up."

"Uncle Jack, get me outta here!"

Everybody ignores me, and I finally give up yelling because it sure isn't doing any good.

After all the sacks have been weighed and emptied, Juan says, "We better weigh this one before it turns rotten."

He lifts the sack up in the middle with me hanging face down, takes me over to the scale, pulls the strap under my belly, hooks it, and leaves me hanging there swinging back and forth.

"Let's see what it weighs," Uncle Jack puts the weight on the tail. "Only forty pounds. I don't know, Juan. If you can't pick any more than this, I guess I'll have to fire you."

"In that case, I'll just take this sack back and stuff some more cotton in it."

"Let me outta here, you guys, please," I beg.

They start to walk away, but Juan turns back and, with a laugh, unceremoniously dumps me out of the bag. I truly believe Uncle Jack would have left me hanging there. I want to tell Juan thank you in Spanish, but I can't.

Chapter 3

At the breakfast table, Dad is telling Mom that the cotton crop was really good. "We'll be able to make this year's payment on the farm without any trouble. I'll be able to get the ground plowed and ready for planting the new crop before Easter. Then maybe I can afford to take you into El Paso and buy you and Sis some new clothes. I'd like to buy the boys each a pair of boots too."

Real cowboy boots! I can hardly wait. Then I remember.

"Dad, something's wrong with ol' Paint. She won't hardly talk to me anymore. She just stands around stomping her feet, switching her tail, and then every few minutes she squats like she's gonna pee, but she doesn't."

"I know. I noticed yesterday. But you're in luck. Vernon Delaney brought Jim over to Bill Harmon's place last week to breed a couple of his mares. If you'll ride her over there, I'll see if we can't get her satisfied. You know the way over to Harmon's, don't you?"

I suddenly remember the gray-haired old cowboy in the barber shop right before school started. I can feel a knot building in my stomach. "Will that Mr. Delaney be there?"

"No, he left his stud there for a few days."

The knot begins to disappear as I try to imagine the great stallion Dad had told me about.

---

* * *

"I've never seen you so cantankerous, Paint. You won't go where I rein you. You keep stopping, and I can't hardly get you to move. What's the matter with you? We're just going over to Harmon's. It's not very far." I don't get any answer.

Dad drives up to the Harmon's house just as Paint and I arrive at the barnyard. Bill Harmon comes out to meet Dad, and they talk a minute before they walk down to where I'm waiting. Dad leads ol' Paint inside the corral next to the barn.

"Take the saddle off Paint," Dad tells me. As I lay the saddle by the fence, Dad takes Paint's bridle off, and Mr. Harmon walks into the barn, opens the gate to a stall, and steps aside. "Y'all better get outta the way!"

"Come on, Scout. Get up on the fence." Dad climbs up beside me.

The big black horse darts out of the barn into the corral, runs all the way around, holding his tail high, shaking his head up and down, prancing like he wants to start bucking.

"Now, that's some stud horse," Dad says. "Look how thick his neck is, how smooth he is over the shoulders, and that powerful rear end. He can run like the devil."

The stallion's slick black coat shimmers in the sun as he stops on the opposite side of the corral from where ol' Paint is standing. She doesn't even seem to know he is there. Shaking his head up and down, he gives a gruff nicker and paws the ground.

Suddenly, he breaks into a run straight toward ol' Paint.

"Look out! He's gonna run over you!"

But he stops almost as quick as he started. Then, stiff-legged, head and tail high in the air, he prances around making a circle with ol' Paint in the center. With ears perked, she's definitely paying attention now. He stops, neck arched, with his nose close to hers, reaches over, and smells.

Paint lays her ears back and squeals a noise I've never heard her make before, bears her teeth, and snaps at the big brute in front of her. But he wheels too quickly and circles the corral again, running stiff-legged, head and tail still high in the air. This time he comes up beside Paint and nips her on the shoulder. Paint squeals again, ears back, tries to kick the stud, and they both break into a run around the corral, running neck and neck together.

It's breathtaking to watch them in a dead run with the stud staying evenly beside ol' Paint no matter what she does.

After two rounds of the corral, they both suddenly stop. Paint snorts. The stud nuzzles Paint on the neck, chews on her shoulder, nips her on the hips, and rubs up against her rear end with his shoulders. I notice the huge shaft stiffened between his hind legs.

Suddenly, ol' Paint squats and raises her tail. Before I can figure out what's happening, the stud rears up on Paint's hind end and drives his shaft into her. They both stand frozen, momentarily joined together, then they slowly slip apart.

The eyes of the stud are glazed. ol' Paint walks away aimlessly.

On the way home, Paint falls into a floating, easy pace. I've never felt her travel along so smoothly before.

Mom and I are the only ones in the kitchen. Dad and Junior have already gone to the fields. Mom is busy cleaning up the breakfast dishes, and I have both of my new boots sitting in front of me on the table. Dad had taken the whole family to El Paso where he bought new dresses for Mom and Sis and boots for Junior and me. We also went to a saddle shop where Dad had shown me a Little Wonder saddle. "One of these days you'll need one like that," he'd said.

I also saw a six-shooter chrome-plated cap pistol at Kress Five and Dime Store which I'd begged for, but Dad said I didn't need anything like that.

I just got through wiping my new boots off with a damp cloth to make them shine, and I can't help sitting and admiring them a few minutes. They still smell like new leather.

I'm roused out of my daydream when I see Uncle Jack walking up from the corrals with a bucket of milk in each hand, and I remember the news he recently gave us. More sad news, I thought.

"Mom, why is Uncle Jack going away?"

"It's time for him to get into something permanent to do for a living. He doesn't want to stay here and work for your father as a farmhand the rest of his life. I think joining the cavalry just like your father did is an admirable thing for him to do."

"I don't want him to go," I say.

Mom shrugs. "Well, since he's my youngest brother, I'll really miss him. But I think it's best for him."

"He could stay here and help Dad. Why isn't that best for him?"

"Now that the planting's done and school is out, Junior is big enough to help your father this summer, so there really isn't that much for him to do around here."

I'm silent for a while, then finally I ask, "When will he be leaving?"

"He's planning on going up to the recruiting office at Fort Bliss week after next. So he'll be with us a few more days yet."

I grab a cold biscuit from the metal plate in the middle of the table to smear grape jelly on as Uncle Jack comes into the kitchen. He sets the milk down by the icebox, comes over, picks up a biscuit, and stands waiting for me to hand him the case knife so he can spread some jelly himself.

We just sit there for a while, and the silence is kind of awkward. Finally, Uncle Jack asks, "What're you gonna do now that school's out?"

"I'll just ride ol' Paint in the sandhills, I guess."

There's another long silence, and I get the feeling that wasn't what Uncle Jack meant to ask me at all. I know that he's really trying to say good-bye. "Why don't you come down and help me feed the livestock?" he asks after a while.

We walk out to the corral together, and I feel like a regular hand, pumping water into the water trough with the red pump. A tin chute carries the water from the pump spout through the corral fence. Although I know the big redwood trough is big enough for five horses to drink at one time, I never thought it took so much water to fill it up. I'm pooped out by the time water begins to lap over the side and run on the ground.

Trying to catch my breath, I climb up on the fence to see where Uncle Jack is. As I pull up on the top rail, Blackie's calf, which is a yearling now, snorts and darts away, his tail high in the air. "What's going on with that crazy calf?" I mumble.

"He's just skittish. You need to gentle him a little."

"How would I gentle him?"

"I'll show you." Uncle Jack lifts a lariat rope from around the fence post next to where I'm standing on the fence. "Go get that cotton rope out of the shed."

As I come out of the shed, I see Uncle Jack with the lariat shaken down to a loop in one hand and the remaining coils in the other. He walks cautiously toward the calf standing in the far corner of the corral. As he comes close, the calf watches him carefully, and as Uncle Jack draws dangerously close, the calf quickly ducks its head and darts past him. The lariat sings as it swings over Uncle Jack's head and snakes around the calf's neck. Running along with the calf to a large post standing in the middle of the corral, Uncle Jack wraps the rope around it in order to hold the calf. The calf stops and stands with all four legs braced against the rope pulling against his neck.

"Get behind him and make him come up close to the post."

I walk up behind him and yell. Tongue hanging out and wringing his tail, the calf bawls and jumps toward the post. Uncle Jack runs backward, pulling out the slack of the rope around the post. Finally, the calf is standing snug up against the post, unable to move away.

"Now, double that cotton rope and hand it to me."

With the calf snugged up close, Uncle Jack is able to throw the doubled cotton rope around the calf's belly, thread the loose ends through the doubled end, and then pull it up snug.

"Now, it's your turn." Grabbing me around the waist with one arm while he holds the lariat tight against the post with the other, Uncle Jack swings me up astraddle the calf.

"Stick your hand underneath the cotton rope." He pulls it snug and then places the doubled back ends in the palm of my hand. "Hold that tight, 'cause if you let go, it'll come loose and you'll fall off. Ready? Ride 'em, cowboy!" Uncle Jack loosens the lariat rope and jerks the loop over the calf's head.

"Stick your free hand high in the air and lean back."

The calf stands there not knowing what to do for a short minute. Suddenly, he jumps to the side, but I'm still with him. Now he lines out, jumping high, trying to throw me off his back. When he comes to the fence, he stops suddenly and ducks back the other direction. I sail into the fence, sticking my head between the top two rails.

I pull myself out of the fence only to see Uncle Jack slapping his leg and guffawing.

"I bet he can't buck me off again," I yell.

After the fifth try, Uncle Jack says, "We better let you and the calf both rest. Maybe you can try again tomorrow." Uncle Jack's shoulders are shaking, and he's wiping tears from his eyes. I don't like the way he's laughing at me. "You're a sight, Scout," he says, between bouts of laughter, "but damned if you ain't a real cowboy."

I'm sore and covered with cow manure, but I don't mind. I don't even mind the laughter any more. Nobody's ever called me a real cowboy before.

Later, I realize that Uncle Jack never did get around to saying good-bye.

Uncle Jack has been gone several months, and it's almost Halloween. It's been a good summer and fall. Our cotton crop is the best we've ever had—stalks so high they're over my head. Dad says it's sure to make two and a half bales to the acre.

Dad's in a good mood because of the good crop. The tall cotton plants are loaded with the white fluff waiting for harvest. I've got other things to think about, though. Halloween. I'm going to be the Lone Ranger for the school carnival. Bubba, Willy, Manuel, and Armando and I have been talking about how we're going to soap up all the windows of the cars and pickups in the parking lot at the carnival.

I'm thinking about the carnival while I wait for the school bus that will take us home after school. Thunderheads are building in the distance, and there is a faint hint of the heavy sweet smoke from burning cotton burrs drifting from the cotton gin in the distance. A cool breeze has come up, and I button my jacket, still thinking about the carnival and the sinister deed we're planning.

Finally, the bus arrives, looking like a big yellow Halloween monster. After we all get on, it rattles down the washboard gravel road, turns north onto the pavement, and as it gains speed, the knobby tires set up a hum that blends with the chatter of Sis and the other girls sitting in the middle of the bus. Since I'm the only second grader on the bus, and the next youngest kid is a fourth grader, I have the whole front seat all to myself.

I stretch out on the bench seat ignoring the scenes of green and red cotton fields sliding by outside the window and slip into a relaxed daydream about the coming carnival.

"Come on, Scout, wake up. We're home," Junior says as he slaps my leg with his coat and steps out the door of the bus. Sis follows him, and they both start walking toward the house without looking back. I pull myself out of dreamland as quickly as I can and dash to catch up with Junior. It's not until now that I realize how dark the sky has become.

I see Dad standing by the corner of the shed. He's waving and yelling something at us.

"You kids get in the house!" he says. "Junior put the dogs in the shed. Hurry now. It's gettin' ready to rain. I'll get the animals in the barn." Dad runs toward the corral, and I run to the house.

I look out the kitchen window. I've never seen such a dark cloud. It has a sort of reddish tint around the edge of the deep purple center. I can see it rolling and churning. The window rattles from the wind.

"Is it a cyclone?" Sis asks.

"No," Mom says. "It's just a big thunderhead."

Suddenly, the window is splashed with water like someone just threw a big bucket full at it. It's raining so hard I can hardly see the pickup parked in front of the house. In just a few minutes, it stops almost as suddenly as it started. It's deathly quiet. Then I see something white fall and bounce on the ground. It's about the size of a marble. Then another.

BAM! BAM! BAM! The noise of them hitting the tin roof of the house is deafening. It sounds like a shotgun going off in rapid fire. I run and grab Mom. Sis is there too.

"Hailstorm!" Mom yells, holding us close. A window cracks, then it shatters on the floor. The white ice marbles pour in. Another window breaks on the same side of the house in the bedroom.

"The bed will be ruined!" Mom says as she breaks away from us and dashes to the bedroom. "Here, quick, help me move it," she calls. I see that a pile of ice has already begun to build up in the middle of the bed.

The hailstones keep pounding at the house for a while, and then, suddenly, it's deathly quiet again. I can hear water dripping somewhere.

"Where's Junior and your father?" Mom asks. Her voice is deathly quiet too. We all run outside. The ground is covered with the white balls of ice so deep that my boots sink down until the toes are covered. The whole world is white. I can see Dad walking up from the barn. The door to the shed opens. Tuffy runs out into the white. Slowly, Junior sticks his head out and looks around.

"Boy, that really scared me," he says as he walks up to us. "I thought that hail was going to come right through the roof. Queenie was shaking like she'd been hit by lightning. 'Course Tuffy's too dumb to be scared."

Mom puts her hand on Junior's shoulder and with the other runs her fingers through his shaggy blond hair, looking him closely in the eyes. Then she looks over his head and starts walking rapidly. We follow as she breaks into a run, going toward Dad, who is standing halfway between the house and the barn. He's holding his hat in his hand, standing slump-shouldered, looking out at the cotton fields. I've never seen him look like that.

I glance at the fields that only a few minutes ago were thick with heavily loaded cotton plants covered with open cotton bolls ready for picking. Now I can only see an occasional bare stalk standing.

Mom throws her arms around Dad, and he holds her close. "We were gonna start pickin' cotton next week," he whispers.

* * *

"Maybe we should start going to church." Mom is washing up the breakfast dishes. She looks tired. I'd heard her and Dad talking last night about what he's going to do since there's no cotton to pick.

"Not today. I promised Mart Osborn I'd help him butcher hogs today. I think he has about eight or ten to butcher, so I'm sure he'll give me half a hog. We're gonna need the meat."

Mom says something sort of under her breath that I don't understand, but it sure gets Dad's attention. "Now don't you go getting down at the mouth. We've seen harder times than this and survived," he says in a much softer and concerned tone.

"I know." A tear is running down Mom's cheek. "But I thought that, with last year's good crop, we had about pulled out of the Depression and were finally going to be able to take it a little easier for a while." She wipes the tear away with the back of her hand and manages a smile. "Well, when you go through town, stop at the store in Acala and get a sack of flour and maybe a pound of coffee. I could use some lard too, but I guess we better not use our credit unless we absolutely have to. If you're getting half a hog, we can render some lard out of it."

As Dad drives away in the pickup, I walk slowly down to the corrals to feed ol' Paint.

"I don't know what to do," I say to her. "Dad sure has been quiet lately. He looked almost sad when he gave me the sack of marbles for my birthday last Friday. From what they've been saying about how poor we are, I didn't expect to get a present at all. And Mom keeps talking about goin' back to teaching school and something about not having anything to put under a tree for Christmas or even to send Uncle Jack at Fort Bliss."

"Well, at least your Dad got the hay cut and baled before the hailstorm, so we don't have to worry about not having enough to feed another mouth," Paint says, as she takes another mouthful of hay from the hay rack.

I look at her huge sagging stomach. I sure will be glad when that colt gets here.

HONK! HONK! It's the horn on Dad's pickup. He's just turning off the highway. He sure came back home quick. I run as fast as I can back to the house.

Mom steps out the front door wiping her hands on her apron just as I get within hearing distance.

"What is it, Boots? What's the matter?"

Dad steps out of the pickup, his face is white as Mom's fresh laundry, "The Japs bombed Pearl Harbor!" He holds up a newspaper. It's the first headline I've ever read. It's only three letters long and covers half the front page. I'll never forget it as long as I live.

"WAR," it reads.

Chapter 4

They just keep coming. Side by side, every man looks just like the one beside him and the one ahead or behind him. From my perch up on top of the kerosene barrel, I strain carefully to look at the face of every one of them, looking for that sharp, thin familiar face with the dark eyes and quick grin that pulls to the side. I've been watching for two days now and have the routine down pat.

"Post!" someone yells. Then they all kick their horses into a trot and raise their butts up out of the saddle and back down again in time with the steps of their mounts. This may go on for a long time, and it looks like their heads make little waves as I look back over the top of the troop train. After a while, someone yells, "Ride easy." Then the horses are slowed to a walk.

Sometimes they stop completely, dismount, and the cavalrymen take time to get a drink from their canteens or smoke a cigarette. Other times, they walk, leading their horses.

It was some time before I realized the saddles don't have a saddle horn like any of the other saddles I've ever seen. Behind each saddle is a set of leather saddlebags with a blanket rolled up and tied on top, across, and behind the saddle. In front on one side, each soldier carries a canteen and on the other a rifle stuck in its boot with the shiny handle running up alongside the horse's neck.

"Maneuvers." That's what Dad had said. "They're going on maneuvers down in the Big Bend country. With the war on now, they have to patrol the Mexican border to keep spies from sneaking into the U.S."

Uncle Jack had written that his troop was planning on a trip down the Rio Grande, but he didn't say anything about the whole cavalry going along. We haven't seen him since he enlisted last June, and I'm anxious to see his horse he'd written about. I can't wait for him to tell me all about the cavalry, but Mom says that with the war on, he might get sent overseas, and if we don't get to see him when his troop comes by, we may not see him again until the war's over. He didn't tell us when he might be coming by. The troops had started coming last week, a few at a time at first. Then more and larger groups. Then whole companies, one after the other, with flags in the lead and wagons and cannons in the rear, stretching out in a long column along the highway as far in either direction as the eye can see.

The noise and rattle of the horses trotting and the gear bouncing is almost deafening as they ride alongside the highway. The highway runs only a short distance from the house, and it sounds just like they're riding right through the front yard.

The dust drifts whichever direction the wind is blowing at the moment, carrying the smell of horse sweat and leather with it. It seems to be mostly right over the house.

Mom had said they might let Uncle Jack stop by to visit a few minutes, so I keep looking. Even if they don't let him stop by, I can wave at him and let him know I've seen him. Ol' Paint is standing sleeping by the kerosene barrel rack with one hind leg relaxed and all her weight on the other three. She doesn't have a saddle on. She's so heavy with foal, she doesn't feel much like being ridden these days. In fact, she doesn't seem to have much interest in anything these days except eating and napping.

Suddenly, I hear a yell among the troops. Ol' Paint raises her head, perks her ears, and nickers. Tuffy starts barking.

"Company, yo-o-o!" The captain raises his hand and the troops come to a halt. "Kimpel, fall out!"

On the far side of the column, I can see a head bouncing up and down as he gallops along the other side of the troops to the front of the line. He stops a moment, salutes, and has a few words I can't hear with the officer at the head of the column. He salutes again then spurs his beautiful bay gelding to a dead run. I stand up on the kerosene barrel waving my hat, yelling as he comes to a sliding stop right in front of me.

"Hidey, cowboy."

I want to jump and throw my arms around his neck and hug him close, but I can sense the other troopers on the highway watching. So, instead, I stand at attention look directly into those dark intense eyes and salute. "Hidey, trooper."

Without another word, Uncle Jack returns my salute, takes me under the armpits, sets me in front of him in the saddle, and lopes around to the front of the house.

"Hey, lady, got any coffee for a tired trooper?" he yells at the front door. As Mom and Sis come out, he dismounts, leaving me in the saddle, and embraces them. Only then do I notice how big this horse really is. His neck is so thick I can't touch my thumbs and span my fingers to both sides at the same time.

The military saddle is shinier than any leather I've ever seen. I look at the rifle and canteen on the front and bedroll and saddle-bags behind the saddle. I imagine myself wearing a flat-brimmed hat, tight fitting pants that flare at the side, and high-top leather boots.

"I've only got a few minutes," Uncle Jack says. "How are y'all doin'?" Then his face changes. He has sensed that something is wrong. "What's happened around here?" he asks, his voice low and quiet.

Tears come into Mom's eyes. "The hail . . ." Her voice tapers off. Only then does Uncle Jack look around at the barren cotton fields. Even though most of the cotton in the valley has been picked by now, the fields should still show the white of some unpicked cotton. I can see the shock in his eyes.

"Why didn't I notice before?"

"It was only a narrow strip that came across our farm and the Gianini place across the highway. A freak storm. We don't normally get hail this time of the year . . . It took everything we had just before we were going to start picking cotton."

"Where's Boots?"

"He left Sunday. Went up to Fort Bliss and El Paso. Although he didn't tell me, I think he's going to try to re-enlist."

"Re-enlist?" Uncle Jack sounded shocked, like he couldn't quite take in everything he was hearing.

"He'd said he had to when he first heard about the war, but I talked him out of it. But then, last Saturday, Mr. Hoover came by and told him that, since we won't be able to make this year's payment on the farm because of the hail, a big farming outfit has offered him cash for the place. Says they can make lots of money with the war now, so he wants us to move."

"Why that no-good son-of-a-bitch! After all Boots done for him. This place is worth a lot more now than it was when you bought it."

"We couldn't make the payment, Jack." Mom's voice sounds tired, worried.

"Hell, Hoover knows nobody can guarantee they'll have a good crop every year. He knew that when he sold the farm to y'all, and he knew there may be some years he'd have to wait for his payments."

I'm listening in shock to things I've never heard before. Move? What does this mean? Move where? Sis's eyes dart to me, meeting my eyes momentarily, then she quickly looks away. I can tell I've heard something I wasn't supposed to.

"I know. I know," Mom is saying. "But, with the war, it seems people and everything have changed. I don't know what we're going to do." She sounds almost hopeless.

Everyone falls silent for a few moments, and I feel an empty sickness in the pit of my stomach. For the first time, I begin to see there's something really wrong around here. Mom's been down at the mouth. Dad seems to have been lost in a daze ever since the crop got hailed out. Now, Mom's talking about having to leave the farm. That can't be right. We can't leave the farm. Things are really getting confusing.

"But look at you." Mom manages a smile and tries to hide her worry. "Don't you look handsome in that uniform?"

"Yeah," says Sis with obvious admiration, shielding her eyes from the glare of the winter sun. Her red hair sparkles shades of copper and gold, "I'll bet all the ladies really chase after you."

In spite of his dark complexion, Uncle Jack blushes, looks down, and watches the toe of his shiny boot working out a print in the caliche dust. "Haven't had much time or chance to meet any ladies worthwhile." Then he looks up at Sis. "But you've grown up. You better look out or one of those troopers will sneak off and try to steal you away."

"Well, every time she goes outside the house, I can hear the whistles and hoots," Mom says. She manages another smile. "Have you got time to come in for coffee?"

"Not really. I need to be getting back or I'll never be able to catch up with my troop." Uncle Jack reaches up to lift me out of the saddle.

I try to put him off. "Will you go over and say hello to ol' Paint? She's missed you as much as I have." I can see ol' Paint standing with her eyes closed and her head down, but I know she's not sleeping. I can tell she's got her feelings hurt.

Uncle Jack won't stay. He gives Mom a hug and tells her not to worry then he rides off. His shoulders are a little slumped and he keeps turning around and looking back until finally he kicks his bay up to a dead run like he's trying to escape. I watch him until he's nothing more than a speck on the horizon.

It's the day before Christmas when Dad gets home. He didn't re-enlist. Forty-six is too old, he says, but he didn't say what he's going to do. He and Mom sit up late talking after they make me and Junior go to bed. From time to time, I can hear the low voices in the dark. Then I hear Sis crying. I get up and walk into the kitchen to see what is wrong.

"Nothing," Mom says. "You get back in bed and get to sleep. Tomorrow is Christmas."

I go back to bed, but I don't feel very excited about Christmas. I can't figure out what is going on, and I can't shake the feeling that something is terribly wrong. Fighting back the sleep that seems to weight my eyelids, I try to listen carefully to the muffled voices in the kitchen.

I can't get very much but I'm able to make out certain words . . . move . . . town . . . Fort Hancock . . . Fort Bliss . . . carpenter . . . teach school . . . Paint . . . Harmon's.

Finally, I can't hold on any longer, and I drift into a restless dream of chasing outlaws and Indians through the sandhills on ol' Paint. There is something crawling on the desert sand. It's the old snake, and the runted puppy is there too. Paint jumps to the side and I'm flying. I keep flying, going higher and higher. I try to get back, but I can't. ol' Paint is standing in the middle of the farm as I soar farther and farther away. The old snake and runted puppy are beside her watching me drift away.

I jerk awake, still feeling as though I've been drifting away. I sit up in bed and realize I'm still at the farm. But it was more than a dream. It was like a message from somewhere, telling me I have to do something. I have to escape.

Everyone else is still asleep, and it's still dark out, but the moon spreads light through the window. As I slip out of bed, the floor is cold, so I put on my boots and a Levi jacket.

In the kitchen, I find a stack of presents on the round table. We didn't get a Christmas tree this year. In spite of the urgency I feel, I take time to look the presents over. I find a box with my name on it. It's heavy and rattles like there's something interesting inside when I shake it. As I stand there shaking it, the wrapping tears and something falls out clattering on the floor. In surprise, I stand there, staring. It's the cap pistol I saw in the toy store, and it's even more beautiful than I remembered, with its artificial pearl handles and a real leather holster just like Roy Rogers wears. I have to bite my tongue to keep from yelling in delight. But I remember my mission and grab it off the floor, stuff it in the belly of my pants, pull my Mackinaw coat off the hook on the kitchen door, slip it over my Levi jacket, and light out as fast as I can to find ol' Paint.

"Come on, Paint. We have to go. We got to hurry."

Paint isn't at all excited. "What's going on?" she asks.

"We have to get away from here. Something terrible is going to happen. They're gonna try to make me move away from here. They're gonna leave you at Harmon's. Just when you're gonna have your colt too."

Without saying anything Paint switches her tail and stamps one hind foot to let me know she doesn't believe a word I've said.

"No, Paint, it's true! You have to believe me. But I don't want to ever leave you. I want to live here on this farm forever where we can ride in the sandhills and chase outlaws." I pull her head toward me. "I'll show you. We'll go away together."

"Where are we going?"

"We'll go up in the mountains and we can live there together, and we can be together always. We have to go now, while there's still time."

I run to the shed and get the big soft cotton rope, tie it around Paint's neck, slip a half-hitch around her nose, and pull her up close to the fence. Then I climb up and slide astraddle her. With the shiny new pistol stuffed into the waist of my pants, we move out slowly.

In a little while the sky is bright red as the rising sun beats back the twilight. I look back down and across the valley from where we had come. I can barely see the house now. Mom will be getting up pretty soon. Maybe she'll cook pancakes. No matter. I'll just have to get by with nothing to eat for a while. I can see dark clouds moving in from the West, but I don't pay them any mind. I'm warm in my Mackinaw, and ol' Paint is moving easy in spite of her added load. Since I'm riding bareback, her body warmth seeps into my legs and butt.

In the dim light, we find the road that travels toward the blue mountains. We seem to have made good time, but the hills are getting steeper and rocky now. The sandhills lay below us, and instead of mesquite and greasewood, there is more catclaw and ocotillo. Now and then I see a mountain cedar.

I'm thinking how quiet it is and that there are no other animals around when a coyote's yelp pierces the air. Startled, I look sharp on all sides but can't see him. ol' Paint doesn't change her pace, so I figure everything is still okay. Then I hear him again. This time the yelp drags out into a long howl. I can see him now silhouetted above us on top of a nearby hill. Then there is another yelp on the other side.

"We're surrounded," I whisper to ol' Paint.

"Don't worry about those scavengers. They won't hurt us, not so long as we're healthy and can fight back. They just haven't seen anyone but jack rabbits for a while and want to visit."

"Hellooo! Coyotes!" I yell. "How are youuuu?" I try to drag it into a howl that mimics theirs.

The one on the hill answers with a long howl that breaks up into a series of shrill yelps which are answered from all around by a string of yelps and howls, some shrill and some deep, some loud and some soft, coming from different directions. I can feel the melody. It's beautiful!

"We've come to live with youuuu!" I don't think I've quite gotten the harmony, but they seem to accept it anyway, and the song goes on.

Suddenly, Paint stops in her tracks, ears pointed straight up the mountain. Just as suddenly, the music of the coyotes stops and it is deathly quiet. I look up toward the mountain and realize I can no longer see it. It has disappeared in a gray haze. A white feather flutters and settles on ol' Paint's mane. Another settles between her unmoving ears. I turn my head around, I can't see where we've come from. It's white everywhere.

"It's snow, Paint! I ain't never seen snow before, have you?"

She just keeps her head down and doesn't answer, but I can't help feeling excited. I've read about snow in the readers at school, and Mrs. Chesser has told us about living up north where the snow got so deep they had to shovel it out of the paths and roads. Just before school was out for Christmas vacation, she had shown us a picture of a horse pulling a sled across the snow and the passengers singing "Jingle Bells." There was another picture of Santa Claus with a sack full of toys on top of a house covered with white snow.

I put my hand out and a large flake settles in, quickly turning to water. It makes my hand cold. I try to dry it on my pant legs, but they are getting wet as the melting snow soaks in. "Come on, Paint." I try to nudge her on, but she won't move.

"I can't see where I'm walking."

"We can't just stand here. We'll freeze!" I kick her hard in the side, but she only moves a few steps and stops again with her head down close to the ground.

I slide off and start to lead her along the road, pulling at the lead rope. Haltingly, we move along. Ol' Paint keeps holding back, and I feel like I'm almost dragging her. My boot slips off a large rock, and I stumble over a small bush. I'm no longer on the road. I can't tell which direction is up the mountain and which is down to the valley.

The snow gets deep fast. As my boot sinks in, the toes immediately become hidden in the white powder. I stop to look around. I can hardly see ol' Paint standing the length of the lead rope behind.

"Come on, Paint. Let's try to find a big rock or bush we can get under."

Now it feels as if I'm walking down a steep hill. Paint snorts and stops so suddenly she jerks the lead rope out of my hand. I try to turn quickly to grab the rope, but my boot slips on a wet rock, and I feel myself sliding, sliding. Rocks are rolling along with me, down, down. I lose touch with the ground. A brief flight. Whump! I can feel and hear the rocks falling on and around me.

With a clatter, I feel something hit me in the middle of my back. I roll over to look at it. It's my silver pearl-handled six-shooter.

Looking up, I can see the top of the cliff I fell off of, but above that, I can only see white flakes swirling around.

I'm in a narrow ravine with another steep cliff on the other side. I can tell the only way out is to walk along the ravine until it flattens out.

"Paint! Can you hear me? I'm okay. You stay there. I'll find my way out of here and come get you."

I hear her snort, followed by a faint nicker. Then I can't hear her anymore.

"Paint, are you still there?"

No answer.

"Crazy old mare, where did you go?"

As I try to stand up, I feel the sharp pain in my knee. The pant leg is torn away exposing a big gash. Blood is spreading out, mingling with the melted snow, soaking into the already wet denim of my Levi's.

I've got to get out of here! I've got to find ol' Paint and take care of her. I stand up and start to walk. One step. The world is spinning. No! I can't!

I don't know why I'm crying. My leg is numb now from the cold, so it doesn't hurt much anymore. But the tears just keep streaming down my cheeks. I've got to stop bawling like a baby and try to get out of here. I've got to find ol' Paint and take care of her. She may be lost. Nobody at home knows where we are. They don't even know we've left. Even if they look, they'll never find us here.

It's quit snowing now. I can see blue sky above the cliffs. Not much snow fell in the ravine, but it's cold down here in the shadows. I shiver. I can feel numbness in my hands and feet. I try to stand up again, but with the numbness, I can't control myself. I manage to crawl on two hands and one knee on the loose gravel in the bottom of the ravine. After only a short distance uphill, I'm faced with another cliff cut out in the solid rock mountain.

Looking downstream, the direction the water flows when it rains, I can see I'm faced with one cliff or large rock after another.

I'll never be able to get out of here on my hands and knees! The tears continue to gush. To hell with it! I don't want to get out of here anyway. I don't want to move into town. I don't want to leave the farm. I don't want to leave ol' Paint. I'll just stay here and die.

But what about ol' Paint?

"Paint!" I yell. "Paint!" as loud as I can. It's almost a scream. The echo off the ravine walls envelops me as I lay sobbing.

Click! Clack! I come quickly awake and look up just as a small pebble hits me right between the eyes. I pull my hat off so I can look upward. The sun has moved low in the sky, but the angle is such that I'm no longer covered by shadow. What caused the little rock to fall? I automatically try to stand up, stumble, and fall, rolling farther down the ravine, rocks and gravel clattering around me.

I hear a yelp. The coyotes! Then I hear a bark. No mistaking who that is!

"Tuffy! Tuffy! Down here!"

I can see his head over the edge of the cliff. The way it is weaving back and forth, I can tell he is wagging his tail wildly.

Suddenly, the sun is blotted out. A giant has covered both me and Tuffy with his shadow.

Even though we've always had horses around, and I know that when I was little he used to take me riding in front of him in the saddle, and that without a doubt he's the best horseman in the world, this is the first time I can remember seeing him sitting on a mount. He's riding Harmon's big sorrel gelding. In spite of my pain and numbness, I can't help but notice he stands taller in the saddle than Roy Rogers or Gene Autry or anyone else I've ever seen.

He puts the horse at ease and lifts one leg over the saddle horn. "You okay?" he asks, as casually as if he'd ridden up to ask the time of day.

"Yeah, I think so. 'Cept my knee's cut, and I'm cold and numb." I can't stop the tears from streaming down my cheeks.

"Well, if you ain't hurt, whatcha bawlin' about?"

I'm surprised by how loud I'm yelling and what I'm saying.

"God damn it! I'm mad. I'm mad 'cause it hailed us out. I'm mad 'cause they're takin' the farm! I'm mad 'cause we have to move to town. I'm mad . . ." I can't go on. I break into sobs pounding the gravel with my fist.

After a while, Dad says, "You through?" When I look up, he tosses a lariat rope down around my shoulders. "Tuck this under your arms and I'll pull you outta there."

Feeling the strength of the rope around me, I struggle to stand up, biting my lip to keep from wincing from the pain, to keep from remembering my tears.

Sitting by the fire, wrapped in the saddle blanket, I feel my hands and feet tingle and sting as the feeling slowly seeps back in. Dad has wrapped his bandanna around my knee so it doesn't hurt so long as I don't bend it. Except in the shadows, the snow is about all melted.

Dad is standing with his back to me, looking out over the valley. "You got an awful long ways up here," he muses. "If it hadn't been for Tuffy, I don't know how I'd ever found you. Your tracks were covered up by the snow for about the last mile and a half." Then, as though it just dawned on him, he turns around and says, "You've never seen snow before, have you?"

"Dad, ol' Paint . . . ?"

"Aw, she's okay. I found her about half way up here tangled to a bush with that damn rope you had around her neck. She'd started back for help when she got tangled up. I took the rope off her neck, whacked her on the butt and told her to get on home. You know riding her up here like that coulda made her drop that colt before she's supposed to?"

"I . . . I guess I didn't think."

"Yeah, well, I guess you didn't."

"Dad, I don't want to move to town."

"You think you're the only one feels that way?"

"No, but . . ."

"You probably don't remember, but when we first bought that place, it was mostly mesquite, salt cedar, and sandhills. Only about twenty acres was in cultivation and fit for farmin'. I grubbed out all the mesquite and salt cedar by hand and leveled the sandhills with a four-horse team pulling a fresno. Now only about thirty-five acres of the entire two-hundred-twenty is sandhills, and it's one of the best irrigated farms in the valley. You think I want to move after all that?"

"No, but . . ."

"Last year, we had our first good crop, and with one more, we'd 'a' been in tall cotton. Now we get wiped out with one lousy freak hailstorm. You think any of us likes that?"

"No," I say meekly.

"But you don't see any of the rest of us runnin' off and bawlin', do you?"

"Do you think God is mad at us?" I ask, almost too ashamed to speak.

Dad's eyebrow goes up. I can tell he's trying to figure what I'm getting at.

"Mom said maybe we oughta start goin' to church."

The big man pushes his hat back, puts one foot on a rock, leans over, resting both elbows on the bent knee, and laughs. "No, I don't think God's mad at us. The Good Book says He rains on the just and the unjust. So, just cause we got rained on a little don't mean He's tryin' to punish us."

"Then why're we havin' so many problems?"

"Well, we probably bring some of these on ourself. Just like you takin' off up here and gettin' in a big mess. We all do things like this, but just 'cause we walk off blind in a snowstorm and fall in a ravine don't mean God's tryin' to punish us. I figure He 'spects us to use our heads a little."

"Yeah, but you or Mom didn't cause that hailstorm."

"I guess that's the hardest kind of thing for anyone to understand. You work your ass off tryin' to do what you think is right, then it's sorta like you get run over by a wild horse comin' outta nowhere. But I guess when God made this ol' world He knew what He was doin', and He made it the way it is 'cause He figured it was best way to do it. Just 'cause we can't tell why things work the way they do don't mean He did it wrong or He didn't know what He was doin'. Leastwise, I don't see it does any good cryin' 'bout it. All I can see is that we have to just keep on tryin' to do the best we can."

"I still don't like it," I say. I still don't want to move. I just hope I don't start crying again.

"Yeah, well, I know change like that comes hard. It's probably the hardest thing of all. Probably causes more pain than anything else in this world. And I know your havin' to leave the farm and move into town is going to be painful. But it seems to me that kind of pain usually makes us stronger. If I didn't know the pain you're goin' through will make you a bigger and tougher man, I don't know as I could stand it. But you got to learn to handle it just like the rest of us."

Tuffy is sitting with his head resting in my lap looking up at me with sad eyes. He wags his tail, sweeping the sand behind him. He whines as I stroke his shiny black head.

"Come on, Scout. We better be heading home. Your mom will think we both decided to go over the mountain."

Sitting behind the big man with my arms around his waist as the tall sorrel gingerly picks his way down the trail in the fading light, I can feel my silver six-shooter tucked in my pants. For the first time on this Christmas day, I feel safe and warm.

CHAPTER 5

"Is it really true what my mom said?" Willy Frazier is following me out of the classroom. "Are you moving to live in town?"

I can feel the hair on the back of my neck bristle and the burning start to rise in my face the way I know it always does when I start to turn red. He takes a step back as I wheel and glare at him.

"Don't be mad . . . That's what my mom said, and I'll be glad when you do 'cause there aren't any other gringo kids our age that live in town, and now I'll have someone to play with."

I know Willy is trying to be friendly, but I still can't help getting mad every time anyone brings up something about us moving away from the farm.

"I gotta go catch the bus." That's all I can say before I turn and start running down the wide hallway.

"You won't have to ride the bus when you live in town," Willy yells.

Biting my lip to hold back the tears, I run out the front door of the schoolhouse, down the steps, and head toward the far side of the playground where we always go to catch the bus home. Junior's already there, and I can tell he's waiting for me, so I stop running, wishing I could go someplace else, because I sure don't want to talk to him now. But I can't think of any place else to go because the bus is pulling up right now, and I'll have to get on in just a minute. When I start walking real slow, hoping Junior will get on before I get there, he starts walking toward me.

"Scout, I've been waiting for you. We aren't supposed to ride the bus today. Mom came by and told me to catch you before you got on. We're supposed to walk to our new house. Dad got a job working as a carpenter in Fort Bliss. He's building barracks for all the troops they're training up there for the war. He has to leave tomorrow, so he and Mom have moved us to a house over behind Franklin's Grocery. Come on, I can't wait to see it. Mom says we'll have electric lights and running water." He turns and starts walking fast in the direction of the trail that leads from school to the main part of town. When he realizes I'm not keeping up, he turns back. "What's the matter? Aren't you coming?"

I'm dumbstruck. I can't say anything. There's a big knot in my throat, and I have that sick empty feeling in my stomach. Where's ol' Paint? Where's Tuffy, and what about all the livestock? We can't just leave them there to starve. When I fed Paint this morning, she was complaining about being so heavy with foal that she can hardly get around. She didn't want to eat much. I told her not to worry. I told her I'd take care of her and be with her when the colt is born. How am I going to know when the colt is coming now?

"Scout, are you coming?" Junior is standing right in front of me, looking me closely in the eyes.

"Sure, I'm coming," I finally manage to say, as I start to walk slowly along the narrow footpath that leads from the schoolyard through a small area of uncleared sandhills and mesquite that lays between the schoolyard and the cotton gin.

"Now that we live in town, we can come play in the gin yard about any time we want to," Junior observes as we walk past the long rows of cotton bales covered with a coarse burlap in the gin yard. Dad had said they are waiting to be shipped to the compress in Fabens where the bales are pressed into a smaller size before they are shipped to the mills back east where the cotton is spun into thread and then finally woven into cloth to make shirts and other goods. Every time I see the gin yard from a distance, with its irregular rows having bales missing here and there, I think of a giant snaggle-toothed mouth opened about ready to swallow the big metal building that houses the gin.

The gin yard makes a great place to play tag or hide-and-seek. But I don't like to play with the big guys because they can climb up on top of the bales and jump from row to row, so they can sneak up on us smaller guys from above. Anyway, getting to play there every day sure isn't worth moving to town for.

Past the gin yard, the trail leads to Zula's Café where we get to go for lunch sometimes. "Now we'll have to go home for lunch instead," Junior says.

Across the highway is Slim O'Neal's Bar next to Levine's Hardware Store. On the other side of the café is the barbershop and then Tolbert's Filling Station. Finally, we cross the highway to the northernmost building of town where Franklin's Grocery is located. The long, one-story red brick building used to be the old fort, and the grocery only occupies the front part next to the highway. The windows and doors of the back part are boarded up. I've heard some of the big kids say there are ghosts and spooks living there, so I get real close to Junior as we walk down the gravel road that runs alongside the brick walls heading down toward the pumping station and big irrigation ditch.

As we pass the grocery building, we can see three small gray houses side by side. The first is where Mr. Hillsboro, the barber, lives. Slim O'Neal lives in the middle one, and at the front of the third, I see Dad's pickup backed up to the front door. Dad and Alfonso Sandoval are unloading furniture into the house. Tuffy has a rope around his neck tied to the front bumper of the pickup. He barks and wags his tail when he sees me. I run and grab him in my arms and hold him close as he whines and tries to lick my face.

Compared to the farmhouse, this one seems big and cold. The unfriendly electric bulb in the center of the kitchen ceiling causes bright light to bounce off the white painted walls, hurting my eyes. I can tell it's uncomfortable as soon as I sit down at our old round table, but it takes a few minutes for me to realize that what's missing is the warmth of the old kerosene lamp we always had at the other house.

Mom has bologna on white bread with mayonnaise and bottled milk for supper. "I haven't had time to cook, so we're just having sandwiches tonight," she explains as she slices some dill pickles onto a plate in the middle of the table.

After washing up at the kitchen sink, Dad sits down and starts to build himself a sandwich. "Well, we got all the beds set up, and the furniture is all set inside the house. Alfonso will come over next Saturday and move it to wherever you want to put it. I'm sorry I haven't got more time, but at least everything is here if you can just find it when you need it."

Mom walks over and pats Dad on the shoulder. "It's okay. We'll make out. You eat and get a good night's sleep. You have to leave early for Fort Bliss tomorrow."

"Dad . . . ?" I hesitate. I'm not sure I want to hear the answer, but when Dad looks at me waiting, I have to go ahead. "Dad, what did you do with. . . ." My voice fails me, but Dad anticipates my question.

"The livestock? I sold old Blackie to John Haskel. He's been wanting to buy her for a long time. He knows a good milk cow when he sees one, and he's tryin' to build up his dairy herd. Mart Osborn bought Sukie and her litter. When we left for town with the last load of furniture, he was still chasing the last two of those little pigs to load in his pickup with her." Dad laughs and shakes his head, takes a bite of his sandwich and continues, "He's going back tomorrow and try to catch all the chickens and move them over to his place too."

I can't hold it any longer, "Dad, what about Paint!" I blurt out. "Where is she?"

"Why, I thought you knew. I took her over to Harmon's. They're gonna keep her over there until we can get some place to keep her."

"But she's about to have her colt," I insist.

"I know that, but Bill Harmon has several horses, and he knows how to look after her. I'm sure he'll let you know as soon as he can after the colt's born, and then we'll try to work it out so you can go up there and see it."

"I promised her I'd be there." I bite my lip to hold back the tears.

"I know, Son. But sometimes there are things we just can't do. It's twelve miles up there from here, and you can't go live at the Harmons'. They're all crowded in that little house with those four girls as it is." Dad reaches over and pokes me in the ribs playfully, "Maybe you'd like to go live in their barn. Then you could play with those girls all the time." Angrily, I try to slap his big hand away, but I can't keep from grinning in spite of the empty feeling in my stomach. He knows I'd never live with a bunch of stupid girls.

I can hear Tuffy whining, still tied to the pickup out front.

"Dad, what about Queenie? Where is she?"

"She went over to Harmon's with Paint. So they'll both be there together."

That was some consolation.

Tuffy whines again. "Why do we have to tie Tuffy up? Can't we at least untie him now?"

"No. Don't you let him run loose around here. He's not used to living in town, and he'll get out on a road and get run over by a car. Besides he might try to go back to the farm until he learns we live here now. I'm sorry, but he'll just have to get used to being tied up."

I'm biting my lip real hard when Mom surprises me. "Maybe we can let him sleep in the house a couple of nights until he gets used to living here."

I jump up from the table and head for the door, "Thanks, Mom."

"But only for a couple of nights now, and tomorrow morning he has to go back outside. You know I never allow dogs in the house," she warns.

When the light is turned out, I hold Tuffy close, trying to ease the pain in my chest and hold back the tears. Tuffy's long shiny black coat feels warmer than the covers of my bed. I can't sleep for worrying about Paint in that strange corral with other horses she isn't used to being around. She probably hates me for not coming to say good-bye.

"Scout, you are just going to have to get hold of yourself. You've been moping around for over a month now. I saw Miss Chenowith at the grocery store yesterday, and she told me you're not doing your work at school. She says all you want to do is play with that toy gun. She told me she had to take it away from you the other day, and if you bring it back to school, she'll take it and keep it until school's out."

I ignore the warning about the gun and get right to what's on my mind. "Mom, when will I get to go see ol' Paint?" I'm surprised how whiny my voice sounds.

"It's going to be a while yet." I can tell Mom is working to be patient. "Maybe next time your father comes home we can drive up to Harmon's place, and you can see her and the colt. Maybe we can arrange for you to go riding on ol' Paint with Jenke."

I wince at the mention of Jenke Harmon's name. She's the only one of the four Harmon girls who's my age. She's real skinny with long blond hair and blue eyes, but she's taller than I am, and she's the smartest girl in the class. I know she thinks I'm a real dummy, but I don't care. I can't stand her. The thought of riding with her is almost enough to make me forget the whole idea, but there's always a chance ol' Paint and I can run off and leave her and that old sorrel hay-baler she calls Star that her dad bought her.

"When's Dad coming home?"

"I'm not sure yet. His last letter said they're working day and night shifts to build barracks at Fort Bliss as fast as they can, and they don't want anyone taking off unless they absolutely have to. Maybe in six weeks or so he'll take off a few days and come home."

"I don't like living in town. Why couldn't we stay on the farm?" I guess I still sound whiny.

"Honey, I know you don't like it." Mom's voice shows she is still trying to be patient. "None of us do. But sometimes there are things we just can't help, and we just have to do the best we can and make the most of it. Besides, it's not really so bad. You don't have to ride the school bus anymore. You can walk up to visit Willy Frazier. You can play with your friends about any time you want to. I hear tell some new people are moving to town, and they're going to put a drugstore with a soda fountain in that old building next to Tolbert's garage."

"I don't care about no soda fountain. I want to go see ol' Paint."

"You're beginning to sound like a spoiled brat now. Why don't you go outside and play with Tuffy? He misses the farm too."

I walk out the back door, letting the screen door slam behind me. Tuffy runs to the end of his chain and whines, wagging his hind end as he holds his tail down between his legs. He keeps putting his head down and then looking up at me. He's always been a happy dog, but ever since we moved to town where he has to be tied up, he's been sad. I unsnap the chain from his collar, and he jumps up against me knocking me over on my butt. I grab him and hold him close. I wish he didn't have to be tied up whenever I'm not with him. I wonder if he'd feel better if I let him loose at night after everyone has gone to bed. I'm sure he wouldn't run away, and he'd be able at least to go out in the cotton field and hunt rabbits.

Tuffy stays in my arms with his head on my shoulder a long time. I sit there holding him and survey the back yard and neighborhood again. The only thing in the back yard is the privy. It's a big double-doored privy with a screen which serves as shade and shelter for Tuffy. His chain is tied to the center post of the screen. Further on west behind the outdoor toilet is a drainage ditch. A cotton field comes right up to the north side of the yard. That cotton didn't get hailed out.

To the south are two more houses just like ours, separated only by the ungraveled caliche ground. I can see ruts in the dry ground where cars have gotten stuck in mud puddles when it had rained.

There doesn't seem to be anything to do around here. I can't go riding like I used to on the farm. How am I going to be a cowboy if I don't have a horse to ride? Even if I had a horse, where would I ride? Even though there is farm land right next to our yard, Dad said I have to stay out of it because Old Man Miller, the owner, will get mad. It seems like Tuffy and I are prisoners. Ol' Paint is a prisoner too, penned up all the time up there on the Harmon farm.

Tuffy breaks free from my arms and starts running around me in circles and barks, wanting to play. Finally, I get up and challenge him to a race down to the drainage ditch.

"Now don't you get all dirty." Mom is pushing me out the door behind Sis and Junior. "I want you walking close to me all the way, and there won't be any pestering one another." Her voice is really firm as we start up the hill to the church with her between me and Junior.

"You look pretty, Mom." I can't remember ever seeing her dressed up like this before.

"Thank you, honey. I'm just sorry your Father isn't here to go with us, but now that we live within walking distance of the church, there isn't any reason for us to not go every Sunday." We've lived in town a year now, but this is the first time we've been to church.

"But, Mom," Sis says, "we don't even belong to this church and you're an Episcopalian."

"Well, it'll have to do. It's the only white church in town. They won't object to our being there anyway. If you kids want to join after you've had a chance to know what it's all about, then I won't object."

"Dad said he wouldn't go even if he was able to," Junior breaks in. "What's he got against church?"

Mom laughs. "He's not against all churches. He just can't bring himself to listen to these hard-shell Baptists preach the way they do. I guess he thinks they're hypocritical."

We walk silently for a while, with Mom holding my hand. Finally, I pull on her arm to get her attention.

"Mom, what's hypocritical?"

She laughs again. "It's a big word. Too big for little boys. You don't worry about it now. You're going to Sunday School, and I want you to learn everything you can. After Sunday School, we'll stay for the preaching. I want you boys to sit quietly, and I don't want you squirming or making any noise."

I'm surprised to see Willy Frazier, Bubba Hillis, and Dee Stotts at Sunday School. Manuel and Armando, I know, are over at the other church where all the Mexican kids go. Betty Lou Gianini, Charlotte Underwood, and Jenke Harmon are here too. In fact, except for the Mexican kids and a few white kids that live too far out in the country, the whole third grade is here.

Seeing Jenke, I can't help but remember the first time I went out to the Harmon's to see ol' Paint. I thought Paint would be real excited and would toss her head and prance around, but she didn't act that way at all. I think it was because Jenke was there watching us, and Paint felt embarrassed acting that way in front of her.

"Paint's doin' all right," Jenke had said. She was kind of hanging back, not coming too close.

I didn't say anything back to her. I just ignored her and wished she'd go away. Pretty soon she did. Paint still acted kind of distracted, though. Maybe it was because she was so busy taking care of her colt. He's a little palomino with a white blazed face. He's cute like all baby horses, but it'll be a while before he's big enough for anybody to ride.

I rode Paint a while when I was there, and I've been out a couple of other times to ride her, but I don't know, things are just different between us now. I know things won't be the same until Dad comes home and we move back to another farm.

So far, I haven't had to ride with Jenke. I hope I never have to. I don't want her around even if Junior did say she's the best rider he's ever seen—for a girl.

Pretty soon I have to quit thinking about Paint when Mrs. Moseley comes in and shows us some pictures of Jesus talking to some kids and tells us Jesus loves us all, and we should love him, and because he loves us, we should be good.

Bubba pulls Charlotte's hair, and they get into a squabble. This gives Mrs. Moseley a chance to spend the rest of the time telling us how boys are made of nails and snails and puppy dog tails but girls are made of sugar and spice and everything nice, so boys have to work especially hard to be good. She didn't mention that before Bubba pulled her hair, Charlotte had taken his chair when he went to get a drink of water.

After a while, Sunday School is over, and we're in the big room Mom calls the sanctuary. Mrs. Moseley is playing the piano and Mr. Moseley, the song leader, is standing up front in the center waving one arm while holding a hymn book in the other. Everyone else is standing, yelling to the top of their voices about seeing "the glory of the comin' of the Lord." It's a good song. I enjoy it.

After the song, Mr. Moseley raises his free hand and says, "Let's pray." Everyone else bows their head and stands quietly. I can't help trying to look around to see what's going to happen. Then Mr. Moseley starts in, "Dear Heavenly Father, we recognize what wretched sinners we are. We know we have disobeyed your commandments, that we have pursued pleasures of the flesh, lusted . . ." and on and on and on . . .

I can't follow it any longer, and then I notice for the first time that nearly every woman there is wearing a hat. Mom has a little white hat that sits in the middle of her head. The lady next to us has a big yellow hat with flowers all over it. The lady in front of me has one with pheasant feathers, sticking out the back.

I turn around and look up into the face of a tall black-headed woman standing with her head bowed and eyes closed tightly. She is wearing something that has flowers, feathers, and ribbons of all different colors. Hanging on her shoulder is a fur of some animal with the head still on it that looks something like a muskrat. The eyes have been replaced with little glass beads. It makes me shiver.

I turn around and look at the people across the aisle. Jenke is standing there with her mother. Both of them have their heads bowed. Jenke's eyes aren't closed, and she sees me looking at her. She sticks her tongue out and then quickly looks away like she can't stand me. That's okay. I can't stand her either.

Suddenly, Mr. Moseley's voice stops and everyone mumbles "Amen" and sits down.

There are more songs and more prayers, and the plate is passed for people to put money in. Mom had given me a dime which I proudly drop in as it goes past me.

Suddenly, everything is deathly quiet. Someone coughs. Another cough. A baby cries. Some lady says, "Shhhh!" Then after what seems to be forever, this tall gray-haired man walks up to the stand in front of the church. His eyes are blazing as he looks straight out over the heads of everyone as though he is speaking to someone hanging to the ceiling in back of the church.

"Sinners!" he shouts. "Listen to me! Listen to me and hear me well! Take my words to heart or you will surely burn in hell!" I almost jump out of my skin as his fist comes crashing down on the stand in front of him, and I can feel the wooden floor and bench we're sitting on shake.

"The Lord Jesus Christ was stripped and beaten. He was made to carry a heavy wooden cross up on top of Calvary Mountain, and there they put a crown of thorns on His head and nailed Him to a cross. Then, when He didn't die, they stuck a spear in His side, and all because of you!"

His blazing stare spreads down upon the congregation, and a long, pointed finger sweeps over us. It seems like he's looking and pointing straight at me. Feeling guilty and scared, but not knowing what I did wrong, I shrink and move in as close as I can to get under Mom's arm.

I don't understand most of what he is saying, but I have visions of bright blazing fires and white hot lava pouring all over me as he continues to pound the podium with his fist and shout about the eternal fires of hell damning us all unless we do exactly as he says.

Suddenly his voice changes. "Now, if you will all turn to hymn number 57 and join me in singing 'Jesus Is Calling' as those who have heard the word of the Lord come forward to confess their sins and rededicate their lives to His service." He is softly inviting us. I almost jump up and run to the podium to plead for forgiveness, but then I still don't know what I did wrong.

Mrs. Moseley is at the piano again and everyone is singing "Jesus is tenderly calling thee home," and I can still hear the preacher's whiny singsong voice pleading for everyone to come up in front of the church to "confess your sins, admit that you have been greedy and selfish, that you have lusted to satisfy your bodily desires, that you have followed the ways of Satan, and that you have not loved the Lord above all else, that without His forgiveness you shall surely burn in hell."

"Amen!" someone yells.

The music stops. "We have here Brother and Sister Jennings who have come forward to accept Christ as their savior," the preacher is saying. I don't know the man and woman standing next to him, but they are both crying, with large tears streaming down their cheeks. "Let us all rejoice and let God know how happy we are that he is willing to forgive such wretched sinners as these." The singing, begging, shouts of "Amen," and rejoicing continues until eventually there is a long line of people standing side by side across the front of the church, all singing as loud as they can with tears streaming down their faces. I don't know what to make of it. I can only stare, wide-eyed and speechless.

Finally, it's over, and we start the walk home. Mom's face is shining like she just stepped out of the bathtub. "Well, how did you enjoy church?" she asks lightheartedly.

Junior grumbles, "I don't see why he has to shout so much."

Sis is mopping the tears that continue to stream down her cheeks. "I think he's the most wonderful preacher in the whole world."

Mom doesn't seem to agree he's that great. "He talked a little loud at times, but it's been so long since I've been to church, I did enjoy it."

I don't say anything because I'm afraid to admit my confusion, but I can't figure out why all those people were crying if they were as happy as they said they were, and they thought the preacher was so great.

* * *

"Just a minute, young man, I want to talk to you." Mom's really got her dander up. "This is the third morning in a row that Tuffy was sitting on the back door step, loose from his chain when I got up. After I found him loose on Wednesday morning, I made a special point to check him that night and again last night before I went to bed to be sure he was tied up good. I couldn't figure out how he'd been getting loose, but this morning when I took him back to tie him up again, there in the loose dust was the footprint of a little bare foot right by the end of his chain. It was a little bare-foot just the same size as fits in one of your shoes."

So she's the one who has been tying him up in the mornings. I had hoped it was Junior, and he wouldn't say anything.

"Mom, I have to go. I'm gonna be late for school."

"No, you're not. You have over forty-five minutes before the bell rings. Besides, you don't have to walk. You can ride over with me."

I hate riding to school with Mom. Now that she's a teacher and sits with all the others at assembly and is seen talking to them in the hallways, all the kids accuse me of being a teacher's pet. It doesn't seem to make any difference that she teaches high school.

I can see there's no point in trying to avoid her. "Tuffy doesn't like being tied up," I tell her. "Besides, he's lived here in town long enough that he knows to stay off the highway. He won't get run over. Mom, he's been real sad ever since we moved here. He may as well be in prison if you're gonna keep him tied up. If we let him loose at night, at least he can run around and play and hunt for bones. He can go out in the cotton patch and hunt rabbits."

"But, it's different here in town, Scout." Mom's look is still stern. "You have to realize we live close to other people. Some people don't like dogs. They don't want them running around loose. The first thing you know, we'll start getting complaints."

"I don't care what people think. Mom, can't you tell he's suffering being tied up like that?"

"Honey, I know. I've noticed how rough and shaggy his coat has gotten. He used to have bright shiny black hair. It seems he's lost weight too. But, he has to learn to adjust and learn to live in town just like you and I have."

"I still hate living here. I feel like I'm in prison too. I never get to go see ol' Paint. I never get to ride out in the sandhills. There's nothing to do around here. Tuffy's the only animal friend I have. He's the only one I can talk to."

"I know you still miss Paint, but you got to go see her three times this last summer. You got to go riding with her twice. Besides you've got your friends here. You see Willy and Bubba all the time. You went swimming in the canal nearly every day. You played war and rubber guns and all kinds of other things. I know you've enjoyed yourself."

"Swimming with Willy and Bubba will never be as much fun as being with ol' Paint. I just don't fit in with those guys. All they want to do is sit around talking about baseball or football, or they want to play marbles. When I talk about riding or roping calves or being a cowboy, they don't understand."

I guess I had a little fun playing war, but I'm not ready to admit it, and besides, because of the rubber shortage and rationing, we couldn't get inner tubes for our rubber guns, so it wasn't any fun after that.

"They never want to play cowboys and Indians either," I whine, "and when we wanted to play with slingshots, you made us quit."

"I certainly did. Bubba got hit in the head with a rock. One of you could have gotten an eye put out or worse. You little boys can play without hurting one another. Well, come on. We have to get to school. It sure wouldn't look good if the typing and bookkeeping teacher was late." She shakes her head. "I just wish you and that dog would adjust a little better."

Mom seems worried about Tuffy and me, and I begin to believe she will agree to let Tuffy run loose, but as she drives to school, she starts in again. "You and that dog are just going to have to get used to being in town and learn that you can't just run wild like you used to on the farm. If you turn him loose again, you'll be punished, and I'll just have to give him away to a farmer who can keep him out in the country."

My heart sinks. I couldn't bear it if Tuffy wasn't here with me. I'll have to be more careful from now on. I'll have to be sure and get up before anyone else does. I hope Dad comes home soon so we can move out of this stupid old town.

I'm rousted out of my sleep by a scream, then I hear a door slam. I lay there a minute trying to figure out what it was, then I realize it's Mom at the back door and she's talking to someone.

"Get the twenty-two. We may have to shoot him." Mom's voice is hushed but excited.

In a flash, I'm in the kitchen. She's talking to Junior. Junior is standing in the corner checking the rifle to see if it has bullets.

"What is it, Mom?"

"Scout, you go on back to bed."

I look at Junior, "What is it?"

With a grim, determined look, Junior shoves the bolt home on the rifle, "It's Tuffy. He's gone mad."

"No! Mom? He was okay last night. He's not mad, he must be sick. Open the door! Let me see!"

Mom stands between me and the door. "Don't you go out there. Look at him out the window. He may have rabies. If he bites you, you'll get them too."

Looking out in the early gray dawn, I see Tuffy staggering in the backyard. He is foaming at the mouth, and it looks like he's choking.

"He's sick. He needs help!" I dash for the front door.

Mom sees me as I come around the back corner of the house in a dead run. She comes out the back door and tries to grab me, but I dodge and slip by. "Tuffy!" I yell. "What is it? What's the matter?"

Tuffy is standing by the toilet, front legs spread to brace himself, head down with his mouth open. Foamy saliva is dripping on the ground. His eyes are glazed over. As I approach, he seems to try to move toward my voice. He takes two staggering steps then falls on his side. As I kneel beside him, he shivers and stretches his legs in a spasm. I can see his throat muscles tightening, and he coughs like he's choking.

"Tuffy, don't die!" I yell, as I take his head in my arms, caressing between the ears and down the back of his neck, trying to comfort him. "Mom, get some help, please." But, as I speak, he jumps in a spasm and slings his head as though he is trying to break free of my grasp, spreading the foamy saliva on my face and bare arms. Then I can feel the life slip out of his body.

I'm sitting behind the toilet, watching the sun setting low on the horizon in a flaming red ball when I hear the sound of a motor. It sounds like a pickup, and I hear it being driven up to the front of the house. I don't even look to see who it is. I don't want to talk to anybody. I just want to be alone. They wouldn't let me bury Tuffy—said he has to be checked to see if he had rabies. If he did, then I will have to take shots. I rub the small place on my arm that was scratched when I was holding him. I may die. I don't care. It's my fault he got rabies anyway. He probably got bit by some wild animal that gave him rabies when he was running loose at night. I can't stand it here without Tuffy anyway. He was the only animal left from the farm that I could talk to, and now he's gone. It's just like when he was born. The little runt born in the same litter was killed because he wasn't strong enough. But Tuffy survived. He was strong and healthy and happy until we moved to town. Then he couldn't stand being tied up. Now he's dead too. I don't care what happens anymore.

"Yes, ma'am, Doc Wilson told me about your dog." I recognize Tony Gianini talking. "Wanted me to come pick him up and take him up to the vet in Fabens so he could check for rabies. I told him I don't think it was rabies. That dog was too healthy, besides he wouldn't die that quick from rabies . . ." His voice trails off.

I start listening closely. Tuffy didn't have rabies. It's not my fault after all.

Mom says something I can't understand.

"I gotta tell ya, ma'am," he continues, "that was one of the finest cow dogs I ever seen. Your boy and that dog walked by my place last summer every time they went down to the canal to go swimmin'. One day we was tryin' to load a big bull, and he was tearin' the corrals down. That dog got after him and put him in the trailer in nothin' flat. Then another time, my old sow broke a panel in her pen, and I had six shoats runnin' loose. I was havin' one heck of a time tryin' to git 'em penned up, and the boy happened by. That dog penned every one of them pigs and was wantin' to do more. Yes, ma'am, he was quite a dog, and I'm really sorry . . ."

This time Mom interrupts in a stern voice. "Why don't you think it was rabies?" she demands.

"Well, ma'am, it . . . I'm real sorry. I knew you always kept him tied up, so I never thought nothin' about it. Doc Watson told me I had to come tell you. If I'd known he was ever let run loose, I woulda told you somethin' about it."

"What are you trying to tell me, Tony?" Mom is almost yelling.

"Strychnine, ma'am. I've had a lot of trouble with these town dogs that people let run loose all the time. They come down at night and chase my pigs and kill my chickens. I've shot a couple of 'em, but there's several I've never been able to catch. So I put some strychnine in some hamburger meat and dropped it around my pens. Like I said, ma'am, if I'd thought your dog might be let loose at night, I woulda told you. If we can find one, I'll buy your boy another one . . ."

The sick feeling in my stomach begins to feel like a big knot as I realize what he's saying. It's my fault after all! I double over in pain. If I hadn't turned him loose, he wouldn't have eaten the poisoned meat. I killed Tuffy.

"If your boy's here, I'll tell him, ma'am."

"No! I want you to promise me you won't tell him anything about it. I want you to go ahead and take the dog and bury him someplace. Then he'll think he was taken to the vet to be checked."

I can hear them walking to where Tuffy has been left since we covered him with a sheet this morning. I've stayed here close to him all day. Mom didn't even suggest I go to school, but she must think I've gone down by the drainage ditch to be alone.

I see the shock in Mom's face when I step from behind the toilet. She can tell I heard them talking. "I want to bury Tuffy myself," I say.

Mom kneels in front of me and takes me in her arms and hugs me close for a long time. "We'll help you bury him. Why don't we bury him down on the ditch bank, and we'll put up a cross for him."

A little while later I'm kneeling by the small grave in the cool evening twilight.

"I killed him, Mom. I let him loose so he could go out and play at night." A dampness rises up out of the drainage ditch causing me to shiver. "I knew he liked to go down around Tony's place because he liked to be around other animals just like me. But he never woulda killed any chickens or chased the hogs unless they got out. Then he would've just put them back in the pen. But he wouldn't have known not to eat the meat if he found it. He would've figured it was okay."

"It's not your fault, son," Tony interrupts, still leaning on the shovel he used to dig the grave. "If I hadn't put out the poisoned meat, or even if I'd told you about it, he'd still be okay."

"But you had to protect your farm, and you can't look out for everybody else's animals," Mom says. I can tell she is grieving too. "No, it's as much my fault as anyone's. I knew Scout was letting him loose, and I wasn't strict enough to make him stop."

I stand up, walk over to the edge of the ditch bank, pick up a big rock, throw it as high as I can, and watch as it sails high in an arch over my head then straight downward, plunging into the deep cut in the earth made to drain the unused irrigation water out of the land. Finally, it hits the shallow stream at the bottom with a dull thunk and disappears into the murky water.

I don't understand why things like this have to happen. It's certainly not Tuffy's fault. He didn't hurt anyone. He was just doing what he thought was the right thing to do, and he got killed for it. It's not fair.

As if she reads my thoughts, Mom says, "It's hard to explain things like this, but I still believe everything happens for the best, even though we can't understand. Tuffy hated being tied up. When we moved here, he had a smooth, black, shiny coat, a bright twinkle to his eye. He was a happy dog. But since we brought him here, he lost weight, his coat got rough, he wasn't happy at all."

"Of course, he wasn't happy," I interrupt, almost yelling. "He was being tortured by being tied up all the time."

Mom continues in her soft, steady voice. "I know. It's as if he would rather have been dead than tied to that chain."

"No, Mom," I yell. "Nobody wants to die. Nobody should ever have to die."

I turn and run away. Mom makes a move as if she's trying to stop me, but I won't let her. I just keep running.

CHAPTER 6

"Those big guys are havin' a Boy Scout meeting up at the church. I'll be glad when we're old enough to join the Scouts," Willy says.

"Yeah," says Bubba. "In big towns, they have Cub Scouts. If they had that here, we'd be old enough."

We are walking up the gravel road toward town. Our burr haircuts have already dried in the hot summer sun. But my shirt is still a little wet because I didn't dry off after swimming in the canal. I like to stay wet because then it keeps me cool for a while longer. We all walk like clowns walking on marbles because the gravel is so hot on our bare feet. Mrs. Frazier had told us we should wear shoes on the hot gravel, but by now the soles of our feet are tough as rawhide, and we'd each rather burn up than admit we couldn't take it.

"I'll be glad when they open the drugstore," Willy says. "Then we can go get an ice cream cone or soda."

"Well, it shouldn't be long now," adds Bubba. "My dad took me by there Saturday, and they already have the counter in and some stools where you can sit. Mr. Silliman told us they will be putting in the fountains this week."

I don't say anything because, even though I believe I've had ice cream before, it was when I was real young, and I don't remember what it tastes like. I've seen pictures of ice cream sodas, but I have never seen a real one. I can't imagine what those things taste like. But I don't want to show my ignorance, so I just keep quiet.

Bubba changes the subject by asking Willy if they have heard anything about his brother, who was wounded during a bombing raid on London.

"I think he'll be coming home pretty soon," Willy says.

"I wish I could be a pilot and fight the Germans." Bubba is back into his dreaming about fighting in the war.

"I wish I could fight in the underground," Willy says.

Bubba objects, "You have to be French to be in the underground."

"I'd rather be in the cavalry," I say, refusing to go along with Bubba's dream.

"Scout, when are you gonna give that up?" Willy teases. "You know there ain't no cavalry anymore."

"I know," I say. I remember when Uncle Jack had written us telling us that, and that they had transferred him into the Army Air Force where he had become a navigator on a B-17 Bomber. "But I'd still rather be in the cavalry," I insist.

"Come on, let's go over and look where the new drugstore is gonna be," Willy says. "We can see through the window."

It seems that all we ever do is daydream and wish and wonder what things are like that we've never seen. I'm getting bored with that.

"My mom told me to come straight home," I lie. "You guys go ahead. I'll see y'all later."

I still can't get used to Tuffy not running up to greet me when I reach the house, even though it's been eight months now, but I try not to think of it as I walk in the front door. As soon as I step inside, I hear a muffled whine as though someone is crying. I stop and listen. It's Mom in the kitchen.

"What is it, Mom? What's wrong."

She is sitting alone at the kitchen table with her hands over her face. She hadn't heard me come in. On the table in front of her is a typewritten letter beside a brown envelope. Embarrassed and biting her lip to stop crying, she grabs a dish towel hanging on the back of one of the kitchen chairs and tries to wipe her eyes dry.

"What's the matter?" I ask again, bewildered.

Still crying, she says, "Well, I may as well tell you. You'll find out anyway. This is a letter from the war department. Your Uncle Jack is missing in action. His plane was shot down over Austria. He may be a prisoner, or he may be dead." I've never seen Mom cry uncontrollably like this before.

She hides her face in her folded arms, face down on the table, sobbing, and I place my hand on her shoulder. "Don't worry, Mom. He's okay. He's not dead, and he's not a prisoner. He's with the underground, and he'll be home safe," I hear myself saying.

Mom stops crying and looks up at me in surprise. "What made you say that, Scout?"

I don't know what to say.

"Are you just trying to comfort me, or—No! That's not it. You mean it, don't you? Scout, you shouldn't say things like that. You shouldn't be saying things you can't possibly know." She sounds a little scared, and it worries me to think I'm doing that to her. I say the only thing I can think of to say—the truth.

"But, Mom, it's true. You'll see. I know. He wasn't hurt when he bailed out of his airplane. When he got on the ground, the underground people took him and hid him." My confidence has returned.

"Scout . . ." Mom is looking at me strangely.

"Mom, you have to believe me. He's okay. Someday he'll be back here with us. We'll all be together again. Uncle Jack and Dad and even ol' Paint will be there. You just wait. You'll see I'm right."

Mom is staring at me, shaking her head, holding the dish towel over her open mouth as though she is scared. Finally, she says, "Scout, I know times have been hard on all of us. This war has made us all think strange things."

"You do believe me, don't you, Mom?"

She doesn't answer at first. She just looks at me, and then she says quietly, "How did you know these things?"

I'm stumped. I don't know how I knew. "I just know," I say. Then, I remember it was sort of like a dream. But I can't remember where or when it was—maybe about a month ago. I saw Uncle Jack's face with that friendly grin that pulls his mouth sideways. He was wearing his aviator cap, and he winked at me, and I knew he had been shot down and was with the underground.

"How do you know?" Mom is asking me again. But I'm afraid she'll think I'm crazy if I tell her what I remember. How can I explain in a way anyone will believe me? I wish I hadn't said anything.

"I just know," I repeat, and again I run away before she can say anything.

* * *

"I'm sorry to hear about your brother, Mrs. McBride," I hear Reverend Johnson telling Mom while he shakes everyone's hand as they leave the church. I'm ahead of Mom in the crowd of people standing around talking and greeting one another, so they don't see me.

"I would be glad to come visit if you need consolation," Reverend Johnson is saying. The last person has just shaken his hand, and he turns his full attention to Mom. "It must be hard, you being alone with your husband in Fort Bliss."

"Oh, I'm okay," Mom says. Then, "I am a little concerned about Scout, though. It seems he is having illusions or something. He refuses to believe Uncle Jack is missing."

"Oh?" questions the Reverend.

"Yes, he insists Jack has gotten into the protection of the underground, and that he'll be home safely."

I can't keep from clenching my teeth when the preacher says in a condescending voice, "Well, young boys have great imaginations." Then he adds with a touch of sternness, "You should keep an eye on him, though, and if it gets too wild, we may have to take some stern action."

"The old goat!" I say to myself. I knew he wouldn't believe me. I wish Mom wouldn't tell other people what I told her, especially the preacher. He'll have me the subject of a sermon next thing I know.

* * *

Mr. Adams, the principal, opens the door and quietly steps into Mrs. Whitley's fourth grade classroom. Mrs. Whitley is explaining how to divide a pie up and get several pieces. Finally, Mr. Adams coughs slightly to get her attention.

"Oh, I didn't see you come in."

"That's okay. I need one of your students." Then looking directly at me, "Scout, will you please come with me?"

I'm scared. I don't know what's happening, what I've done to get in trouble.

"You're not in trouble, Scout," Mr. Adams says, as if he's reading my mind. I relax. "It's your father. He's dying. I hope you can get there before it's too late."

I feel as if someone has hit me in the stomach, and I don't remember much of what happened next—how I got to the hospital—who brought me here to his room.

I don't recognize him at first. His face is a sickly gray. His eyes are partially open but appear to be clouded. His breathing is rapid and uneven, and he is breathing into some sort of mask with a balloon on the bottom that keeps blowing up and down every time he inhales or exhales. His thinning hair seems wet from sweat and is plastered back on his head.

Mom is holding his hand, looking at him intently. I go over and sit in a steel folding chair in the corner. Sis reaches over and touches my hand, her face streaked with tears. "Pray, Scout. Pray like you've never prayed before."

I don't feel like praying. I'm too mad. I'm mad that I can't cry like she does. I feel like I would rather cuss than pray. I pull my hand free, slip out of the chair, and walk as quietly as the rage inside me will let me out into the long white hallway with its shiny white linoleum floor. The odor of alcohol and ether is everywhere. I feel I have to get some fresh air, or I'll be sick.

I find my way past the admitting desk, out the front door, and down the tall concrete steps onto the lush green lawn in front of St. Anthony's Hospital.

The smell of the fresh cut green grass makes me feel a little better. All of that green soaks up some of the anger. I haven't seen many lawns like this. With the heat and lack of water in the desert, only rich people or hospitals can have this kind of grass. Leaning against the lone elm tree in the middle of the green, I look up at Franklin Mountain back behind the hospital and then at the puffy white thunderheads building beyond in the blue desert sky.

"Pray . . ." Sis had said. I've never prayed in my life. Oh, I always bow my head and close my eyes in Sunday school or church when the teacher or preacher prays, but I've never prayed myself. I never tried to talk to God like the preacher had said we're supposed to.

I've never asked God to forgive me when I've made some stupid mistake. I always figured He knew what happened, and He knew if I felt guilty or if I needed forgiving. I never asked God to give me anything or to do something for me. I've sure wished and hoped awful strong a few times. But I never figured there was any need in asking. He knew what I wanted, and if He thought it was the right thing, my wish would come true. If not, then I'd just have to learn to live without it.

To tell the truth, I don't even know what God is. There have been several times when I felt that presence, that magic that makes me feel good and that everything will be okay. Is that God? I wonder. It sure hasn't been anything like the way Reverend Johnson describes God when he's preaching and yelling up in front of the church. He makes God sound like a mean old man. Mean as old Vernon Delaney maybe.

Now, am I supposed to all of a sudden ask him to let Dad live? Would God let him live just because I asked?

If I had asked God, would that have kept our family from losing the farm and being torn apart at the beginning of the war? If I'd asked, would that have kept Dad from having to go to Fort Bliss to work? Would it have kept us from having to move to town? Would it have kept me from having to leave ol' Paint behind at the Harmons' or Tuffy from dying? Would it have kept us from getting hailed out in the first place?

But how could I have known to ask, since I didn't know it was going to hail before it did?

In the shade of the big elm tree, looking up at the rolling clouds, I ask aloud, "What am I supposed to do? If getting down on my knees and goin' on like Preacher Johnson will save Dad, I'll sure do it. What should I do?" I can feel my voice quiver.

I stand very still staring at the clouds, trying to get an answer. Suddenly, a dust devil whirlwind kicks up by the tree, bends its branches, and blows my hat off. The hat is carried high in the air, and then, as suddenly as it started, the whirlwind stops. My hat settles in the middle of the highway that runs beside the hospital. I dash to pick it up.

Spat! Fwoop! Too late. A big shiny black sedan speeds right on by, without any indication it saw the hat. Looking after the disappearing black monster, I stand in the middle of the road and try to shake out the creases and dirt. Rubbing my elbow on the mutilated brim to wipe off some of the black marks, I look back at the clouds, "If that's supposed to be some kind of message, I sure didn't understand it," I say out loud.

I'm standing at the bottom of the high concrete stairs leading up to the front door of the hospital trying to figure how I'll explain what happened to my hat when I feel it. It's that same presence, that same indescribable closeness that I feel from time to time. It doesn't talk out loud, but sometimes it tells me things in very clear unmistakable words. It's the same presence that told me about Uncle Jack, and now, suddenly, I know Dad will be all right.

I run up the stairway and through the front door so I can go tell Mom and Sis and Junior, but when I hear the loud "clack" of my boot heels on the hard white linoleum floor, I stop dead still. I can't tell them, I remember. If I do, they'll ask how I know, and then they won't believe me.

I sneak back in the alcohol- and ether-soaked room to find Mom has dozed off, still sitting in the straight backed chair with her head resting on the edge of the bed, still holding Dad's hand in hers.

Sis and Junior have gone to the cafeteria to get a coke.

On the other side of the bed, I stand watching the balloon grow big and then shrink, grow and shrink. It seems the breathing has slowed some and is more regular.

I reach out and touch the big calloused hand lying limp on the white sheet. I put one of my hands inside the huge palm, and with my other, I close the limber fingers so that it looks like my hand has disappeared. Suddenly, the big hand becomes tense, and the fingers tighten on my hand.

Dad stirs and opens his eyes. He looks at me blankly as though he's getting his bearings. Then, after a long while, he winks at me.

"Dad, they said you may die," I whisper.

He turns loose my hand and, taking care not to wake Mom, pulls off the ugly oxygen mask. A familiar twinkle appears in those gray eyes.

"Not today, Son. Not this time. I got a few more cats to skin and a few fish to fry yet before I check out of this old world." His whisper is slow and raspy.

"I was scared."

"What were you scared of?"

"I thought you were gonna die just like Tuffy. I don't think I could take that."

"Sure you could take it." There's a touch of surprise in his voice.

"No, I couldn't, Dad. If you died too, I know I just couldn't take it."

He replaces the oxygen mask over his face and breathes like he is gathering strength. Then, when he takes it down, he looks at me hard. "What you gonna do, die too?" He places the mask back on his face, but he continues to look at me hard, daring me.

Finally, I look away. "Dad, do you believe in God?"

His face starts to get red. As he pulls the mask away, his whisper is harsh. "What is this? You gonna try to get me saved before I die?"

"No, Dad, no, nothing like that. It's just that . . ." The words stick in my throat.

Dad's expression softens a little, and I think, for just a second anyway, that he understands. He breathes in the mask, then his look gets hard again. "You gotta understand that just because I didn't die this time don't mean I won't die someday. We all die sometime, and we never know when it's gonna be. If that happens, it's no reason for you to stop livin'. You'll die someday too, but your life is still ahead of you, and you gotta keep goin' till that time comes, no matter what happens to me." He squeezes my hand hard and pulls on it making me look at him. "You understand that?"

What he really means is am I man enough to face it? When I hesitate, he jerks my arm again for emphasis.

"Yes, sir," I whisper, as I meet his gaze, but I'm not at all sure I mean it.

* * *

Crash! It sounds like glass on the cement floor. "God damn it, I can't do nothin' right any more."

Mom and I both appear in the kitchen at the same time. Dad is standing in the middle of the kitchen with the broom in one hand and dust pan in the other, looking down, at the broken china cup, cursing to himself.

"Let me clean it up," Mom offers.

"No, you get outta the way. I broke it; I can clean it up."

Mom steps back, putting her hand out in front of me, signaling for me to stay out of the way and keep quiet. "The doctor doesn't want you bending over like that. Let me get it swept up off the floor," she insists.

"To hell with that damned doctor! What am I supposed to do, rot doin' nothin' for the rest of my life? I been sittin' around so much waitin' to get well, I can't even pour myself a cup of coffee without makin' a mess. I think if I'd get out and do some work I'd feel a lot better."

"Now, you know they said if you try to do too much too soon you may have another attack, and next time it could kill you. Besides, getting all upset like this is just as bad. Now will you please sit down over there, calm down, and let me clean this up?"

Resignedly, Dad hands the broom to Mom and the dust pan to me. "Here, help your mom." Then, more to himself than to me or Mom, as he moves toward a chair at the kitchen table, "I don't know. They tell me to keep calm, but it seems to me just sittin' around like this is more aggravatin' than if I was out doin' a hard day's work." Then, instead of sitting down, he turns to Mom. "If I don't do somethin', I'm gonna explode. I don't care what those damned doctors say. I'm gonna get outside and at least walk around and get some fresh air. Scout, get my tobacco and cigarette papers outta the bedroom, and we'll walk down to the drainage ditch."

I look at Mom. She'd told all us kids to not aggravate Dad and be sure he doesn't overdo. She looks at Dad a long time, then finally turns to take the dust pan out of my hand and nods assent.

"Just to the drainage ditch and back. You stay right with him all the time. If he has any problems at all, you come get me, no matter what he says. You understand?"

I'm back in a flash with the cigarette makings. I'm not sure who is more excited, me or Dad. He's been home from the hospital for almost a month now after spending six weeks in the hospital. I was really glad when he first got home, but he's been getting more and more restless. He's no fun to be around when he's like that. Maybe now he'll be a little easier to get along with.

As we walk out the back door, I try to take Dad's arm to steady him, but he shoves me away. "I'm not that weak," he says. He walks the short distance from the house to the edge of the cotton field that borders the north side of our yard where he stands slump-shouldered rolling a cigarette.

The field has been a dull red color since the crew of pickers came through with their long sacks trailing over their shoulders as their fast-moving hands stripped away the white fluff. I can see an occasional wisp of white that was missed or a dried leaf flapping in the fall wind still clinging to its stiff, unbending stalk. The growing season is all over now. I remember during the summer how I would notice every day that a plant had grown or see a new bloom or boll had appeared, and later it would burst open revealing its white fruit, the precious cotton which was the reason for it all. But the stalks have stopped growing and changing. They no longer bend with the wind; they are dead now, skeletons, waiting to be plowed under to make way for the new crop to be planted in the spring.

As he takes a deep drag on the cigarette and blows the smoke out, I can tell Dad is thinking about our hailed-out cotton crop and the farm he worked so hard and loved so much. That's all over too. Nothing can be done to change what happened now. I want to say something to comfort him, but I know I feel the same pain he does, and I can only bite my lip.

After a while, he squares his shoulders and turns his back on the field, facing toward me and the bare ground lying behind the house. "You know," he says, pointing behind me, "there's a lot of unused ground here. If we had a little chicken wire and a few cedar posts, we could build a chicken pen, and then maybe next spring we can get some baby chicks and even dig up some of this ground and plant a garden. It won't be much of a farm, but at least we can get something growing around here."

It sounds like a good idea, but Mom's warnings are still ringing in my ears. "Dad, Mom said you're not supposed to overdo," I hear myself saying.

"Well, how's about you do the work, and I'll be the foreman. You know, foremen don't work anyway. They just boss people around." With a wink, he puts his arm around my shoulder, and we walk slowly down to the drainage ditch.

* * *

By spring the twenty-five little yellow baby chicks have been ordered from the Sears Roebuck catalog. Dad has rounded up some setting hens too. Bought them from Mrs. Hillis. Dad said the hens would adopt the chicks we ordered, and we wouldn't have to buy a kerosene brooder to keep them warm until they got big enough live on their own.

Dad brought home some wild duck eggs too, and put them under the old setting hens. He found the eggs under a bridge while he was working on his new job. The job, which he took over Mom's protest, is ditch rider for the conservancy district.

People who don't know better think a ditch rider is someone who rides a horse up and down the ditch bank. They don't know that Dad's district is over thirty miles long. It would take him three or four days to cover it on horseback. Sometimes he needs to travel from one end to the other and back again in one day. That's the reason he drives a pickup. Besides, he has to haul head-gate boards and hooks and other materials with him.

To the farmers, the ditch rider is an important person because he is the only person in the county with authority to give them permission to use some of the precious water from the community canals.

I really enjoy going with Dad when he travels up and down the valley in the old pickup, rattling and bouncing over the rutted dirt roads, checking the canals, the water levels, talking to the farmers, deciding when they can use the water to irrigate their cotton crop. Then sometimes he will lower the head gates to back the water up so a farmer can open the flume that lets water run from the canal into his own irrigation ditch which carries it to his field and thirsty crops.

There's usually a lot of other talk too—talk about the best time to water, how often to water, what kind of fertilizer to use, how much, when to put it on. Then, of course, there's always talk about the war.

When I'm with Dad on his runs, I can tell he likes to linger, remembering and missing our farm over by Acala, wishing he could farm his own farm again. Sometimes, he will pick up a hoe and chop cotton along with the other hands, or help an irrigation hand get his ditch set to distribute the water just right. Watching him makes me miss the farm that much more.

I guess riding the ditch is second best. Anyway, I'm always glad to do anything to get out of town. It sure beats sitting around wishing ol' Paint was here and wishing we could go riding in the sandhills.

Today, though, Dad seems anxious to finish his rounds and get back home. He even says we're leaving early. "I want to get to the post office before it closes. Those baby chicks should come in today," he says.

Junior is waiting for us as we drive into the front yard. "The ducks are hatchin'!" he yells as soon as we're close enough.

"Well, those ol' hens are gonna have more than a few ducks to worry about," Dad says as he reaches in the back of the pickup and lifts out the flat box with holes all the way around the sides and hands it to Junior. "Put these in the kitchen to keep them warm, and then after dark, we'll put a few under each hen so they'll think all their eggs are hatchin.'"

"Oh, Rosie!" Junior says to the grumpy old Rhode Island Red hen as he reaches into her nest and she pecks him on the hand. Lifting her gently, Junior points, "There, see." Looking over his shoulder, I can see a small yellow fuzzy duck sitting among broken egg shells. He shakes his head and blinks his eyes to adjust to the light let in when Junior lifted Rosie. "See that broken egg there? The little duck in it keeps wiggling to get free. Pretty soon he'll be out too. And, look, you can see where all the other eggs have at least a little hole pecked in them from inside."

Suddenly, the duckling in the broken egg Junior had pointed to struggles violently, causing the shell to break further, and he falls out, flopping on the bottom of the nest. "Hello, little duck," I say. "Welcome to the world." I want to reach in and pick him up, but Dad has told us not to be picking them up until they are up and walking around good.

As I crawl in bed, I try to dream about the golden little ducks, but the dream is blurred with the image of that old rattlesnake wanting me to see something I can't understand and the little runted puppy that never got a chance to nurse his mother. Then I see ol' Paint, and I want to go to her and tell her about the little ducklings, but she fades away before I can reach her.

"Look, Rosie's coming off the nest!" Junior yells. He and I have been taking turns watching all day. Dad had said she might come off if she thinks all the chicks are hatched. We had put five of the ordered chicks under each hen last night, and then we put the rest of them with the hens this morning early. Several of the chicks have wandered out of the nest to eat and drink from the trays we had set out for them.

As the big red hen clucks and steps carefully out of the nest, a flurry of white and yellow fluff dashes out ahead of her. The chicks all head for the feed tray and the ducks for the water, stumbling over one another, trying to climb in and trying to swim in the shallow tray. Rosie strides away from the trays, clucking to call her big unusual brood, scratching in the dust to find food for them. A few of the chicks follow, pecking where she has scratched, but the ducklings stay at the water, and the other chicks, obviously hungry, scratch and peck at the feed tray for the grainy chick mash Dad bought for them.

Clucking and scratching furiously, Rosie is obviously flustered because she can't seem to get the attention of most of her young ones. Finally, she returns close to the feed and water trays and settles down, clucking softly. One yellow duckling struggles out of the water tray and runs under her wing for protection. Soon the others follow, one at a time, until all are safe under the mama hen. Then one sticks his head out to look around at the strange world of the chicken pen we have built for them. Rosie continues to cluck softly as the chicks and ducklings learn to make their way from under her umbrella of protection to the feed and water trays.

Mom and Sis have joined us to watch the miracles of new life taking place in what was barren ground last fall.

Mom jabs Dad in the side playfully. "I might have known. There's no way you can be kept from farming. But I have to admit I didn't see how you were going to get anything started in this place."

"We should put up a sign calling it McBride's Chicken and Duck Ranch," Sis says.

I can't join in their excitement completely. "If it's gonna be a ranch, we need a horse," I say. "We ought to build a corral and bring ol' Paint to town too." I can see the pain in Mom and Dad's faces as they try to smile like I was joking, but their silence tells me they know as well as I do that a few chickens and ducks don't make a farm. They'll never replace ol' Paint or Tuffy.

Sis wheels quickly and walks into the house. As she goes in the door, I can see her wipe a tear from her eye.

Junior kicks a small rock loose from the bare adobe dirt and chunks it over the chicken pen as hard as he can. Then, with his head hanging down, bouncing as he walks, a hand in each pocket, he heads off toward the drainage ditch. I glare at Mom and Dad watching Junior walk away. For a minute it feels good to punish them, to make them understand how I feel. But then, when I look back at Junior sadly going off alone, I suddenly feel ashamed and guilty for what I'd just said. Why don't I keep my mouth shut and my feelings to myself? Why do I have to try to make them feel empty and miserable all the time just because I do?

CHAPTER 7

I'm sitting on the back step, and the smell of chicken frying for Sunday dinner drifts through the screen door. Along with it drifts the sound of Mom and Dad arguing in the kitchen.

"Just because I'm a woman is no reason why I can't do that job every bit as good as any man."

"Well . . ." I can tell Dad is trying to think fast. "It just don't seem right, a woman working for the railroad."

Mom is livid. "They said taking the census was a man's job too, but when I got through, they didn't find near as many problems with my reports as they did with all those men that did El Paso and Culbertson counties."

"Well . . ."

"Nobody ever said it doesn't seem right for me to be a school-teacher. Now you tell me why? What's the difference?"

"You know I don't like you workin' anyhow—no matter what . . ."

"I was working when you met me. Teaching school. And it makes no difference what you like. I've had to work from time to time just to make ends meet. Just like you do. Now what's the difference?" She doesn't even give Dad a chance to answer, she just starts in again. "Being a stationmaster requires a good head, and you always said I've got a good head. The pay's good too, Boots. Not only that, they have living quarters above the station, so we can save on the rent."

That clinches it. I can only hear Dad mumbling, but I know Mom will be going to work for the Southern Pacific Railroad, and we'll be moving into the depot at McNary, Texas.

I try to remember what McNary is like. I know it's a lot smaller than Fort Hancock. At least there won't be as many people there. I'm sure it'll be a lot better than this place. I don't like this big town. It must have two hundred people in it.

*   *   *

By Thanksgiving we've moved to McNary.

Sitting in the kitchen of our second story living quarters above the depot, I look out over the settlement where we live now.

There's Hank's Grocery Store, which also serves as post office and filling station. Then there's Tally's Café and Orville's Garage. Across the highway is the cotton platform which sets real close to the railroad spur, and then on the other side of the tracks is an old abandoned cotton gin.

The depot where we live is about a quarter mile south of the cotton platform. The huge wooden frame two-story yellow building with dark brown trim can be seen for several miles in every direction because McNary sits on the crest of a hill up above the valley where all the farms are. Few people know that this little wide spot in the middle of the desert up above the Rio Grande Valley on Highway 80 is the shipping point for one of the largest cotton-growing areas of the world. At least that's what Mr. Akins, the ag teacher, told us. During cotton-picking season, all the cotton gins in the valley haul their bales up here and place them on the platform so Mom can make arrangements for having them loaded into boxcars, and the trains take them back east to the mills that weave it into all types of cloth.

McNary is also a major siding for the Southern Pacific Railroad. There are three tracks. One is the spur for the boxcars to be parked by the platform so the bales can be loaded. Then the second track is used for trains to pull off the main line for passing trains going the other direction.

There's a telephone outside on the northeast corner of the station for train conductors to call the dispatcher for orders. Sometimes at night I can hear them shouting over the phone, reading back orders and getting the exact time so they can check their watches. It won't do for their watches to be off, even a few seconds, because if they're off on their time, they might meet a train coming the other direction in the middle of the night.

Across the tracks from the depot is an old car garage with the roof blown off and some small pens where someone had kept a horse or cow sometime in the past.

Beyond the town limits all I can see is desert extending eastward toward the blue mountains and westward toward the valley farms. The greasewood and mesquite bushes with an occasional yucca plant sticking its green daggers toward the sky here and there give the sandy desert a grayish-green color.

As I look out over the distance, I feel relaxed and comfortable. It's the most comfortable feeling I've had since we left the farm. At least here, there aren't a lot of people around watching everything you do. If I had ol' Paint, we could ride eastward all day and not see another person.

I've been thinking about just that for days, and finally, at this moment, I manage to screw up my courage enough to bring it up.

"Dad, if I fix up that old abandoned garage and those pens across the tracks, do you think we could bring ol' Paint up here to live with us?" It's been three years since we had to leave the farm, and although I've seen Paint from time to time, it's just not the same as having her with me all the time.

"Son," Dad says, dragging his words out like it makes him sad to have to say them, "do you know what it costs to feed a horse? It's different when you live on a farm. You have other livestock to feed, and you grow most of your own. But, up here on the mesa above the farmland, we'd have to buy and haul every bit of hay and oats to feed her."

"I'll get a job and earn the money to feed her. I'll haul the hay myself."

To my surprise, Mom becomes my ally. "Why don't you think about it, Boots?" she urges. "If we fix up those corrals, we could get another milk cow too. I think I miss the fresh milk and butter we had on the farm more than anything else."

"Do you realize what it'll cost to feed a horse and cow too?" Dad asks.

But Mom is insistent. "If we get another good cow like old Blackie, there will be more milk than we can drink, and we can sell the extra to some of the folks here in McNary. Scout can deliver it."

I get so excited I want to jump up and down and yell, but I bite my lip instead. It seems too good to be true, and I'm afraid if I get too excited something will go wrong. With a straight face, I quickly excuse myself like I have to go to the toilet, and instead of heading for the privy behind the depot, I cross the tracks to examine the old garage made of used crossties to see what it will take to get ready so ol' Paint can come home. Don't get too excited, I keep telling myself. But it's impossible to still the excitement in my chest, and I can't help trying to imagine what it will be like when it's fixed up and ol' Paint is here.

I can see ol' Paint in the big semitrailer full of cattle now, and a tingling sensation runs down my spine. Is it really about to happen? Festus Gibbs is taking a load of cattle to Van Horn, and he's agreed to bring Paint along and drop her off on the way. He is backing the big cattle truck down in the barrow ditch and up against the railroad berm where the bank is especially steep. That way Paint will be able to walk out of the trailer without even having to jump.

Suddenly, I realize I don't know how to feel. I've been so scared something would go wrong I've been unable to let myself feel anything. So many things have happened since ol' Paint and I were separated, so many disappointments, so many times I wanted to cry but couldn't, so many times I gritted my teeth and swallowed my feelings, that now I can't remember how to let myself feel.

When she sees me, Paint sticks her head over the side board and nickers. Then, when Festus removes the rear panel, she trots off the trailer and across the railroad tracks to where I'm standing with Dad. I don't know what to say, but I guess that's just as well, because anything I might try would probably stick in my throat.

"Bill Harmon gave this to me to bring along too, but see'n as how you've growed, I don't see where it's gonna do you much good," Festus says as he stands there holding my old saddle.

"You may as well take it on down to Van Horn with you, and see if you can sell it to someone who's got a little kid," Dad says, and he reaches over and bops me on the shoulder. "This one ain't so little anymore."

Paint nudges me and says, "Aren't you gonna get on?"

I can tell she wants to feel me on her back just as I have longed to feel that fullness, that closeness and communication of having her between my legs. Taking a hand full of her mane just at the base of her neck, I surprise myself by jumping flat-footed, to land astraddle her back in that comfortable place just behind her withers. We stay there a minute feeling each other, then I nudge her with my left knee, and we ride off toward the sandhills, feeling as one again, just like old times.

"Hey, ain't you even gonna use a bridle?" Festus Gibbs yells. But we don't pay any attention. We're absorbed in feeling that old oneness, that old closeness, that freedom again as she moves at a fast trot through the sand dunes, turning here and there as I lean one way or the other, faster or slower according to the pressure of my knees.

We cross the arroyo that runs just south of the depot and ride into a mesquite grove out of sight from everyone where I put my hand on Paint's neck and she stops. I slide off and walk along side her. "Welcome home, ol' gal," I'm finally able to whisper.

"You have gotten a lot heavier," she grumps, as she hangs her head over my shoulder so I can hug her neck. I get a feeling like I want to cry. Which is strange. It doesn't seem right to want to cry when you're so happy.

It's nice and cool sitting on the freight cart here in the shade of the depot. I like to hang around here during the heat of the day and count cars on the trains as they fly by. Across the tracks, ol' Paint is standing with all her weight on three legs, her left hind leg relaxed, sleeping in the shade of the barn we made out of the old garage. It's too hot to be out riding, particularly since I have to ride bareback now that I've outgrown my saddle. When I ride bareback, Paint sweats and my Levi's get wet. Then Mom makes me take a bath and change clothes.

I've been saving the money I earn sweeping the store and stacking groceries on shelves for Hank. I have forty dollars saved now. All I need is ten more dollars, and I'll have enough to buy that Little Wonder saddle from Barney Farrell. I had admired it when we lived in Fort Hancock because it's just like one Dad had shown me at the saddlery in El Paso a long time ago. Since he hurt his back and can't ride anymore, Barney had told me he'll sell it to me if I can raise fifty dollars. Ever since then, I've been saving nickels and dimes that Mom and Dad have given me to buy candy and sodas. Working for Hank at ten cents an hour has helped a lot, but I only get to work about five hours every Saturday, so it will take almost the rest of the year before I'll have enough. I've got to keep saving, though. Whoever heard of a cowboy without a saddle?

"Hey, kid!" It's a soldier leaning out a window of one of the passenger cars on the troop train that's pulled into the siding to wait for the 2:30 mail flier. There have been a lot of westbound troop trains sending more help to fight the Japs now that Germany has surrendered.

"Hey, kid!" he says again, as I look up from my daydream, "Is that a café over there?"

"Yeah, why?"

"Go get me some candy."

"I ain't got no money!" I stand up and pull out my pockets so he can see.

"Here! Here's a dollar. Go get me all the candy that will buy. Hurry, before this train pulls out!"

I dash up, and as I reach for the dollar, three more are thrust in my hand. "Get me some too" I hear from voices at the end of each arm.

I'm running as hard as I can, but every time I pass a door on one of the Pullman cars, I get another three or four dollars stuck in my hand. "Hurry, kid!" they yell, as they stick the bills in my hand.

I can hear the whistle of the flier as I pass the cotton platform and start to cross the highway. The troop train will be moving out in just a few minutes. I look at all the money in my hands. There has to be almost ten dollars here. Maybe there's enough for me to pay for that saddle. I stop in the middle of the highway and look back. The troop train hasn't moved yet. I see what looks like a thousand heads sticking out the doors and windows of the olive-green Pullman cars all looking at me, waiting. What difference does it make if I keep the money? I think to myself. They don't know me. That train will be pulling out in just a minute, and they'll never see me again.

I start to stick the money deep in my pocket and walk away, but I can feel all two thousand eyes on my back. I stop and turn around and see them all looking at me. They're all wearing uniforms, and one of them has a lopsided grin that kind of reminds me of Uncle Jack. Again I start to walk away, but I know I'll never forget what I've done if I don't help the troops all I can. It's the only chance I've really ever had during this long dreary war to do anything to help. I dash for the store.

The candy counter in Hank's store is right by the front door. I'm so out of breath I can hardly yell. "Hank! Quick! Give me all the candy this money will buy!"

"How much you got? What's this for?"

Between puffs, "I don't know how much. The troop train. The soldiers. Hurry, the flier just went by. It'll be pulling out quick."

Somehow Hank understands my breathless, excited speech. He takes the wad of dollar bills in his hands as though he's weighing it to see how much is there, then he drops it on the counter behind him and grabs some boxes.

"Here! Here's a carton of Milky Ways and two cartons of Almond Hersheys. Can you carry all that?"

I grab the three boxes and run out the door. Thank goodness, the troop train is backing out to the east instead of going straight west out the other end of the siding. I'd forgotten the local is sitting on the west end of the siding, blocking the troop train, waiting for it to get out of the way.

I cross Highway 80, pass the cotton platform, and when I get between the tracks, I run as hard as I can, carrying the candy. I see the engine clear the switch and stop while the brakeman throws the lever and the clear signal is given. I can see the steam shoot up above the smoke stack as the fireman comes down on the whistle. A few seconds later, the scream hits my ears. I'm still running as hard as I can. Black smoke comes out the chimney, steam spurts out on both sides by the wheels. I can hear the first "huff" and see a smoke ring rise above the chimney as the big eight wheels spin on the steel track then a short pause and another "huff" as the engine starts to move toward me.

"Go slow, go slow!" I yell. But I can't wave my arms. If I do, I'll drop the candy.

The engine is moving slowly as it huffs by me. "What ya got there, kid?" I hear the fireman yell as he goes by. Beyond him, I can see heads and waving arms sticking out all the doors and windows of the line of Pullman cars. The heat waves make it look eerie.

I stop and put the candy on the ground as the first Pullman gets close. A soldier is on the step hanging on to the hand rail, with his free hand reached out as far as he can. I put a Milky Way in it.

"Hey, kid! What about mine?" I hear from inside the car. I try to toss one in the window, but there are so many heads, it bounces off one and lands on the ground.

I put three bars in the next hand that comes close. I can tell by the clickety-clack of the wheels, the train is picking up speed fast. I start tossing the bars to the hands sticking out the windows and doors. Most of them are caught.

I look down, and I have a whole carton of Hershey bars left. The last car is about to go by. The train is really moving now. I can feel the wind pulling me with it, and the wheels make a steady roar instead of the slow clicking. I pick up the whole box and throw it. My aim is good. It sails over the head of the soldier standing on the step in the door and skips over the heads of the troops inside. I can see candy bars flying, arms and hands grabbing along the full length of the Pullman.

I stand gasping for breath, watching the last Pullman speeding away from me when the back door opens. A soldier steps on the rear platform and waves at me. Then he throws something in the air and points for me to get it.

I'm too tired to run, but I walk, keeping my eye on the little brown package that has fallen between the rails as the train disappears to the west.

With the train gone, the desert is quiet again. A dust devil kicks up and makes its way over the sand dunes away from the tracks. Even though it's hot, the breeze stirred up by the dust devil feels cool and refreshing on my sweat-covered face. I hear some crows having a squabble. I look up to see one land on the tin roof over the cotton platform. He's got a piece of a candy bar he's picked up by the tracks in his beak.

I pick up the brown thing the soldier had thrown. It's a ten-dollar bill tied around a Hershey's almond wrapper.

CHAPTER 8

"Have you heard?" Willy Frazier is peddling his bicycle as fast and hard as he can over the ruts in the hard dry adobe ground.

"Heard what?" I'm standing on the only sidewalk in town in front of Silliman's Drugstore and Soda Fountain. Dad has brought me into town with him so I can get a haircut while he goes to a meeting of the conservancy board. He dropped me off, and I have an extra dime, so I'm trying to decide whether to get a frosted coke or a strawberry sundae before I go to the barber shop. I hate going to that barber shop more than anything, so I want to put it off as long as I can. I'd rather be home practicing my roping with Paint.

"They dropped a bomb," Willy says, "a great big bomb. Big enough to wipe out a whole city. They dropped it on the Japs. The war's gonna be over real quick."

That means Uncle Jack will be coming home, I'm thinking. We still haven't heard a word from him, and sometimes I see Mom looking at his picture and crying. It has been over two years since she got a letter saying he was missing in action after his plane went down.

The way she looks makes me feel so bad I can't keep from telling her not to worry, that Uncle Jack will be home someday. I tell her that even though I know it upset her the first time I did it. Maybe it even scares her a little. But lately, it seems like it makes her feel better, so I keep telling her that I know he'll be home some day.

"They call it an atom bomb," Willy is saying, still peddling away, still going on about the end of the war. "It's only about the size of a baseball, but it's so powerful it blew up a whole city."

"How can they make a bomb that small?"

"I don't know, but they say with all the new science there's gonna be a lot of changes now, changes we never thought of."

"Things sure do seem to be happening fast in Fort Hancock now that the war's over," Mom is saying, as she cleans the breakfast dishes. "Henry Brown bought the old Franklin store and tore out all the inside walls. He's going to install benches with a screen at the lower end and a projector room by what used to be the front door, and Hudspeth County will have its first picture show."

She's trying to put on a good front, trying not to show how much her mind is still on Uncle Jack. It's been almost three months since that bomb was dropped and nearly two months since the war was officially over, and we still haven't heard a word from him.

"I know," says Dad. "They've paved the road up the hill to the railroad track, so now it's real easy to get up to the post office, and Old Man Hoover is a big businessman now. He's building a new fancy cotton gin on the south edge of town."

Junior joins in, "Yeah, and at school, they're building a new woodworking shop and home economics center."

"Now they're building more and bigger ditches too," Dad observes as he rolls a cigarette. "They're trying to reach land with the irrigation water that's never been farmed before. With the high price of cotton, everyone has gone crazy trying to clear new acreage. Bob Hillis is clearing that bunch of sandhills just east of the old Henson place. He'll never get nothing to grow in that sorry ground."

"I heard they're going to start opening the gate on the bridge across the river on Saturdays so the people from Mexico can come over here and trade at the stores on this side too," Mom says.

"Yeah," says Dad, "and we need lots of field hands over here to farm all this new land. It's got to where the border patrol hardly ever comes around anymore, and John Adiss is fixing up all those old adobe barracks down there on his place where Camp Ninety used to be, so there'll be some place for them to live."

"What's Camp Ninety? Was it an old fort?" Junior asks.

"No, it was an old CCC camp during the Depression. There's several other camps like that down the valley."

"Dad, with all this new land bein' put in . . ." I hesitate, I'm afraid to ask.

"What, Scout?" Dad's voice is impatient.

I swallow and blurt it out, "Will we be able to get another farm?"

Dad's face starts to get red, and Mom interrupts before he can say anything, "I don't think that's very likely. With your father being so sick, we haven't been able to save enough money to buy one, and since he's had a heart attack, no bank will ever give him credit. I think we're going to have to just get used to the idea that we're not going to be able to get another farm."

I look at Dad. The pain in his face tells me it's true, and I have to look away.

There is a long dead silence in the kitchen, but Dad's no quitter. "I talked to John Haskell the other day," he finally says. "He wants to get out of the dairy business. He wanted me to take three or four cows off his hands. He'll sell them to me on credit. I didn't think much about it at the time, but with all the new people coming into the area, they're gonna need all the milk they can get. If you boys'll do the feeding and milking, I'll see if I can work something out."

Mom seems excited. "This won't be like the chicken farm in town, Scout," she tries to reassure me. "You already have Paint and one milk cow. It'll give you a chance to earn some extra money."

"There's something else I been thinkin' about," Dad says with a quick glance at Mom. His look is so sheepish she can tell he's scared she won't agree. She looks at him hard, and he looks away, but he keeps talking. "Cold weather's coming on, and there's a meat shortage. People need meat as bad as they need milk. This is a great chance for us to buy a new ice box and stove. If we butcher a few beeves, I'm sure we can make enough in a few weeks." There's a sign of the old enthusiasm in his voice.

"You know you're not in any condition to go lifting big halves of beef around or to be bending over to skin a steer. Next thing I know we'll be having to haul you back to the hospital." Mom's got her stern voice working.

"Well, I've been doin' pretty good. I've only had two flare ups since my first attack. That's a hell of a lot better than those damn doctors ever thought I would. If it was up to them, I'd still be layin' in bed. Besides, I can have the boys help me do the liftin'. We can get a tripod so we can hang them with a block and tackle. I can carry it and all my butcher knives in the pickup. When I'm ridin' ditch, I get a chance to see every beef on every farm in the valley, and whenever they're ready to butcher, I can buy it, and with the pickup fixed up right, we can butcher it on the spot. We can quarter it and hang it in the warehouse here at the depot till it cools, then peddle the meat to the work camps on Saturdays and Sundays."

I can tell by looking at Mom that she's losing this one. She looks at him hard, and I can see the concern in her face, but she's come to accept that he feels better working and feeling useful than sitting around on his butt doing nothing. "You have to promise me you won't kill an animal without having one of the boys or somebody else to help you," she says finally.

"Okay. I promise," Dad says too quickly as he looks at her, trying to hide his surprise that he didn't get more argument.

Mom turns to Junior and me. "You heard that. I want both of you to help me keep tabs on him and be there whenever he slaughters anything."

I'm sitting on the front step of the depot trying to sort out all the talk. We're not ever going to get another farm, Mom said. I can't bring myself to go tell ol' Paint about this. I know she still hopes we'll get a farm someday. She likes it here a lot better than she did at Harmons', but she wants us to have a farm where we can all be together.

We'll probably enjoy milking and feeding the new cows. I already do most of the milking of Betsy now. But I know I can't tell her about Dad doing butchering. I've seen him slaughter a few animals before, and I don't like it. When Dad killed chickens for frying, sometimes he'd made me help pick them clean after he cut their heads off and dipped them in hot water to make the feathers come loose. I had to grit my teeth to keep from getting sick. He's never made me help butcher a beef, but I've watched enough to know it'll make me feel bad. I understand they have to butcher animals if we are going to have meat to eat, but it still doesn't seem right to me that anyone should ever have to die.

I'm so deep in my thoughts I hardly notice the 8:30 Greyhound as it stops down by Tally's Café and throws off the morning papers and then roars in a cloud of diesel smoke as it heads on east. But just as it draws even with the depot, it pulls off on the opposite side of the highway and stops. I watch as it sets there a minute then roars off in another cloud of smoke. I'm so engrossed in my misery that it doesn't dawn on me how unusual it is for the big bus to stop like that until I see a figure standing in the smoke on the other side of the highway.

"Hey, cowboy, you reckon a feller can get anything to eat around here?"

I'd know that voice anywhere! Then as the smoke clears, I see the sharp features, dark eyes and sideways grin. I can feel the tears welling up behind my eyes, but I bite my lip. "Uncle, Uncle Jack!" I shout so they can hear me up in the kitchen. I meet him in the center of the highway wanting to hug him, but I stop and salute because he's still in uniform, and because cowboys don't hug other men.

Uncle Jack grins and salutes me back. Mom, Dad, Sis, and Junior spill out of the depot while the two of us are still standing there like that, so close, yet not touching. Mom and Sis are both crying as they run up to him and throw their arms around him. I swallow the lump in my throat and drop my salute, but then it seems like I don't know what to do with my hands. Finally, I fold my arms in front of me so they won't ache so much from wanting to put them around Uncle Jack.

Dad shakes his hand. He seems unable to say anything for a moment, then he says, "Good to see you, Jack. You doin' all right?"

Just like it hadn't been more than a week since he'd seen him. I can see a muscle twitch in Dad's jaw.

"Doin' fine. How 'bout you, Boots?"

"Can't complain," Dad says.

I'm struck by that phrase, by how much there is that he feels is unnecessary to say, and I suddenly know there's plenty Uncle Jack may never say either.

"I guess you're surprised to see me, aren't you?" he asks, with that sheepish sideways grin as he turns back to Mom.

"Not really," Mom says through her grateful tears. "Scout has been so insistent that you'd be here, I had come to believe it myself."

"I was scared," Sis says. She's still crying too. "I was scared you were dead. When we heard about your plane crashing, and then we never heard from you . . ."

"I never wanted you to worry," Uncle Jack says. "But there was no way I could contact you after I was rescued by the underground. I was with them until the war ended, and then after that—"

I don't hear anymore after that, and I don't think Mom does either. She's looking at me with a funny expression. I don't know if she's scared or what.

* * *

Uncle Jack pulls off the highway and parks across from Rojalio's Bar. "You wait here," he says as he steps out of the '37 Chevy he bought from Dale Tolbert.

"Why can't I go with you?"

"'Cause your Mother would skin me alive if she found out I took you in there."

"Why do you drink so much?"

"Look, Scout, you're a wise kid for your age, and you're growin' up fast, but there's some things ain't any of your business, and you wouldn't understand if I told you. Now you just wait here, and I'll be back in a minute."

"Is it because of what happened in the war?" I persist.

"Just mind your own business," he says between clinched teeth as he slams the car door and strides across the highway into the bar.

It seems like an eternity before Uncle Jack comes out of the bar, but when he finally does, he's carrying a paper sack and some of the hard light in his eyes is gone. He smiles at me as he opens the car door, puts the beer on the floor behind the seat, takes one bottle out of the sack, and pulls an opener out of his pocket. I hear the gush of air as he peels the cap off. "Ahhh," he says after taking a long drag on the bottle. The malty smell of the beer fills the car, but I can smell whiskey on his breath too. He must have had a shot while he was in the bar.

Suddenly, the bar door swings open, and I'm surprised to see John Moseley, the song leader from church, come out with a bottle stuck under his left arm. Hanging on his right arm, giggling about something funny is Isabel Domínguez, her long black hair flowing over her shoulders. I'm surprised I didn't recognize Mr. Moseley's car parked by the side of the bar, but then I'd never expect to see him here anyway. In church he's always talking and praying about how bad it is to drink and dance or enjoy "pleasures of the flesh," as he puts it.

They're laughing and talking so much when they get in the car they don't know anyone else is around. They sure don't give any sign of seeing Uncle Jack and me. The blue sedan pulls out from the bar, but instead of heading toward town, it crosses the highway and heads east on the dirt road that leads through the sandhills up to the old Underwood place.

I'm wondering what they're going to do out there in that direction. It's about seven miles to the old abandoned ranch house, and there's nothing in between except sandhills. Uncle Jack takes another drag on the beer bottle as we sit watching the rising dust trail following the Moseley car as it disappears into the desert. "That old hypocrite son-of-a-bitch!" Uncle Jack says with a laugh.

Suddenly, but obviously too late, the bar door swings open again and Rojalio appears, white apron around his waist, waving frantically. "Hey, Señor Moseley," he yells. "You owe me ten bucks."

"Y'all comin' to church this Sunday?" Willy asks. He's leaning against the trunk of the big cottonwood as we wait for the bell to ring to tell us the lunch hour is over.

"Not if I can help it," says Bubba. "But my maw will probably make me. You gonna be there, Scout?"

"I don't know yet. Mom tries to make us go every Sunday even if she's too busy to go herself. I know that if he can, Junior'll probably try to make me go with him. He goes every time he gets a chance so he can sit and hold hands with his ol' girl friend. How come you ask? Somethin' special goin' on?"

Willy turns to face away from us as though he's embarrassed. "Naw, nothin'. I just wondered."

Mrs. Moseley doesn't come to our Sunday School class like usual. It's just me, Willy, Bubba, and Dee. The girls have all been put in another class. For some reason somebody decided boys and girls shouldn't have Sunday School together. Dee and Bubba are sparring in the corner, doing a little slap boxing. Willy is just sitting there kind of quiet. I ask him what's wrong, but he just tells me to shut up and leave him alone.

"Is this the intermediate boys class?" Mr. Moseley has just walked into the room. Dee and Bubba stop their horsing around and look at him. Bubba nods. Willy slumps down in his seat.

"Mrs. Moseley won't be here today, so I thought I'd take the opportunity to talk to you boys about something Brother Johnson asked me to check into," Mr. Moseley says. Willy turns and looks out the window. "You know, you boys are growin' up now, and it's about time you start lookin' ahead thinkin' about what you're gonna make of yourselves. It's also time you think about givin' your life to Christ and askin' Him to forgive you of your sins. You never know, you might get killed tomorrow, and if you haven't been baptized, you'll burn in the eternal fires of hell."

I steal a glance at Willy. He's still intent on looking out the window, but I can tell he knew this was coming.

"You boys are big enough to go up before the church and renounce your sins now. So, when Brother Johnson gives the invitation today, I want all of you to come on up to the front, and then we'll have a baptism next Sunday," Mr. Moseley says. Now all of us are shifting around uneasily in our seats. "Now let's have a word of prayer," Mr. Moseley says.

Everybody bows his head except me. I look at Mr. Moseley while he asks God to "lay a burden on these boys' hearts to renounce their sins and to give up their sins of the flesh." In my mind's eye, I can see the soft, brown flesh on the bare arms of Isabel Domínguez when she was all over him coming out of the Rojalio's Bar that day.

Finally, the prayer is over and Mr. Moseley leaves. All four of us are quiet, like we've just been hit with about two hundred pounds of cow manure. I look at Willy again. I can tell he's really worried. Finally, he looks at me and the others. "You guys goin' up to the front of the church?" he asks.

"Not me," Bubba says emphatically. "You wouldn't find me dead up there in front of all those people."

Dee's indecisive. "My mom's been talking to me about it, but she says I don't have to right now if I don't want to."

They all look at me. I don't know what to say, so I just look back at them. We file out of the classroom, and I begin to get a nervous feeling in the pit of my stomach because I'm wondering what's going to happen. I'm all mixed up. I need time to think about this thing. Mom's never said I have to join the church, and I don't feel like I've done anything bad that I need to be sorry about. I don't feel like getting up in front of the church and crying. Well, maybe I feel like crying, but it's sure not because I'm happy I've been saved. I'm scared.

The church service goes pretty much as usual. Reverend Johnson goes on about how, if we don't come up in front of the church and confess our sins, we'll all die and burn in hell. If we do come up, he promises we'll see heaven with its streets paved with gold where the lion lies down with the lamb and there is no pain or suffering or death.

No death, I think to myself, and I'm kind of interested. Tempted to go up there.

Now the congregation is singing, "*While Jesus whispers to you, come sinner, come! While we are praying for you, come, sinner, come!*"

Reverend Johnson continues to make his plea, speaking louder than the singing, his hands raised above his head, his eyes closed.

"Come up and take the load off your heart. Come up and accept Jesus as your savior . . ."

Willy, Bubba, and I are sitting together in the last row in back of the church. Dee has gone to sit by his mom. Willy is sitting next to the center aisle. Suddenly, Mr. Moseley appears, standing by Willy.

"You boys come on up now. Jesus is calling you."

Without looking back at us, Willy slips off the bench and walks up the aisle. I think I see his shoulders tremble as he walks up to the front.

Mr. Moseley takes Bubba by the arm. "Now is the time, Bubba. You go on up there too."

Bubba looks back at me questioningly, but the pressure is too strong. He slowly trudges up the aisle, a little runt with tall giants standing on each side of the aisle, singing loudly, and Reverend Johnson standing at the end of the aisle, shouting for him to confess his sins and be saved. Seeing how scared Bubba and Willy are, I feel like crying for them. Then I wonder if that's the reason people always cry when they go up front.

I can feel myself trembling as Mr. Moseley turns to me. "Come on, Scout." The command is so strong, I feel myself being pulled toward the aisle by some unseen force. But it's not the quiet magic force I've experienced sometimes. This one seems scary. Evil, maybe. I grab the seat and hold on. Mr. Moseley has captured me with his eyes, and I can't make myself look away from him. He reaches and grabs me by the arm. "Come on. Give your life to Jesus. It's time for you to be saved."

"No!" I yell.

I jerk my arm free and dart past Mr. Moseley. But, instead of turning down the aisle, I dash for the back door. I push the door open so hard it slams behind me. I can hear the singing and Reverend Johnson praying loudly, and I can hear Mr. Moseley. "Come back, Scout!" But I don't look back. I run past the parked cars, head down the hill, turn toward the cotton gin and don't stop or look back until I've lost myself in the gin yard where I know no one can find me.

Mom and Dad are sitting in the main office of the depot when I come in from school.

"Brother Johnson came to see me today. Why didn't you tell me you ran out of the church last Sunday?" Mom asks in her stern voice.

My stomach sinks. Ever since last Sunday I've been worried about what happened. Am I really sinful like they say? Am I one of those people they talk about being possessed by the devil? Maybe it was the devil that made me run out of church, and I'm going to be his evil servant instead a servant of God. Maybe that's what they mean by "being saved." Maybe I should let them dunk me under the water. Maybe that will save me from the devil, and I won't do things like that anymore.

"Aw, it was nothing. They were just tryin' to force me to be baptized, and I'm not ready yet." I hear myself trying to be casual.

"Well, don't you think we better talk about it?"

"Aw, Mom. I just can't understand it. They all go up in front of the church and cry and say how happy they are. It don't make sense. And what's getting dunked underwater got to do with anything? Is that supposed to make me a better guy? It sure don't seem to have done Mr. Moseley any good."

"What's that crack mean? Mr. Moseley's a fine man. He's the main deacon at the church. If it weren't for him leading the singing and helping with the prayers, Reverend Johnson would probably have to do it all himself. Mr. Moseley's a good family man, and I don't know anything you can say bad about him."

"Well, it seems to me all they talk about is how you shouldn't smoke or drink or dance or anything that's fun, and if you do, you're sinnin'. I don't see how having fun can be a sin. And, even if Mr. Moseley says it's a sin, it don't keep him from doin' it."

"Scout, you don't know what you're talking about."

"Yes, I do! About two months ago, me and Uncle Jack saw him come out of Rojalio's Bar with that Mexican girl, Isabel, and he had a bottle under his arm. They got in his car and headed for the sandhills."

Mom turns white. She glares at me with both hands on her hips. "Look at me, Scout. Are you lying to me? Don't you ever say something like that about someone if it's not true."

"Why would I lie about something like that? Ask Uncle Jack if you don't believe me. Or ask ol' Rojalio. He came out of the bar after they had drove off, and he was cussing about Mr. Moseley not paying his bill."

Mom hands go up to her face as she stands there wide-eyed and open-mouthed. Dad has been real quiet all this time, but he breaks in now. "Scout, are you sure about what you're saying?"

"Dad, ask Uncle Jack."

"You know good and well we can't ask him right now since he's in Fort Hood. I just want to be sure you're not making that up."

"Do you think I'm possessed with the devil?" I'm almost shouting.

Dad puts his hand up to calm me down. "No, I don't think anything like that."

"Do you think I'll go to hell if I don't go up in front of the church and let them dunk me in the water like they want?"

Dad laughs. "Well, if you go by what they say, I'm already gone and done for, so I may not be the best person for you to ask about that."

I turn to Mom, looking at her, asking the same question with my eyes.

"No, Scout, I don't believe your father is doomed for hell, and I don't believe you are either. I would just like for you to keep going to church for what you can learn. It's a good thing for you to learn about the Bible."

"I don't want to go back to that place, ever," I say between my teeth.

"You don't have to," Dad agrees.

Mom starts to say something then changes her mind. After a moment, she says, "I don't want you to tell anyone else what you said about Mr. Moseley. People will say you're spreading gossip if you do. Besides, if he's doing that sort of thing, word will get out soon enough anyway."

I couldn't care less about Mr. Moseley right now. I'm just glad to be off the hook for getting myself baptized.

"Did you get baptized last Sunday?" I ask Bubba. He, Willy, and Dee are sitting in Junior's Model A Ford admiring the way he's fixed it up. I'm standing on the running board leaning in the window. We're waiting for the school bell to ring after lunch.

"Yeah. Mama bought me a new suit and the dye came off in the water and turned it all blue," Bubba says and laughs.

Willy isn't as lighthearted about it. "It ruined my suit too. I don't see why they wouldn't let us wear Levi's or something that couldn't get ruined."

"How'd it feel when they dunked you under?" Dee probs.

"That stupid preacher pulled my hand when he put me under, and my fingers slipped off my nose, and I got water up it. I 'bout choked to death," Bubba grumps.

"I mean, how'd it feel? Did you feel saved? Do you feel cleaner now? Do you feel any different?"

"Naw." Bubba spits out the window. "I wouldn't 'a' done it if Willy hadn't."

We all look at Willy.

"My dad made me do it. He told me when Mr. Moseley came for me that I had to go up and get saved and baptized. I can't tell as I feel any different. It was just embarrassing to have to get up in front of all those people. But now I'm glad. I'm saved now. I know I won't go to hell. When you guys gonna get saved?"

Dee is sitting in the middle, and he works the gear shift intently. "I guess I'll do it next Sunday. Wanna come with me, Scout?"

"Naw, I guess I won't be going to that church no more. My dad said I didn't have to if I didn't want to."

"What?" It's Willy who speaks, but they all look at me in surprise. "You rather go to hell than go up in front of all those people?"

The bell rings, and I dash for the classroom. How can I explain to these guys how I really feel? I can't tell them about Mr. Moseley, but even if I could, that wouldn't make any difference. They'd just say he's possessed by the devil, and he needs to rededicate his life to Christ. I just don't know how to explain that I've got more questions about God than I have answers, and that maybe I really *would* rather go to hell than get all emotional up in front of a church full of people.

CHAPTER 9

I've learned to block out my feelings totally on this thing we are doing.

Dad's arguments about it being right because of the rule of "survival of the fittest" went over my head, but when he talked about what cowboys do, he got my attention. "You gotta understand that the main goal of bein' a cowboy is to put meat on every table in America. If all those cattle aren't slaughtered, where's that meat gonna come from? What difference does it make who does the killin'? They're still gonna be just as dead. The one who can do it quick and painlessly and produce the cleanest, finest beef—now that's a real cowboy," he had argued wearily.

"All right, let's see how good you boys are." Dad stops the pickup a short distance from where the steer he'd just bought from Rex Carr is standing, munching from a block of alfalfa we'd thrown out for him. He's a big, fat shorthorn, roan in color.

Junior takes the .22 from the rack behind the pickup seat and cautiously steps out of the pickup on the side away from the steer. The steer doesn't pay any attention until Junior is a few yards away. Suddenly, he stops eating and looks intently at Junior, head held high so as to sniff his scent. Junior quickly lifts the .22 and takes aim. No matter how hard I clinch my teeth, I still can't help flinching when I hear the pop that drops the steer to his knees.

Dad pulls the pickup beside the quivering body, steps out and hands Junior a skinning knife.

"Here, Junior. Cut his throat. Scout, you get the tripod set up and then help with the skinning." Junior and I already have the routine down pat, but it makes Dad proud to watch us work quickly and efficiently, and he can't keep from telling us how.

With the sharp knife, Junior quickly makes a slit across the quivering steer's neck and sticks the knife in deep, moving it back and forth until it slices the jugular. Steaming dark red blood gushes out over Junior's hand onto the ground, and the body slowly becomes still.

With a shovel, Dad digs a hole by the steer's head "so the blood'll drain into it and not make a big mess."

I pull the tripod out of the back of the pickup and lay it out by the steer's hind legs, ready to raise, then I get a skinning knife from the bucket Dad had set out for us.

The steer is rolled on his back now and, starting at the hind legs, I make a slit in the skin along the back of the leg down to the center of the crotch. The same with the front legs. By now, Junior has made a slit down the neck, across the brisket, down the belly, and between the hind legs to the butt hole.

I take the right side and Junior takes the left. Now it's a contest to see who can skin down to the center of the back first. I cut off the fore and hind legs at the knee and place the singletree between the hocks while Junior skins out the head and cuts it free from the neck.

Together we raise the tripod over the beef so the block and tackle are centered over the singletree. It takes both of us pulling with all our weight to lift the big carcass. When it swings free of the ground, I cut the hide free from the tail and skin it free from the part of the back we couldn't reach while he was on the ground. Dad places a tub on the ground underneath to catch the entrails when Junior slits the belly open. It's all we can do to lift the full tub into the back of the pickup.

Dad hands me the saw, but I'm too short, so Junior starts sawing down the middle of the back to cut the carcass in half. After he's gotten it down low enough, I take over. I give out when I reach the neck, and Junior takes over again. When the two halves swing free, we cut them in quarters and load each in the pickup, cover them with the tarp, and load the tripod.

"Forty-seven minutes. Not bad for a couple of knuckleheads," Dad says with a grin.

I notice as we drive away that Dad has covered the clotted blood and smoothed the ground. By tomorrow after the wind blows our tracks away, you won't be able to tell we've ever been here.

There was ice on the water trough this morning, almost an inch thick. I had to break it with an ax so the livestock could drink. Most people don't realize how cold it gets in the desert during the winter. It gets a lot colder at night up here on the mesa than it does down in the valley. The wind blows a lot more up here too. In spots where it's wet, you can still find green grass growing in the valley, while up here, the cold January wind has turned everything a dull brown. Even the greasewood, which doesn't lose its little green leaves, looks like it has shriveled up so you can only see the black stems from a distance. As I gaze out over the barren landscape, everything looks gray right up to the foot of the dark blue mountains. All the snakes, lizards, and a lot of the varmints are in hibernation now, so about the only wild life you'll see is an occasional jack rabbit and sometimes a coyote. When you get up in the mountains, you'll see some mule deer.

It's cold, even though the wind isn't blowing this evening. I brought warm water from the depot to wash the cows' udders, but it turns cold as quick as I splash it on them, and by the time I finish rinsing them off, my fingers feel like icicles. The only way to keep warm is to move fast and keep contact with the tits and udders. Sometimes, when my hands get to cramping, I will stick them up in the cow's flanks to warm them up.

I'm sitting on my T-stool milking a Holstein we named Blackie, just like the one we sold nearly seven years ago. I hear Socks meowing to my left and behind me. The big old black cat with white stockings on all four feet is sitting up waiting for a shot of fresh warm milk. I level a stream right at his mouth, and he drinks it down without losing a drop. I get back in rhythm with each hand on a tit. Swish. Swish. The milk builds up a thick foam in the pail. Sometimes I try to write my name in the foam with the stream of milk, but it's too cold tonight.

It gets dark so early this time of year, the sun was hanging low when I got off the school bus. By the time I changed clothes and heated up the water, got the cows in, and started milking, it'd already started getting dark. I still have five more cows to go.

Socks cries for more.

"All right," I say. "One more shot, then you get the hell outta here."

What's left of our chicken flock is already up on the fence as high as they can fly with their stubby wings, getting ready to roost for the night. Their clucks and quiet squawks have a soothing effect on the cows as they munch their evening feed. We've only got six hens and one rooster left out of the second batch of twenty-five chicks we got from Sears Roebuck by mail two years ago.

Junior and I did a real good job with them, having learned how to do it when we lived in Fort Hancock. We only lost three raising them up to grown chickens. By fall, we were able to kill a fryer for dinner every Sunday, and the hens were beginning to lay enough eggs so we didn't have to buy any.

But then, in the winter when things got really dry and cold, the coyotes got hungry and started raiding. We'd set traps every time we butchered a calf or hog, using some of the entrails as bait. Nearly every time, we killed three or four coyotes and hung them on the barbed-wire fence around the pasture. Festus Gibbs had said that would scare off the live ones, but it didn't seem to make any difference. They just kept on raiding the chicken coop.

One cold, windy night, Junior sat himself up in a shelter he made out of bales of hay and laid in wait for them. He killed three that night with the old 12-gauge. But they still kept coming. By the end of last winter, we had a dead coyote hanging on every fence post for over a mile, but those old stupid desert dogs wouldn't take a warning. If their pelts had been worth anything, we'd have made some good money.

They even ganged up and attacked the dogs. Bemo's a big bloodhound pup George Title gave us, and we thought he could keep them away for sure. But they had him and another dog we named Spot both hiding under the door stoop of the depot, afraid to come out unless one of us was with them.

Thank goodness, we haven't had any raids so far this winter. Dad is in the hospital again, the third time since his first heart attack, and Junior is staying up there with him. I don't know how I'd handle a coyote raid alone. It's all I can do to keep all six cows milked and fed and deliver the milk. But I've heard a few yelps and howls the last few nights. It feels like they're moving in closer again. ol' Paint has been staying in closer to the barn at night instead of out in the pasture like she did during the summer. The coyotes generally won't hurt horses or mules or grown cows, but they'll scare them and chase them if they can.

I still have to block out my feelings about killing animals, but Dad's argument about survival of the fittest has begun to make a lot more sense. Also Mom explained that in this case it is a struggle between us and the coyotes as to who gets to kill and eat the chickens. She said that in ancient times hunters and fighting men always respected their opponents regardless of who won the fight and that therefore the coyotes would respect us for fighting to save our chickens.

By the time I've finished the two Holsteins, Blackie and Bossie, and moved to Ginger, the little Jersey, I realize it's gotten dark, and I'm working mostly by feel. But I can see a bright glow in the east. A new full moon will be rising.

Ginger looks back at me still chewing a mouthful of the bran and grain mixture, her lower jaw jutting out like she's smiling and trying to show off her lower teeth. The sweet smell of the ketones on her breath mixed with the bran remind me of pancakes and hot maple syrup. As I wash her udder, I can feel her giving down the milk. I can tell she's content.

"What d'ya mean, wait here till midnight?" I'm roused out of my daydreaming by a conductor yelling on the telephone at the corner of the depot. "God damn it! We're supposed to be in Valentine by midnight," he says, still shouting into the phone.

I can't get it all, but it sounds like the dispatcher on the other end of the telephone shouts right back, and there's trouble down the line, so his train is going to have to wait quite a while before they'll be allowed to move on. He hangs up the receiver with a bang, and I can hear him cussing to himself as he walks back toward the engine. Until now I hadn't noticed the freight train sitting right beside the cotton platform. Apparently, it had come in on the spur at the west end and moved slowly and quietly up to where it's now stopped. Sometimes they'll do that if they're ahead of schedule or have to wait for instructions.

It really feels cold now that it's gotten dark. Steam seems to spurt from the mouth of each cow. I hurry as fast as I can to finish the milking, saving Rebecca, the orange-colored Guernsey, till last. She's such a bitch. If I don't treat her just so, she'll try to kick me and refuse to stand still so I can milk her. I pour her feed in the trough and rub her back.

"Sawww, be still, babe." I bend over and ease my head into her flank so she can't kick me as I wash off her large tits. She stamps her feet and moves around.

"Sawww, sawww, babe." She settles down as I slowly start milking the close front tit. I move the bucket in under her as I continue to milk slowly, all the time keeping my head up against her flank. Finally, I'm able to pull my T-stool up and ease my butt down on it.

"Sawww, Sawww, babe," I keep talking to her gently. Then sure enough, about halfway through, just when I begin to think everything is going to be okay, I do something wrong. I don't know what, but the half-full bucket of milk goes sailing across the corral, and I fall backward on my butt, landing in a fresh pile of cow plop.

"You ol' bitch!" I whack her across the ribs with my T-stool, and she runs to the back of the barn, snorts, and stands there looking at me with her head down. There's a dare in her eyes, but it's too cold to fight, and I figure I got enough milk out of her so she can wait till morning.

"Maybe by then you'll be tight enough so you'll be glad for me to milk you clean, you ol' hussy."

I grab a gunnysack hanging on the fence to wipe the manure off my Levi's and get ready to make the four trips across the tracks and up the stairs of the depot to carry the milk in so Mom can strain it and fill the round long-necked bottles.

Mom says I shouldn't carry two bucketfuls at a time, but I figure I should carry as much as I can. Carrying five gallons of milk at a time all that distance and up the stairs will make me strong. By the end of the third trip, I can feel the muscles in my arms and legs swelling.

As I start the last trip, I notice the moon has risen in all its fullness—a bright orange, shedding light across the cold desert. It's so bright I can see my shadow as I walk westward toward the depot carrying a milk bucket in each hand.

Just as I step between the main-line tracks I hear it. Three quick yelps followed by a long shrill howl. I turn and look, trying to see him on one of the nearby hills, but I know he's a long way off. I stand motionless for a long while between the main-line rails shimmering off to the east and west in the cold bright moonlight on either side of me, waiting. Waiting to get a glimpse of movement. Waiting for a second wail to give me a better direction. Nothing. Finally, I relax, watching my breath drift on the still air.

Chung! Chung! It's the water pumps on the big steam engine waiting down by the cotton platform, the only sound I can hear in the cold stillness. I go on upstairs and help Mom finish with the milk by pushing the cardboard caps into the tops of each full bottle and wiping them clean before placing them in the metal carrying racks.

We set the warm bottled milk out on the landing by the kitchen window so it can cool overnight.

After a bite to eat, I fill the coal buckets and stoke up the fire in the two potbellied stoves before going to bed.

My bed is upstairs by the east window looking out to the north and east over the railroad tracks. As I crack the window before crawling under the covers, I can make out the barn across the tracks in the bright moonlight. The rails on the main line still shimmer, two parallel lines that disappear in the distance to the east and west. I can see the big eight-wheel driver still sitting on the spur down by the cotton platform. A distant train whistle breaks the silence of the crisp desert air. I can tell he's waiting at the Finley

Siding four miles to the east. It's a long, shrill whistle, followed by two short toots. Almost immediately, it's answered by a series of distant coyote yelps and howls.

The engineer sitting down by the cotton platform can't resist getting into the act. He answers the train at Finley with another long, loud scream that he tapers off slow to a deeper, lower, husky whistle, which is again answered by a chorus of the desert varmints. They're closer this time.

As the coyote chorus dies out, the train in Finley comes back again, starting with a low, deep whistle that grows into a loud shrill response. This time he is answered by a small group of long, deep, mellow howls that seem to be located on top of the sandhills across the draw to the south and east of the barn.

Now it's McNary's turn again. Three quick toots from the engine by the cotton platform is mimicked by a series of three quick barks from a group of coyotes that seem to be over by the nearby gravel pit a short distance to the north. Soon everyone catches on. The coyotes will mimic and elaborate on any sound the trains offer. At first sad, then happy, then mellow. Sometimes the coyotes in the east will add their own different refrain to the song of a group on the south side. Then a group from the west will add their interpretation. Sometimes it will end with everyone joining in at the same time.

Mom is beside me now, kneeling by the open window. With her arm close around me, we listen as the two steam engines, first one and then another, lead an endless chorus of what seems like the voices of a hundred coyotes spread in every direction over twenty square miles in a beautiful winter concert, a lonesome tribute to the bright yellow moon, made crystal clear upon the cold dry air—an enchanting, captivating, and inspiring serenade by the largest, most powerful machines made by man in harmony with the lowliest scrawny, cowardly scavengers of the desert.

I'm not cold, but I can't keep from shivering. I can feel Mom shiver too.

"This is the real beauty of the desert, Scout. Look at it, feel it, listen to it carefully and remember it. All the secrets of life are here."

CHAPTER 10

I can hear Mom and Dad talking in the kitchen about the meeting Dad went to last night. I can smell bacon and coffee cooking, so I know Mom is making breakfast. But it sounds interesting, so I just lie in bed listening.

"They organized a roping club. Sonny Walsh has a set of plans for a roping arena, and Robert Hillis is donating that old salt flat over north of Rojalio's Bar just off the road that leads up to the old Underwood place. Harold Rigsby got the Southern Pacific to give us a bunch of railroad ties, and Tom Jefferson is having his hardware store provide the net wire at cost." I can tell Dad is really excited.

"They're gonna start buildin' on Saturday and figure they can have it finished by the seventh of June. That weekend they want to have a matched ropin', so Festus Gibbs and Vernon Delaney each donated a beef, and they want to have a barbeque to get everything started off right. They want me to take charge of the barbeque. I'll do the butcherin', make the sauce, and see to the cookin'."

Mom has to put in her usual word of caution. "Now, Boots, you've only been out of the hospital a little over a month. The doctors said what got you into trouble was that you kept on doing more than you should. I know you want to help out, but I'll not have you gettin' yourself into anything where you're going to over-exert yourself again."

"Naw, naw, don't get all upset," Dad says, with a wave of his hand. "You don't have to worry about any of that. The boys can do the butcherin' for me, and they'll get some of those young bucks like Jay Byrd and Harold Simms to dig the pit and cut the mesquite. Once it's all set up, all I'll have to do is supervise the cookin' and see to it the sauce gets put on just right. I'm not gonna have a heart attack from just mixing up the sauce. If I do, then maybe it's time for me to give it all up anyway."

At this last comment, I come fully awake in alarm. Mom is quick to react. "Just what do you mean by that last remark?" I can hear the concern in her voice.

"Oh, I don't mean nothin'," Dad retreats. "I just get tired of those damned doctors telling me I just have to lay around like a vegetable. If that's what I am, then I'm not worth much, and I feel a lot better doin' somethin' that makes me feel worthwhile, even if it does bring back the chest pain a little bit."

They're quiet a few minutes while Dad is sipping his coffee. I can feel the tension ease slowly, and Dad's enthusiasm returns. "Besides, helping on this thing is the least I can do. It looks like this ropin' club is finally gonna give that kid a chance to see a real ropin' match and learn a little bit about what a rodeo is. You know, I've always hated I couldn't show him those things myself."

I can't take it any longer. The whole kitchen seems to glow with brightness when I ask, "Dad, will you enter the ropin' match?"

Dad really lights up. "Well, that . . ."

Mom cuts him off. "I should say not! That's just what I need—your father to climb on some crazy horse and go chasing and roping cattle. It'll kill him for sure. Scout, I don't want you encouraging him at all. You promise me you'll not let him get involved in anything like that. Promise me now or I won't even let you go to the roping."

"Aw, I promise," I say with disappointment in my voice, but I'm so excited about the roping, I have to run out and tell ol' Paint all about it before breakfast.

The sweet smell of fresh-dug dirt makes me want to get down in the pit and dig with my hands so I can feel the damp coolness of the clean loose soil, but I promised Dad I'd stay out of the way. I watch them back a pickup loaded with cut mesquite up to the pit and begin to fill it with the firewood. When it's about half full, Jay Byrd splashes a little kerosene over the wood and throws in a match. Soon the smell of the damp dirt is overcome with the odor of smoke from burning mesquite. The fire is hot, so I walk over to the back of Dad's pickup where he's busy making the sauce.

He chops up five pounds of butter into a big pot, pours in a jug of vinegar, then turns to me. "Scout, get that case of ketchup off the pickup seat and start opening them for me."

I'm glad to be busy, but I've never seen this much ketchup in my life. Once I get the bottles open, I help shake the red sauce into the big pot as Dad stirs and adds a variety of spices. Soon the ominous mixture begins to smell inviting and takes on a smooth, dark brown consistency. Dad opens a loaf of white bread and tears a slice in half, handing one part to me as he dips his half in. "Have a taste. Tell me what it needs."

I really like the tangy sauce and reach for another slice of bread.

"Nope, no more right now. We have to save it to be sure there's plenty to go 'round." Dad quickly seals up the open wrapper protecting the bread. Seeing my disappointment, he adds, "Maybe you can have some more later when we start spreading it on the meat."

* * *

"You awake, Scout?"

I yawn. "Yeah, I guess so."

"Come on. I better take you home so you can get some sleep and rest up for tomorrow."

I sit up on the saddle blanket Dad had laid out for us to sit on by the barbeque pit. The glow of the hot coals in the bottom of the pit is the only light now. In the dry cool desert air it feels good to sit close to the pit and feel the warmth float up past the meat cooking on the hog wire which is spread over pieces of pipe laid across the pit. The smoke mixed with the smell of cooking beef and barbeque sauce wraps around the small group tending the fire. The men occasionally turn the meat while spreading sauce generously.

The delicious smell is less inviting now that I've eaten almost a whole loaf of bread dipped in the pungent sauce, along with an occasional sliver of beef someone has sliced off to "check the flavor."

The group has been passing a bottle of Old Crow around for an occasional nip, or to spice up a cup of coffee as tall tales of cowboys, roundups, cattle drives, and cow horses are boldly spun, each cowboy adding his special flavor to the hodgepodge of experience.

The whole bunch is spellbound when Dad tells of his favorite Tar Baby, a coal black stallion he won in a poker game. "When I was sergeant in charge of the remount station at Fort Bliss," Dad explains, "Pancho Villa pulled his raid on the little town of Columbus, New Mexico. The general, old Black Jack Pershing, picked six of us to scout for his troops when they chased that ol' bandit down in them rugged mountains of northwestern Old Mexico. That black stud saved my hide several times when me and a couple other scouts got cut off from the main troops. We had to ride three days an' nights to make it back across the border without gettin' caught by Pancho's men. Ol' Tar Baby was the only horse to make it. The horses them other two was ridin' plumb give out, and we had to steal horses for 'em twice, so's they'd have mounts that could keep up with ol' Tar Baby." Dad laughs as he remembers it. "We left the tired ones in trade, though."

Mart Osborn joins the group, pours about half cup of coffee in a tin cup, then fills it with Old Crow. Once he's settled cross-legged by the fire, Dad continues, "Once we was ridin' right into a big ambush in a narrow canyon, and I thought that stud had gone crazy as a peach-orchard borer when he just balked and wouldn't go in there. Finally, when they saw we wasn't gonna ride into their trap, the Meskins started chasin' us. After about a mile, I could tell they was gainin' on us, so I told my partners to pull off in some bushes an' hide. Then me an' that Tar Baby flat outrun 'em all."

I notice everyone is quiet and still as Dad takes another drag on the Old Crow. A hot mesquite coal pops real loud in the barbeque pit as a signal for him to continue. "We hadn't had any water for two days, and the next mornin' we was in the middle of that desert out there northwest of Chihuahua. I thought we was done for. Perkins wanted to turn back, but if we did, we'd ride right into Pancho's hands. Finally, I was about to give up myself and head back when that damned stud took the bit in his mouth and started off at a trot headin' due south. I tried to stop 'im and turn 'im, but he wouldn't have any of that, so I finally decided to trust 'im one more time. After about a mile and half, he took us into a little ravine with a spring in it where we had all the water we could drink. That night we crossed the Rio Grande just west of El Paso."

"I hear tell you went back, Boots," Mart Osborn says after Dad quits talking. Mart presses harder when Dad looks at him sharply. "I hear tell you got to know ol' Pancho Villa pretty good. Even rode with him."

The sharp look on Dad's face lasts only a second then he breaks into a laugh, "Ah, now you know how tall tales like that can get started," he says as he helps himself to another swig of whiskey.

I notice how Dad didn't exactly deny riding with the old bandit, and I wait for him to tell more, but when anybody tries to prod him he just laughs again and says he's talked enough.

I drift off to sleep soon after Dale Tolbert starts telling his tale about his own horse, because I'm sure the wonderful deeds of the mighty Tar Baby could never be surpassed by any other four-legged animal.

I'm brought out of my reveries by Dad's urging, "Come on, Scout, don't go back to sleep. Go get in the pickup, and I'll take you home."

As I come fully awake, stand up, and stretch, I notice all the whiskey is gone and the fire has burned down to coals. The circle of men is breaking up, some of them already headed for their pickups.

I take one last look at the glowing embers and the smoke rising into the darkness. For just a second I can clearly see the form of a big black horse rearing and tossing his head in that swirling, dancing smoke.

"We're goin' down to the ropin.' We're gonna get to see the way they do it in the rodeo."

Paint is as excited as I am. "Bring the rope," she says. "Maybe we can catch a calf ourselves."

I slip the Little Wonder on her back, cinch it snug, and tie the rope with the laces. I have to step back one more time to admire the special saddle I worked so hard to buy. I've soaped it and spread a thin layer of Neat's-foot oil on to make it shine like new. I bet it's going to be the best-looking saddle at the arena.

Paint is so eager she starts out at a lope without any urging from me as I step in the stirrup and swing aboard. Then she settles into that smooth, easy, ground-covering trot that she does so well, keeping her ears pointed at our destination. We cover the two miles to the arena in no time.

"Boy! That's some big corral," she says, as we top a small ridge, which gives us a wide view of the entire layout.

"Yeah, wait till you get inside. It even looks bigger from inside than it does from out here."

Cars have begun to drive up and park around the outer edge of the arena. Inside the big fence, there are several men riding their horses at an easy pace, swinging loops over their heads, and occasionally tossing a loop at an imaginary calf, stepping off, instructing their mounts to stop quickly and back up to hold the rope tight like they have roped a calf.

Paint stops and watches from across the fence. She knows how to do that real good since we've been practicing.

Bubba Hillis comes over riding his big bay horse that he says is a great cow horse. "You see that guy there?" He points to a slender man standing in the saddle, swinging a loop over his head as his large blue roan lopes around the arena. "That's Dusty Rhodes. He's a champion roper from Marfa. Dad says he's the best roper west of the Pecos River."

In awe, I watch as the cowboy lopes by just on the other side of the fence. His saddle has very little swell, and I notice that, in addition to the rope he has in his hand, there's another rolled up and tied to the saddle horn with a small cotton string. A loop is already built, but it's stuffed down into the breast harness. Around his shoulder, he has a small rope with the end hanging loose, reaching almost down to his knee.

A small strap runs from the cinch between the roan's front legs, through the breast harness, and clips to a hard-twisted rawhide noseband above the bit of the braided leather bridle. The roan's nose is bleeding where the band cuts into it as he steps high, prancing, holding his head up. Whenever the rider reins him, he swings his nose upward so that it hits the band hard.

Ol' Paint heaves a sigh. "Boy, that looks like a dude getup if I ever saw one."

"Aw, you don't know what you're talking about. You never saw a real calf roper before."

Sonny Walsh climbs up in the announcer's stand above the chutes. "Okay, you men. To get things warmed up, we'll have a little jackpot. Five dollars each, one calf. Everybody put your money in the hat. Bob Hillis will hold the money. Let's get ready to roll."

In a little while he yells, "All right, we got six ropers in this first jackpot. Anybody else want in? We're gonna close it up in about five minutes."

Finally, the action starts, and Jay Byrd is first up, riding his big brown-and-white paint into the box below the announcer's stand, backing around to face the chute where the calf will come out. Tom Jefferson, serving as "barrier man," pulls a string tied on one end to a screen-door spring, stretching it across the opening of the box, placing the ring tied on the other end between two staples. He inserts a nail through the staples and ring holding the string tight. He then pulls out the small cotton rope tied to the nail about ten feet to the barrier line where he holds the flag up ready for action.

Byrd nods "ready," and the chute gate is opened. A floppy-eared Brahman calf darts out. As he crosses the barrier line, Quincy drops the flag, releasing the string across the box, and the race is on. The big paint gelding with Byrd leaning forward, swinging his loop over their heads, catches up with the calf just before it reaches the far end of the arena. Byrd throws, the calf ducks, and the loop falls empty on the ground. Car horns honk, hands clap. Someone yells, "Tough luck, Byrd."

I clap my hands, excited. "See, Paint? You have to give the calf a head start. You can't come out of the barrier until the guy drops the flag."

Paint snorts but doesn't say anything.

Festus Gibbs is next on his slick black mare that holds her tail high as she trots into the box. She's quick to start as soon as the calf's head appears, and she breaks the string before the flag is dropped. But she catches the calf quickly. In fact, she gets there so quick, Festus isn't ready, and as he starts to swing his rope, the mare runs on past the calf. Festus starts cussing.

"God damn crazy mare! How you expect me to rope a calf if you run past 'im?" He brings the loop of the rope down hard across the mare's tender flank then swings it back, coming down hard again on the other side. Whack! Whack! I can hear the rope find its mark. The mare kicks up her hind legs in reaction to the whipping, throwing Festus forward over her head.

Horns honk and the crowd laughs. Free from her owner, the mare races back to the box, looking for a way to escape, but old Vernon Delaney appears out of nowhere and grabs her rein, putting a steady hand on her neck. I can tell he's talking to her, but I can't hear what he says. The mare becomes quiet in almost an instant. Hat in hand and embarrassed, Festus Gibbs walks up to the box. "I'm gonna kill that bitch," I can hear him say, but Vernon Delaney holds up his hand and stands between them. I still can't hear what he says, but Festus calms almost as suddenly as the mare did, and the three of them move out of the way over into a corner of the arena.

"Juan Garcia is up next!" yells Sonny Walsh.

Juan is riding a slick little Grulla Dun he has been breaking. The peach-colored, almost pink horse has a dark red mane and tail that are connected by a stripe the same color running down the middle of his back. He's well built too, with a well-developed rump, deep, wide chest, and low withers. He travels easy with his head low.

Juan isn't one to treat a horse hard. He's breaking him with a handmade hackamore using a piece of lariat rope woven for the noseband instead of a hard bit in his mouth.

The Grulla shies and balks at the box. Juan encourages him with a whack across the rump, and the Grulla breaks in two, exploding high in the air, stiff-legged. But Juan is ready and able for the task. Juan isn't very tall, but he's stocky and strong. Riding a Little Wonder just like mine, and with his legs drawn up against the swell, it's amazing how quick and smooth he can move with every buck of the bronc between his legs. The horse is jumping so high that underneath them on the other side of the arena, I can see the top of a car. Finally, the Grulla lines out, jumping and kicking along the fence all the way down to the far end of the arena where he breaks into a dead run. Juan doesn't try to check him but spurs him on three times around the arena.

Finally, feeling the bronc has gotten the kink out of his back, Juan pulls him to a sliding halt and reaches over to pet him on the neck, talking easy to him. Car horns honk, and the crowd cheers.

Moving in that easy trot, Juan heads the Grulla back up toward the box. I try to stifle a shiver as I thrill at the sight of the two of them melded together, first in conflict, now in union, as they again prepare for the contest. Ol' Paint feels it too. She's watched the whole episode with her ears perked, and as they move by close on the other side of the fence, she lets out a low deep nicker. I don't know for sure what she says, but I can tell it's filled with encouragement and admiration.

The Grulla quickly breaks out of the box and falls in behind the racing Brahman calf. With a long, reaching throw, Juan snags the calf and steps off as the Grulla slides to a stop. The horse stands firm with the rope tight as Juan throws and ties the calf.

Again the crowd cheers.

"Twenty-seven-point-nine seconds!" yells Sonny Walsh. "Now let's all go eat. We'll finish the ropin' after that."

Just as the crowd starts to move where Dad and the others have set up the tables to serve the food, someone pulls up in a shiny '49 Ford coupe with a loudspeaker on top. They drive up next to a big flatbed truck parked just west of the tables and High Pockets McKenzie climbs up with the microphone in his hand.

"All right, folks. We're gonna git the band up here for a little bit to give you a sample of what you're gonna hear at the dance tonight at the high school gymnasium. Then I think we got a few people here want to talk about the upcomin' election. Come on up here, Johnny."

A little man struggles to lift up a big bass fiddle as another man, plump and jolly, climbs up with a regular-sized fiddle in his hand. After some confusion, cussing, and groaning, they get all their instruments in place and set up a beat with the bass and guitar. Then the fiddle breaks out with "Boil Them Cabbage Down."

High Pockets pulls a French harp out of his shirt pocket and demonstrates his version of "Orange Blossom Special." Then they change to a Mexican beat and several cowboys yell as High Pockets starts singing "El Rancho Grande" as loud as he can.

As the music ends, Tom Jefferson climbs up and takes the microphone.

"Folks, as you know, we have a primary election coming up here in a few days, and since there ain't any Republicans in this county, the outcome will tell us who our government will be run by for the next couple years. I thought this would be a good chance for you to meet some of the candidates."

"Well, God damn!" says an old cowboy, standing close by where Paint and I are watching at the back of the crowd. "If I'd know'd they's bringin' politicians, I'd stayed at the ranch."

"Oh, hush, Henry," says a plump woman standing next to him.

Tom Jefferson goes on, "Now I think you all know I'm your candidate for mayor, but that's such a lousy job, nobody else wants it, so I don't have any opposition. But it gives me great pleasure to introduce someone who needs no introduction, your Democratic candidate for re-election to the United States Senate, Woodrow Wilson Bean! Come on up, Woody."

A man in a black suit climbs up on the truck, takes off his coat, picks up the microphone, and waves amid clapping, yelling, and car horns honking.

Obviously basking in the cheers, after a bit he raises a hand for silence.

"Thank you, folks. As you know, I've been in Washington with President Truman helping put together the programs to put this country back together after that devastating war.

"Now let me tell you what we're gonna do when I go back up there for my next term. . . ."

The drone of the loud speaker fades into the background as Paint and I meander back to the roping arena.

Finding the gate open, we go inside. This is the first time I've seen it on the inside from horseback.

"Come on, Paint. Let's see what we can do." I tie the end of my lariat to the saddle horn and shake out a loop on the other end. I steer Paint into the box and turn her around to face the chute where the calf will come out.

"You can do this, can't you, Paint?"

"Of course I can. You think I'm a dummy?"

"Let's try it."

I nod my head, and the imaginary calf is let out of the chute. Paint dashes up behind him, and I deftly lay the loop around his neck and step off as Paint slides to a stop. I run down the length of the rope and grab the end like I'm a calf pulling on it. Paint backs up, holding the rope tight, acting like she's watching to see if the calf is going to run to one side or the other. I jerk the rope, and she takes a step back. I throw my hands up like I've just tied the calf, and Paint eases the tension on the rope.

As I walk proudly back to my mount, I catch a movement in the corner of my eye off to the right.

"You and that old hay baler couldn't catch a calf if your life depended on it."

I turn to face the figure that had been standing by Festus Gibbs's little black mare that is tied to the fence. I can feel the red building from my neck upward until my whole face and ears are burning. He stands there smiling, puffing that hand-carved pipe with the bull's head and ivory horns.

"We can too!" I yell. "We can rope and tie any steer west of the Pecos River."

"I'd like to see that," he says, as he starts walking toward us. I jump, quickly putting my foot in the stirrup and wheeling Paint at the same time. I spur Paint to a lope, and we leave the arena with the uncoiled rope flying behind us. We head for the nearby sandhills and don't stop until we're out of sight of the arena and the crowd.

I step off Paint and lead her across the desert sand. Why does that old man have to be so mean? Why does he think I can't be a good roper? I know I can. I've been practicing with my rope every time I get a chance. All I need is a chance to prove I can. All I need is a chance to rope some calves and show them we can do it. I'll show that old man some day. I'll show him I can. I'll figure out a way.

I turn and look at Paint.

"Boy, you sure got mad back there. Why didn't you tell that old man to let a calf out, and we'd a' showed him."

Paint's as mad as I am.

"I tell you what, Paint. I don't know when or how we're gonna do it, but we're gonna be the best ropers in the country. We're gonna be the champions. We'll show 'em all. Let's go back down there and watch real close. Let's see how they do it. Then we'll practice till we're better than all of 'em."

By the time we get back, the speeches are over, and the roping has started again. Paint and I slip silently up to the fence where we had been watching from before. I'm surprised to see Dad sitting on the ground inside the fence right in front of us. I'm even more surprised to see old Vernon Delaney sitting right beside him. I start to ride away but decide to stand my ground. I let Paint stand quietly behind them. With the action in the arena, they don't know we're behind them.

"The next and last roper up is Dusty Rhodes!" yells Sonny Walsh.

The slender man on the blue roan rides out to the center of the arena and stops and shakes out a loop, checks his horn knot, and pulls the little rope from over his shoulder. He builds a small loop in the little rope and places it between his teeth and tucks the end in the side of his belt. Ready now, he spurs the roan into the box.

In the box, the roan quickly swirls on his hind legs and backs into the far corner. Tense and with ears perked, he sits back on his haunches and kind of dances with his front hooves, waiting.

Dusty nods. The calf is freed, and the roan starts running at the same time so as to reach the barrier just as the flag drops. Perfect timing. In a split second, the roan is right behind the Brahman.

With one quick swing over his head, Dusty lets go of the rope, trying to make a quick snag, but the rope falls short on the ground. I hear moans in the crowd, but without losing a second, Dusty jerks out the extra loop he has tucked into the breast harness, and he is ready to rope again. This time, after two swings of the loop, the lariat snakes out and clamps around the neck of the calf like a bull snake stealing quail eggs.

At the same time, Dusty dismounts and the roan slides hard on his hind legs, leaving skid marks in the loose dirt. When the calf hits the end of the rope, he is running so hard the sudden stop jerks him over backward. Dusty is standing by him as he regains his feet. With surprising strength, Dusty lifts the calf and lays him on his side. Then with lightning speed, he places the loop of the little rope on one front foot, places the two hind legs across it, and in a blur of motion, wraps them up tight, throwing both hands in the air.

"Twenty-one-point-eight seconds. That's the fastest time, and Dusty Rhodes is the winner of the jackpot!" Sonny shouts.

Horns honk and some clap their hands. Someone yells, "That 'a way, Dusty."

"I don't think much of that high-headed horse, do you?" It's Dad talking to Vernon Delaney.

"Naw, I don't much like them high-headed, prancin' nags. Look at his nose. It's all bloody where he keeps swinging his head up and hittin' that noseband. A horse like that just wastes a lot of energy and punishes himself. I prefer a horse that handles hisself more natural-like. That blue could run a lot faster and would be a lot better ropin' horse if he'd lower his head and quit ringin' his tail. But, with that kid spurrin' him one minute and jerkin' his head the next, can't expect 'im to do much else."

Sonny Walsh is yelling again, "All right, we're gonna do something here with the kids. We're gonna have a barrel race. This is to see how well these kids can handle their horses."

A barrel race? What's a barrel race? I've never even heard of that. I wonder what they do. The way Paint's ears twitch I know she doesn't know what it is either.

"All right, all you kids under fifteen come on in the arena and put your name on the list. Some of the club members have kicked in a little change, and we have two dollars and fifty cents for the winner. We got a dollar for second place."

Vernon Delaney is talking to Dad, "I bet that kid of yours don't even have the guts to get in a contest like that."

"I do too!" I yell at the mean old man.

Dad turns to me. He grins at old man Delaney and twitches one eye like he got something in it. "Oh, hidey, Scout. I didn't know you were there. You want to enter the barrel race?"

"Sure I do." Then after a moment's thought, I say, "Dad, what's a barrel race?"

"Well, you watch. They'll set up some barrels out there, and all you gotta do is ride ol' Paint around them as fast as you can."

As we ride into the arena to put my name on the list, Sonny Walsh is saying, "Okay, kids, you watch. Jay Byrd will ride around the barrels and show how it's done. You start from back in the ropin' box, and when you cross the barrier line, Quincy will drop the flag, and your time will start. You ride around the barrels in a figure eight and then back across the line, and when the flag drops again, your time stops."

As we watch Jay Byrd riding his big paint around the barrels and back across the barrier, Sonny adds, "If you go around the barrel the wrong direction, you'll be disqualified. If you knock a barrel down, you'll be fined ten seconds."

"You can do that, Paint. We do that all the time when we're lopin' around among the greasewood bushes. All you gotta do is go wherever I rein you."

Bubba Hillis is up first. His big bay lumbers across the barrier line, past the first barrel, then turns around the second, but the bay is running so hard, he can't turn very close, and he swings wide almost to the edge of the arena before he heads back toward the finish line. Bubba is barely able to get him to turn enough to go to the other side of the near barrel so as to make a complete figure eight.

"Twenty-seven-point-two seconds!" yells Sonny Walsh.

I'm shocked to see who's up next. It's Jenke Harmon riding ol' Star. Her dad is standing next to her in the box, talking to her. "Okay now, you do this just like you been practicin'. Slow down before you get to the second barrel so you can turn tight against it, and then whip 'em to run hard back across the startin' line."

Star comes out running hard with Jenke spurring him all the way. Then, just before reaching the far barrel, she stops spurring and jerks the reins. Star checks his speed, but he misunderstands the cue and turns too quick, going past the barrel on the wrong side.

"You make him go around the right way before you come back across the line," Bill Harmon yells.

Only after stopping Star dead still can Jenke get him to turn and go back around the barrel on the correct side.

"Forty-eight-point-five seconds," yells Sonny Walsh after she finally crosses the starting line. "That's okay, Jenke. That pony just needs some more trainin'."

I watch Jenke ride out of the arena. She's got her head high, and you would have thought she had the highest score, the way she looks. Stupid girl. It sure didn't look like they had been practicing.

Dee Stotts, Herby Cook, and Charlotte Underwood go around before it's my turn. Bubba Hillis still has the fastest time.

My heart is pounding like a hammer in my chest. "Okay, Paint, just take it easy." I can tell she's nervous too. "Follow my lead and go where I rein you. We'll show that old man with the pipe in his mouth. Okay, let's go!"

I can tell Paint is running as hard as she can, even though all I did was drop the reins. She wants to show him just as bad as I do. She doesn't need any whip or spurs. After we pass the first barrel, I rein her slightly wide to the right of the second, leaning over so as to move with her and make it easier for her to run. Then, just as we come even with the second barrel, I shift my weight and rein hard to the left. It's natural and easy for Paint to change directions. She turns so close on the barrel my leg brushes against it, causing it to rock back and forth. As I lean forward again, I can tell Paint's giving it all she has.

"That 'a way, girl. We'll show that old bastard. Come on!"

"Well, whadda ya know. That's the fastest time yet!" yells Sonny Walsh, as we slide to a stop in the roping box. "Nineteen-point-nine seconds is the winning time."

I hear a horn honk and some clapping of hands, but Paint and I are too excited to pay much attention. "We did it, Paint! We won!" I say as we ride out of the arena.

"Hey, Scout, come back and get your money," Sonny Walsh yells.

I'm still holding the cash in my hand, too excited even to stuff it in my pocket as I ride out of the arena. Jenke is standing by the fence holding Star's reins. For a second, I think about turning around and riding the other way. I don't know why, exactly. It's just that she bugs me. It's already too late, though. She's already seen me. She's probably going to give me a hard time for beating her so bad. "You did good, Scout," she says as I ride by. "I'm glad you won."

That's not at all what I expected, and I don't know what to say, so I just don't say anything. I don't even look at her. I ride away as fast as I can to greet Dad, who's beaming. "We won, Dad . . ." I start to say more, but old Vernon Delaney interrupts, poking his pipe at me.

"Well, you may go do the barrel race all right, but that's really just sissy stuff. I bet you'd be skeered to enter the calf ropin'."

"I am not! You just watch."

"Okay, I'll be watchin'. I'll see if you got the guts or not. Tell you what. We're gonna have another ropin' here in about two weeks. I'm willin' to bet you're skeered to show up and enter. I got five bucks here." He takes the green bill out of his pocket and waves it at me. "I'll bet you ain't got the guts to show up and enter. If you do, I'll pay your entry fee."

"I'll be here. You just bring your money," I say between clinched teeth as I wheel Paint, spurring her to get away from the old man as quickly as we can.

As we ride home that night, the anger is still a burning lump in my chest. "We're gonna practice, Paint," I whisper. "We're gonna practice till we're better'n anybody else. We'll show that old bastard."

CHAPTER 11

D r. Stevenson walks out of his office laughing. Dad is walking behind him still buttoning his shirt.

"Well, your old man's still as mean and ornery as ever. Just you keep your eye on him so he doesn't overdo. I think, as long as he doesn't strain himself, he's gonna be okay now." The gray-haired old doctor puts his hand on my shoulder. "He's lucky to have a strong strappin' young man like you to take care of him. Y'all drive careful goin' back down the valley, now."

Dad's in a good mood as we leave the doctor's office.

"Let's stop by Morgan's Saddlery, and I might buy you a new lariat rope before we go home," he says.

I always love the smell of new leather that fills a saddle shop, and I thrill over the new saddles and bridles of various types that are on display.

"If you're gonna be a calf roper, you need a saddle without any swell, so's when you rope a calf, you can get off and tie the calf faster," Mr. Morgan tells me. But I still love my Little Wonder with the large swells that I can grip with my thighs if a horse bucks or turns too quick. That way I can ride with my legs and knees and keep both hands free, and I don't have to hold on to the saddle horn like a sissy. Having both hands free can be mighty handy if I get caught in a real mess where a horse gets a rope tangled under his tail or around his hind legs or something like that.

All too soon Dad makes the purchase of thirty feet of three-eighths Manila hemp, and he's pushing me out the door. "Thirty foot's awful short. Most ropers get thirty-three foot. After you put a hondo on one end and a horn knot on the other, you'll only have about twenty-eight foot of rope," Mr. Morgan warns.

"That's all my boy needs." I can hear the pride in Dad's voice now. "That extra three foot only means a couple extra coils of rope to get in the way."

I'm glad I've been practicing using a small loop so I can be more accurate and don't need such a long rope.

Dad is silent, but I feel proud as I drive the pickup, making our way through the city traffic with the new rope laying on the seat between us. Out at the edge of town, I head the pickup south on Highway 80. I drive slowly because it makes Dad nervous if I drive very fast, especially since I just started driving. Cars keep honking and passing because of my slow pace down the two-lane highway. Traffic is so heavy that sometimes as many as three cars build up behind us, waiting for a clearing of oncoming traffic so they can pass. A couple of times, I pull off on the shoulder so the crowd of cars can clear out. It helps Dad relax when I do that.

"Want to stop in Clint for a sandwich?" I ask.

"Naw. Let's get on home. Your Mom will be worried about us. Turn your headlights on. It's gettin' dark."

"Why don't you relax and take a nap while I'm drivin'? It's still another fifty miles home."

"You know I can't sleep ridin' in a car. You just keep your eyes on the road, and I'll be all right."

I turn on the radio. Maybe a little western music will make Dad relax some more.

"Eques, eh, ele, o. Cuidad Juárez, Cuarta Chihuahua, República Mexicana," barks the announcer. "This is XELO, your fifty-thousand watt station at Clint, Texas, broadcasting from Juárez, Mexico, bringing you the best in western music. Now here's T Texas Tyler singing 'Remember Me.'"

After we pass Fabens, the traffic has thinned to only an occasional car going the opposite direction. The radio announcer is extolling the benefits of Carter's Little Liver Pills and urging us to take advantage of the special offer by mailing our money to "Clint, that's Clint, C-L-I-N-T, Texas."

The cowboy music seems to be working for Dad, because the atmosphere in the pickup has changed from one of tension to a relaxed, almost happy feeling. Now Dad is tapping his foot in time with the guitar on the radio as it picks out "Oklahoma Hills." We're about halfway between Fabens and Tornillo.

Suddenly, a black sedan passes us, going so fast it runs its left wheels off the pavement on the other side of the highway and kicks up a big cloud of dust before the driver is able to get it back on course down the highway. About a quarter mile ahead, I can see the headlights of a pickup heading toward the pavement from a dirt road that comes from a farm house off to the west.

But the pickup doesn't stop! The driver must not realize how fast the car is going. Without slowing at the intersection, he pulls onto the pavement in front of the speeding car. The taillight on the car brightens, and I can see it move to the left then suddenly back to the right. I can hear the screech of tires on the pavement then a sickening thud followed by the scraping of metal. Both vehicles move off the highway into the barrow ditch in one twisted mass of metal.

My heart is pounding in my throat, and I have a sick feeling in the pit of my stomach as I stop our pickup on the opposite side of the road so it's even with the wreck. A cloud of dust slowly drifts away, leaving everything still and quiet.

"You check the ones in the pickup. I'll check the car." Dad is giving instructions as we both get out of the pickup and dash across the highway. I can hear someone crying in the car now. It sounds like a woman.

I approach the driver's side of the pickup to see what looks like the driver's head in the darkness. The window is gone. The head moves, and I hear a moan.

"Take it easy! I'll get you out of there!" I say as I try to find the door handle so I can open it. The pickup and car seem to be welded together in a perfect T, with the pickup being the cross at the top and the car being the stem. The head keeps rolling and the moaning gets louder. Suddenly, I realize the door handle is gone. I pull on the door. It's jammed.

I can hear Dad on the other side of the car. "Take it easy, miss. I'll have you out of there in just a minute." The wailing from over there is almost a scream now.

"Take it easy, mister." It sounds like he's having a hard time breathing. I reach in the window and try to hold the head steady. I can feel warm wet blood as I touch the short hair. With the other arm I reach under his chin, and something hard, wet, and slick falls into my hand. In the dim light I make out a plate of false teeth.

I remember to reach in the man's mouth to be sure he hasn't swallowed his tongue. I learned that at first aid training in the Boy Scouts.

The smell of gasoline is strong, and suddenly there's light from underneath the car. Fire!

"Let's get them out of there quick before the fire spreads!" Dad says. He is standing beside me now.

"This pickup door is jammed!" I yell and run to the other side of the pickup. The door is already open, but the seat is pushed up blocking my way. I can't reach the man inside.

"This door's jammed too!" Dad shouts. "This driver's out cold, if he isn't dead. Quick, Scout, get the crowbar and shovel out of the back of the pickup!"

I'm able to find the crowbar quickly in the tool box in back of our pickup, but in the dark it seems to take forever to find the shovel.

"Hurry, Scout!" Dad yells. "You throw sand on the fire while I try to pry these doors open." He takes the crowbar from me.

In the bottom of the barrow ditch, I find loose sand and throw it wildly. Soon the fire on the ground under the car is out, but I can see a light under the hood, which is bent upward. I swing the shovel as hard as I can, and as it clangs against the hood, the motor is no longer covered. Two quick shovelfuls of sand on the motor, and it's dark again.

Dad is cussing, "I can't get either one of these doors open. Take the crowbar and go around on the other side and see if you can get the seat out of the way enough to get him out. I'll try to find another way to get this damned driver out."

With the crowbar, I'm able to rip up the seat and throw the stuffing on the ground. Finally hooking the claws into the spring, I'm able to give a hard pull, and the seat moves toward me.

Suddenly, there's light again!

"Git the shovel quick, Scout! There's gas all under the car!"

It takes me forever to find the shovel again. By now the fire is inside the car. I throw sand on Dad and everywhere, but it doesn't seem to do any good.

With superhuman strength, Dad reaches inside the window, grabs the still-unconscious driver under the armpits, and pulls him out the window. He's surprisingly small. Looks like a kid.

The driver of the pickup is fully awake now and screaming at the top of his lungs. As Dad carries the car driver away from the inferno, I dash back to the other side of the pickup. Now I have superhuman strength too. I pull the seat completely out of the pickup. The old man is still screaming. The stuffing from the seat is now on fire under my feet.

I grab the old man's arms and pull.

"My leg's caught between the brake and clutch," he suddenly says very clearly to me. Kicking the burning seat stuffing aside, I grab the crowbar and dive head first into the floorboard of the pickup. The man screams in pain as I jam the bar against his leg between the bent brake and clutch peddles. Dad is behind me now with his arms around the old man's chest pulling. Suddenly the leg comes free.

"Git outta there quick, Scout!" I hear Dad yell as he drags the old man down into the barrow ditch.

I'm clear of the pickup and running hard when the gas tank on the car explodes, spraying burning gasoline in the air. The concussion knocks me down.

Dad is beside me. "Are you hurt?"

"Naw, I'm okay. How's the old man?"

"I don't know. I think he's hurt pretty bad. Let's get them all loaded in the back of the pickup, and we'll head for town."

Dad carries the old man by the shoulders, and I carry his legs as we move him to our pickup and lay him out on the pickup bed.

A car approaches from the south, stops, and the driver offers help.

"I think we got everyone out. If you'd go ahead to Fabens and tell the sheriff or state patrol to send someone out and have them call an ambulance, we'll meet 'em in Fabens. I think some of these people need to go to the hospital in El Paso," Dad explains, and the car speeds off.

We find the car's driver lying on the ground where Dad left him. He's snoring lightly in a deep sleep. When I get close, I can smell whiskey on his breath.

"The son-of-a-bitch is drunk," Dad observes. "I shoulda left him in the car."

In the firelight, I can see he's much older than I had thought before. In spite of his small size, the man's face shows the lines of age. Suddenly, I'm reminded of the woman when I hear her whimper. She's sitting on the ground by the front wheel of our pickup.

We load the car driver, still snoring, on the pickup bed beside the other driver. As we're putting up the tailgate, I notice Dad is breathing hard and fast. His face is dripping wet with sweat. Suddenly, he grabs his left arm, doubles up and slumps to the ground.

"Dad!" I kneel over him.

"The whiskey under the seat," he whispers.

In a flash, I grab the pint bottle that Dad has always carried since his first heart attack. He's unconscious by the time I'm back by his side.

"Dad, wake up!" I slap him hard, lift his head and pour some of the whiskey in his mouth. He swallows, then coughs and spits, but he doesn't wake up.

I try to lift him, but he's too big.

I hear the woman whimpering behind me. I grab her by the arm.

"Help me lift my dad in the pickup!"

"I can't. My leg hurts."

I jerk her to her feet.

"You help me, you bitch, or I'll kill you right now!" I scream.

Slowly she moves, limping. I lower the tailgate and together we lift Dad in beside the other two men.

"You ride back here with them!" I yell, as I shove the woman in and put the tailgate up again.

I've never driven this fast before. Eighty-five miles an hour, as fast as the pickup will run. I see a sheriff's car with a red light flashing heading toward me just as I reach the edge of Fabens. I blink my lights, stop, and get out to wave them down.

"I got the people from the wreck, and my dad's had a heart attack!" I yell as the sheriff slows and rolls down his window.

No matter how many times I'm here I'll never get used to this smell of ether and alcohol. It always makes me feel queasy. Sitting here on this small white bench with white walls all around me, I feel out of place in my dirty, greasy clothes. I have to squint my eyes against the glare of the electric lights bouncing off the shiny white linoleum floor. A tall skinny nurse in a white uniform walks by, carrying a tray with stainless steel knives and needles on it. Her hard leather heels against the floor make a loud clack that echoes off the walls. I can't keep from shivering in this cold, sterile hospital atmosphere. The bench is cold and hard on my butt. As I watch the nurse disappear around the corner, a door opens and closes behind me.

I turn to see Sis take one look at me with red eyes and tears streaming down her cheeks then turn and run down the hall. I start to follow her, to comfort her, but Junior appears at the doorway.

"Dad wants to see you now."

I hesitate at the foot of the bed. Junior pushes me on up where Dad's hand reaches over and takes mine in his. The oxygen mask is working hard, the balloon quickly filling and shrinking with his rapid breathing. But the pale gray eyes still have that usual flicker. His hand tightens on mine.

"I thought you were dead. I . . ." His face blurs as tears fill my eyes.

There's a flurry of motion and the mask comes off his face.

"You remember cowboys don't cry," he says in a low, hoarse whisper. "I don't want nobody cryin' over me. You understand?"

"Okay, Dad. I won't." I swallow hard, choking back the pain, fear, and anger.

"Now you listen to me," he's talking between quick short breaths. "I want you to promise me you'll take care of your mom. She's gonna need you real bad now. You take care to see she don't overwork herself. I want you to sell any of the livestock you can't take care of all by yourself, and I want you to help her in her work for the railroad wherever you can. And help your sister too. And stay out of trouble. You hear me?"

"I hear you, Dad." He's squeezing my hand so hard it hurts. "But, Dad, you're gonna be okay. You've always—"

"No! I did it up right this time. This is it. Those damned doctors would love to keep me flat on my back from now on. I ain't goin' for that, you understand?" When I don't say anything, he again asks, "You understand?"

I don't, and I don't want to. I want him to get well, but I don't say anything. I just look at him.

"You're gonna have to take it from here without me." Though he is whispering, his words are hitting me hard in the face. "Junior will help you, and you can do it."

"Dad . . ."

"No! I don't want no cryin' now."

I swallow the lump again before it can erupt in a scream of the anguish frothing inside me.

His grip on my hand falls limp. He struggles to put the mask back on his face. Junior hurries to help and gets it put in place.

After a few minutes, the rapid breathing slows. The eyes open again. The usual flicker slowly returns as he focuses his gaze on me and winks.

Junior takes me by the arm and leads me from the room.

"You go out and stay with Sis. I'll get Mom from the coffee shop. Mom will stay here with Dad, and we'll go stay the night with some friends of Mom's here in town."

A light comes on in the strange little room. I must have dozed off to sleep because it takes a minute for me to remember where I am.

"It's three-thirty," I can hear the lady saying. "Your mom called. Your daddy's gone on now. He doesn't feel any more pain."

We're all silent a moment. Then Junior asks, "Where's Mom? I better go get her."

"No, that's not necessary. Mr. Bogardus has gone to get her, and he'll take her on home. You kids go on and sleep until daylight, and then after breakfast you can go home."

She turns the light out and closes the door.

I can feel the heavy darkness closing in on me as I lie in bed in the little guest room with Sis crying softly beside me. The events of the day before replay themselves in my mind. If only—if only I'd remembered and kept Dad from getting so excited and working in a frenzy to save those people. If only I'd made him wait in the pickup while I got them out myself or, better still, if I'd driven on to Tornillo to get help. I try to visualize making Dad stay in the pickup or getting him to agree for me to drive on into Tornillo, and all I can see is him telling me to help him save those people. No matter how guilty I feel, I know he wouldn't have let it be any other way.

Then we're at the hospital. His words jump out at me: "Those damned doctors would love to keep me flat on my back from now on. I ain't goin' for that," he'd said.

I roll over in the bed. What did he mean, he ain't goin' for that? Suddenly, the old snake and little runted puppy from years ago appear. "Don't you see now?" the old snake asks.

I'm about to scream back that I still don't see, when Junior, who has been lying silently for a long time on the couch, hits it hard with a fist, making a loud "whack." Then he starts cursing.

"God damn it, I can't sleep. Are y'all asleep?" he asks.

"Let's go home," Sis says.

Nearly every farmer, rancher, and businessman and their families for fifty miles up and down the Rio Grande Valley have come to pay their respects. Even Mr. Silliman has closed the drugstore, and Mr. Tolbert closed the filling station. I bet the post office is the only place in town left open. Even Mr. Hendricks, the school principal, called the school board and got permission to use a school bus to take any of the forty-three high school students sixty miles into El Paso for the funeral.

There are more people standing outside the funeral chapel than can fit inside. It seems like it's taken hours for each person to pass his coffin and pay their respects. They've set up speakers outside so the overflow of mourners can hear the eulogy. They add a scratchy crackle to what's intended to be soft organ background music.

"There sure are a lot of people gonna miss that guy," Uncle Jack says to me in a hushed voice, causing that lump of pain and anguish to swell up in my throat again. We're sitting in the family cubicle watching the single-file line coming in the back door, down the aisle, past the open casket, up the other side, and back out the door.

Each person seems to approach the open casket with a mixture of anticipation and disbelief. It's hard not to expect the waxy expressionless face to break into that familiar good-natured grin and a twinkling eye to look up and wink as if to say this is all a joke. Few people have ever seen Boots McBride with a blank face, but this time it remains motionless, and, as they come close, they're assailed with the faint odor of embalming fluid. At that moment, the bitter reality hits them in the pits of their stomachs like an invisible fist. The expression of anticipation and disbelief fades from their faces and is replaced with pain and despair.

It doesn't surprise me to see Vernon Delaney in the line, but it does surprise me when he breaks out of the line, walks into our private cubicle, and gives Mom a big hug. "You just let me know if there's anything I can do," he is saying. Then he turns to a tall, dark-headed woman and a short, skinny man that followed him. He points at me, "There's the young man you're lookin' for."

The rather pretty woman approaches me with the little skinny guy following close on her heels, nervously fingering a big wide-brimmed straw hat he's carrying in his hands. He has a black eye and a healing cut across his cheek. The woman's face becomes familiar when she leans over and puts her hand on my shoulder. "I'm Billie Jean Boyd. This here's Johnny Scott. You may have heard of Johnny. He's a jockey. We're the ones you pulled out of that wrecked car." I must have recoiled because her eyes widen as she drops her hand from my shoulder and steps back.

But the jockey finds his voice now, as he steps close and says quietly, "You may hate our guts, and I don't blame you if you do, but I had to come here and pay my respects to the man that saved my life. I want you to know that if there's ever anything I can do—any-thing—all you gotta do is ask." With that, before I can say anything, before I can figure out whether to be mad or not, he turns and walks away with Billie Jean following close behind.

As soon as the last person passes the casket, Buster Bailey steps up to the podium. Buster is big and round, and it seems strange to see him with a necktie, black coat, and shiny shoes, instead of his customary blue denim bib coveralls and brogans. He's even shaved his scraggly whiskers off, and his hair is combed back slick. I'm probably not the only person there thinking he's the last person one would expect to get up and talk in front of a big crowd like this.

"All right, folks, I've more or less volunteered to do this. So lis-ten up, please. I'm sure nobody's surprised these services ain't bein' held at the church at home. Boots McBride never made any secret of his disdain for what he considered to be the hypocritical ways of the people that run that church, and I guess, next to me, there ain't nobody those people consider a bigger sinner. So, we're gonna get a cavalry chaplain down here in a minute to say a prayer, and then we're gonna take him out and give him a proper military funeral. But first, I'm gonna tell you what I know about Boots McBride."

He takes a deep breath and stands silent for a moment as though he forgot what he wants to say. Everyone is waiting, silently urging him to go on.

Finally, he starts. "Boots McBride was quite a character. He used to break horses for the cavalry remount station at Fort Bliss, and later he rode as a personal scout for General Black Jack Pershing as he chased Pancho Villa into Mexico after the Columbus Raid in 1916. After that, he became a personal friend to that Meskin bandit, and rumor had it he had his finger in a little caper where several wagonloads of supplies, gunpowder, and munitions disappeared from the fort and found their way through Vernon Delaney's big spread down to the Big Bend country, where they ended up in the hands of the Meskin Revolution."

Buster is getting his second wind now.

"Boots lived by the code of the west: 'You can do anything you're big enough to,' he'd say, whenever I doubted we could do something he was talkin' about. But he showed a touch of tenderness when he said: 'You don't do nothin' that'll hurt anyone else, 'less, of course, it's necessary to keep them from hurting you or your'n'. And when the goin' got tough, he'd say, 'You do what you gotta do.' I seen him kill a boar hog by cuttin' its throat, and then a few days later he spent several hours tryin' to save a baby ground squirrel that a horse had accidently stepped on."

Buster stops to scratch his gray head. He seems to have forgotten the crowd he's talking to. With his left hand in his pants pocket and still scratching his head with the other, he finally continues.

"I guess, like most of us, Boots had his ups and downs. Over the last twenty years, he's owned and lost three of the best cotton farms in the valley. Durin' the bad times, he's worked as a common laborer, cotton picker, and cowhand. But no matter how bad things got, there was always food on the table for the three kids. He was always good for a handout, and he would buy drinks for the house when his luck was high. He always had time to spin a yarn for the kids and give them some change to buy candy."

There is a hushed conversation among the people outside, like someone is filling in a late comer.

"There's hardly a family in the valley he hasn't lent a hand to at one time or another, sometimes with loans that never got repaid. Or maybe he just pitched in to help with the work when they were short, or maybe he nursed them when they were sick. Next to me, he was probably the best horse doctor in the whole county. I seen him fight men he thought was tryin' to take advantage, and I seen him nurse a sick starvin' hobo for two weeks before sending him off with a fistful of dollar bills."

Buster pauses as he reaches up and wipes the back of his hand across his right eye. "Now he's dead. Killed hisself to save three people he didn't even know. I talked to Laura and found out that, at the present time, his material goods comprise a 1946 Chevrolet pickup, one outlawed horse, a Jersey heifer, and six milk cows, which are gonna have to be sold to pay for this funeral and his doctor bills. I guess by most standards, people will say he died a poor man, but his legacy to all of us has been a rich one. Now the Good Lord's seen fit to take Boots from us, and all I can say is I hope the Lord takes him serious 'cause he's the finest man I ever knew."

Buster Bailey suddenly stops talking and blows his nose on a big white handkerchief. Finally, he continues, "Now we're gonna get Molly Harmon up here to sing 'How Great Thou Art.'"

After the song, the young chaplain sent by the cavalry stands up, looking sharp in his uniform with its polished brass and his shiny shoes. He reads briefly from Dad's military record, says he was a fine man and his friends will miss him, says a short prayer, and marches out to lead the procession to the military cemetery.

The organ plays "Amazing Grace" as we follow the pallbearers carrying the casket out to the long black limousine hearse. Uncle Jack, Mom, Sis, Junior, and I are ushered into another limousine that follows the hearse on the long drive to the cemetery at Fort Bliss. At one point, as we're going around a curve and up a hill, Uncle Jack points out the window and says, "Look, I bet the motorcade following us is over two miles long."

At the military cemetery, with all the headstones just alike and placed in straight rows so that you see a line of headstones every direction you look, Dad's coffin, with an American flag draped over it, is placed on a bracket over an open grave. The chaplain ushers us to a row of metal folding chairs by the grave.

There are seven soldiers commanded by a master sergeant standing at parade rest on the opposite side of the grave. I notice each is wearing a Seventh Cavalry patch on his shoulder. At the end of the grave, opposite from where the chaplain stands, is a corporal with a shiny bugle tucked under his arm.

The chaplain reads from a Bible, says a few words and a long prayer, after which the master sergeant yells:

"Tenshut! Port, arms! Ready. Aim. Fire!"

My ears feel like they split as all seven rifles fire over our heads at the same time. I hold my ears as the same process is followed two more times.

Now the bugle splits the air with its shrill rendition of "Taps."

The sweet music seems to pierce my heart and let some of the pain slip out in the form of a few tears. "I can't help it, Dad," I say under my breath, and I do my best to hide the tears and make them stop.

The sergeant takes the flag off the coffin, brings it over, and asks me to help him fold it. I look at Junior. He jumps up and takes the other end out of the sergeant's hand, and we fold it together. Junior then turns, hands it to the sergeant, and salutes. The sergeant returns the salute, turns smartly, and marches in front of Mom, lays the flag in her lap, steps back, salutes, does an about-face, and marches back to his troops.

The casket is lowered into the grave, and the assembled crowd stands quiet and motionless. Finally, Mom stands up, walks to the edge of the grave, picks up a handful of the loose dirt, tosses it on top of the coffin, and walks proudly toward the car we had ridden in. Sis, Junior, and Uncle Jack do the same.

By the time it's my turn, I've choked back the tears, sadness, and pain. I take a big handful of dirt and toss it on the coffin. As I watch it fall, I whisper, "Bye, Dad. Don't worry, I won't cry again."

CHAPTER 12

I t seems odd, but before Dad died, the only time I could talk to
him was when I was with him. But since he died, I've felt his
presence with me just about all the time. In fact, I find myself
talking to him about as much, if not more, than I talk to ol' Paint.
Sometimes, I find myself talking to both of them at once.

Sometimes, it feels like Dad's leading the way for me. Occasionally, when I'm in doubt and don't know which way to go, I get
a glimpse of him riding that big black stallion, Tar Baby, he always
used to talk about—the one he rode when he was a soldier for
General Pershing, chasing Pancho Villa. I see Tar Baby switch his
long, flowing black tail as he steps gingerly over a rocky ledge, and
Dad waves for me to follow as they disappear over the ridge, and
I know which way to go. I've seen them at night when I'm getting
ready for bed. I've seen them at school when I'm trying to figure
out a hard problem. Once I saw them when I was running to catch
the school bus.

I see them most often at times like now, when I'm riding
ol' Paint. When this happens, I keep nudging her onward to catch
up until she complains. But now, I can feel her resisting my urging.

"What's the matter with you—don't you want to keep up?"

Paint suddenly slows to a walk. "What are you talking about?
What's the big hurry? I've been traveling as fast as I can," she says
grumpily.

Only now does it dawn on me she hasn't seen what I've been
seeing. I had assumed she saw them just like I did and knew why

I kept wanting to hurry along, but now, as she complains in an angry way, I realize she doesn't know what's been going on.

"Okay, ol' girl, take it easy. We'll move along at a comfortable trot," I say, as I head her out of the sandhills along the highway heading into Fort Hancock.

As we come into town, we enjoy watching the usual Saturday morning stream of people from Mexico who have come across the Rio Grande to trade at the stores—people walking, some horseback or riding mules or donkeys, some in wagons, and now and then an old Model A Ford chugs by. They carry all sorts of trade goods, chickens, pigs, leather goods, ropes, an occasional saddle blanket or rug. A few have hand carvings of saints or other such knickknacks. It's always fun to see what they've brought.

Finally, we head up the hill to Manuel's house. Paint isn't very happy when I leave her tied to the front fence made of two-by-four frames and chicken wire, but I promise I'll be back as quick as I can get away.

* * *

"Come on, don't be bashful." Manuel is urging me in the front door of his house.

Even though we've been friends since we were in the first grade—since that time we both got a whipping for speaking Spanish on the school grounds—I've never been to Manuel's house before. He lives up on the hill in Fort Hancock, the part of town the Anglos usually call Meskin Town. He lives close to the Mexican church, the railroad depot, and the post office.

It's the usual adobe flat-roofed house like most others in that part of town. But it has a fresh coat of stucco on the outside that hasn't been painted or colored, so it's the blue-gray color of cement.

As I step in the door, I can smell the cleanness. The cement floor is shiny like it's been waxed, and it's covered with Mexican throw rugs here and there. The adobe walls have been whitewashed.

I'm surprised how big the house is. I expected it to be only two or three rooms, but beyond the front sitting room I can see a hallway that leads to the kitchen and several other large rooms that appear to have been added on from time to time.

From the kitchen, I can smell frijoles and pork cooking.

"Wait here." Manuel leaves me standing uncomfortably in the front room as he disappears down the hallway. I can hear a commotion of voices, and I immediately wish I hadn't given in to his insistence that I come to his house for lunch. He has been asking me for a long time, but now, since Dad has died, he has been more and more insistent. I finally decided if I didn't give in he'd drive me crazy.

"This is my mama," Manuel says, emphasizing the Spanish accent, as he ushers in the short, plump woman with a pleasant face. She is light-skinned like Manuel and has dark brown eyes and black hair like his.

"Hello, Scout. How are you?" I'm surprised as she speaks in clear, unaccented English. I'm glad she's speaking English, though, because although I can still understand it a little, I haven't spoken Spanish in years, and I'm not sure I could. It's like old Miss Harbour whipped all the Spanish out of me.

"I'm very glad you have finally come to our home," Manuel's mother says. "Manuel has talked so much of you that I feel I know you already. Come into the kitchen. I have already made ham sandwiches for you boys to eat. Will you drink milk or would you like a coke?"

Now I'm really surprised. I'd expected beans and tortillas or maybe tamales or tacos, certainly not a ham sandwich and a glass of milk.

While Manuel and I eat, Mrs. Espinosa stands by the kitchen counter explaining that Mr. Espinosa was called out to fix a railroad switch. Being a signal maintainer, he is on call all the time. Then she chats about the weather, school, and how wonderful it is that Manuel and I have been friends all these years.

After I've eaten, I stand and start to thank her for the good food and tell her how much I appreciate being invited, but before I can say anything, she interrupts.

"Before you go, there is someone else who wants to meet you. Manuel will take you to her house. It's just back behind ours."

The small unstuccoed adobe house in the back of the lot looks old and weathered. There is an old cement walkway of a few feet before a concrete step down to get to the smaller-than-usual solid wood door. There's a vine of some sort I can't recognize growing up the wall and hanging over the entrance. Manuel knocks, and after a long silence, he knocks again.

"Abuelita!" he calls.

After another long silence, the wooden door slowly opens into a dark room. A very small, wrinkled, and old-looking woman with her head covered with a dark heavy shawl stands behind the door, gazing at us without speaking.

"This is Scout. Boots McBride's son, Granny," Manuel says in Spanish.

The old woman's eyes light up and the expressionless face breaks into a smile.

"You are Laura's son?" she says in Spanish. "Do you speak Spanish?" she asks.

For a moment I don't answer, then I surprise myself by saying "*Un poquito.*" Her smile broadens. "Come in."

Manuel indicates for me to step into the room ahead of him. I have to duck my head under the vine and the low doorway to get inside. I'm immediately struck by a pungent smell I've never smelled before. It's so strong it almost burns my eyes and nose. As my eyes adjust to the darkness of the room, which is furnished with old Mexican-style furniture, I can see smoke rising from a small clay pot sitting on a corner table.

"Come with me."

I look at Manuel questioningly. He nods, so I follow her into an even smaller dark room lit only by a small candle sitting on a table in the middle of the room. Along the wall, I can make out numerous figurines on the shelving. Some of them I can recognize: crucifixes and the Virgin Mary or the Virgin of Guadalupe. Many of the others that I don't recognize seem grotesque, strange, and frightening. One is a carving of a man holding a snake over his head up to the sun.

"Sit down." Still speaking in Spanish, she indicates a woven cane chair on one side of the table as she sits on the other side.

"Give me your hands."

I look over my shoulder at Manuel standing behind me. He nods, so I swallow hard and place both hands on the table, palms up. The old woman takes the right one in both her hands and holds it close to the candlelight, studying every line carefully. After what seems like a long time, she takes the other hand and examines it the same way. Then, she examines both hands together, comparing one with the other.

The smell of the incense is heavy in the air. I feel dizzy and queasy, almost like I've had a drink of whiskey. I can't figure out what's going on.

Suddenly, she looks me directly in the eyes for the first time. "Yes, you're Laura's son," speaking in broken English now. "It is as I have said."

I'm wondering what this old woman is talking about, but apparently she sees the look in my eyes and tries to explain.

"I know your mother when she first come to this valley and lived with the Bean family before she meet Boots McBride. I live with them at the same time. I teach her Spanish, and I see she has the good heart. I teach her to understand the ways of our people. I read her hands too. I tell her she will have two sons. The younger will do many special things and will have a special sight. Now that I read your hands, I know it is true."

"What d'you mean?" I start to stand up. "I don't know what you're talking about."

The old woman holds tight to my hands and pulls me back down into the chair. I look over my shoulder at Manuel. He's standing with his arms folded over his chest, grinning. I don't know what's going on, and I resent this old woman's invasion into my private life. How do I know she's telling the truth?

The woman pulls my attention back to her. Her piercing eyes feel like they drill right through my heart.

"I see it in your hands. I see it in your sad eyes. You have a great hunger to learn the many secrets of life, and you have many questions. You must find the answers if you are to have peace. You will find the answers, but you will find them in a place you do not want to look.

"I must tell you these things so you will know. If you are to find peace, you must listen to those you do not think are wise. I must tell you these things so you will not feel so much sadness."

We sit for a long while in silence with her holding my hands tightly, her intense eyes continuing to burn into me.

I feel like I'm under her spell, but finally I have to take a deep breath, and then I begin to relax a little bit. She slowly loosens her grip. After the long silence, I jump when she starts to talk again.

"You will not want to believe me. You will deny what I have told you. But it is true, and you will see it happen. Then you will remember what I have said, and you will know it is true.

"You need not fear. Your papa is with you, and he will lead you for a while."

How did she know that? I look at her carefully. She's crazy. She can't know I've seen Dad.

"Yes, I know," she says aloud, nodding in answer to my thoughts.

I head ol' Paint back into the sandhills toward where the railroad track runs. We'll strike the road that runs along the tracks and follow it home. My head is still reeling as I go over what the old woman said.

I remember being blinded by the bright sun when we left the old woman's house, but it felt good to be out in the fresh air again.

"She's my grandmother. Her name is Magdalena Gonzales," Manuel had explained before I could assault him. "She made me bring you here. She believed it was very important, and she said she must talk to you now because she is very old."

"Why in hell didn't you warn me?"

"There was no way I could. If I had said anything, you wouldn't have come."

"Yeah, but she's crazy. She doesn't know what's going on. How can she know anything about me?"

Manuel takes hold of my arm and squeezes it firmly. I can tell he's holding back his anger. "She knows," he says, as he looks me directly in the eyes. Then he pushes me away. "You don't have to believe it if you don't want to. But you will. You'll see she's right."

I feel scared and sick at the pit of my stomach as I mount ol' Paint and ride out of town.

Now I try to talk to Dad but he's not there. I ask ol' Paint if she knows what happened back there, but she just heaves a big disinterested sigh.

I don't want to think about it either. I won't let myself think about it. All I care about is being a world champion cowboy. That's what I'm gonna do, and that's all I'm gonna worry about.

CHAPTER 13

I can feel Paint tremble between my legs. She is squatted against the corner of the roping box with her ears perked, concentrating on the chute gate. I nod, the gate swings open, and the floppy-eared Brahman calf darts out all within a flicker of a second. Paint is running hard, trying to catch the calf. I lean forward to help her run, poised, ready, holding the loop out from my body, ready to swing it over my head and toss it out to snare the calf around the neck. I can tell Paint is running as hard as she can. She wants to show that old bastard with the bull's-head pipe how good we are.

We've been practicing every day, leading Betsy's Jersey calf out away from the barn. Then I'd turn him loose, and as he ran back to his mama, Paint would chase him, and I'd rope him just like we'd seen the ropers here at the arena before. We've gotten so good that I haven't missed a loop in the last fifteen tries. I know we won't have any problems. All I need is for Paint to get me close enough.

Just a little closer. I start to swing my loop, and the calf sees us closing behind him. In a blink he ducks to the right and runs away from us like we're standing still.

"Come on, Paint. Catch him," I urge. But the calf keeps moving away. I stop swinging my rope and look down at Paint, "Come on, gal! Run faster!" But I see she has her ears laid back against her stretched out neck, obviously running as hard as she can. The calf is still moving away from us.

The calf reaches the end of the arena and stops in a corner, looking for a way to get out. As we catch up, he darts past us, running back toward the other end of the arena, and I snag the loop around his neck. The action is so quick Paint is caught off balance when the calf hits the end of the rope and I dismount. She doesn't fall, but it's all she can do to keep her legs under her and not let the calf drag her down the arena. As I try to take hold of the calf to throw and tie him, he darts away, pulling hard against the rope tied to my saddle horn. Paint isn't strong enough to hold her position, let alone run backward, which is what I need her to do.

Finally, I come back to Paint's head, throw my arm over the rope, then move down it to the calf's head. Just as I grab him to throw him, he ducks his head, hooking me in the chest and making me stand up straight. Then, before I can react, he butts me in the stomach and ducks under my legs, throwing me up over his back. I do a compete flip landing hard on my back as the calf scampers around Paint, who is still trying to hold the rope tight.

As I pull myself up gasping for breath, Juan García gallops up, steps off his Grulla Dun, takes the rope at Paint's head, runs down, and quickly throws the calf. Paint is too tired to hold the rope tight any longer, and he easily slips the loop off the calf's neck and turns him loose.

As I walk up trying to decide whether to thank him or cuss him, he turns to me. "Hell, that calf was gonna kill you and your horse both. Maybe you can swing a loop all right, but you got a lot to learn about throwin' and tyin' a calf." As he strides back to his horse, "You better get yourself a bigger and faster horse if you're gonna rope these big Brahman calves."

It takes me a few moments to I realize I'm standing there with my mouth open as he mounts the Grulla and rides away.

I can feel the shame building as I slowly coil my rope and hang it on the saddle horn. Paint's clearly worn out standing with her head down. "I'm sorry," she says. "I just can't run that fast."

"It's all right, gal. It's all right. It doesn't matter." I look up at the end of the arena and see Vernon Delaney squatted against a fence post, puffing his pipe. I look at the other end of the arena to see if there is a way I can get out without having to go past him. Bob Hillis closes the wooden gate behind the calf after letting him into the holding pen. That's no way out. I can't go hide in the holding pen until everyone leaves. I can't just stay down at this end of the arena because everyone will see me and think I'm too embarrassed to go back up there where they're all standing around. Just as I accept the fact I'm going to have to walk past Vernon Delaney, Sonny Walsh calls out the next roper. Maybe I can get by while everyone's watching him. Maybe he'll have a worse wreck than I did, and everyone will be laughing at him instead of me. I walk fast, leading Paint close to the fence, trying to become invisible.

Vernon Delaney is watching the other roper. It doesn't look like he's too interested in me. I move to the other side of the arena, hoping I can get out without having to face him. I'd saved enough money from the milk deliveries to add to my winnings from the barrel race to have enough to enter the jackpot roping, and I had gotten here early to put my entry in before Vernon arrived. When he saw me he offered to pay my entry fee, saying he'd make good on his promise, but I refused. "I don't need your money," I retorted. "Besides your offer was for two weeks after the matched roping." He knew I couldn't be here then because that was the week Dad died.

"Okay," he'd said. "If that's the way you want it." He turned and walked away without saying any more. It had felt good to see his disappointment.

Now I know he's thinking he was right all the time. He believes Paint and I can't tie a calf. We'll still show him. We'll find a calf that can't run so fast. We'll find one that's smaller, and we'll show him. We can still do it.

The other roper has tied his calf and is now riding back up to the box amid car honks and clapping. I pace myself to walk along beside him, keeping him in between us and Vernon Delaney until we reach the gate to go out of the arena. Just as we get to the gate, Juan García rides up to Vernon and catches his attention. It's my chance to slip out of the arena.

I walk, leading Paint until we're in the neighboring sandhills. Just when I mount Paint, and we start the long ride home, the words of Juan García begin to eat at me. "You better get yourself a bigger and faster horse," he'd said.

"He's right, you know," Paint says reading my thoughts.

I dismount, stand directly in front of Paint, and look her in the eye. "No!" I yell at her. "Don't you say that. You're the best horse in the whole world. We've been together all our lives. That will never change. We're still gonna be champions. You and me. No one else. You hear me?"

"Champions rope those big fast Brahman calves," Paint says.

"I don't care. We'll find a way."

Paint looks away. "Let's go home," she says.

I can tell she's not saying what she's really thinking. I can tell she doesn't want me to ride another horse.

CHAPTER 14

"Know why I like you?"

"Eh, whyzzat, Doc?" He's imitating Bugs Bunny.

"'Cause you're the only guy I know that has redder hair and more freckles than I do," I lie. Fact is, I think red hair and freckles are ugly.

If I admitted the truth as to why I like Doc Cummings, I'd have to say it's because he's cool. He lives in the city. In El Paso. He knows all the things that make a guy cool. Instead of having his hair cut in a burr like mine, he has a flat top with the sides long, combed into a duck tail at the back. He has a black leather jacket too.

When he came to see me this time, he brought a pack of Lucky Strikes. This is the first time I ever smoked a ready-rolled cigarette.

We're sitting in the pickup, parked across the highway from Rojalio's Bar, passing the cigarette back and forth between us. I pull at the cigarette and watch the lit end glow bright red in the dark. Then I open my mouth and draw the smoke deep in my lungs, feeling the relaxing reaction of my chest that tends to mask all the confusion and hurt I carry there. I understand now why Dad smoked. The nicotine has a way of settling that frustration, the upsets, the storms that boil within me that I'm afraid to let slip out for fear I'll be embarrassed. It gives me a small amount of comfort and lets me feel more in control.

There's plenty of light from the red and green neon lights that run around the big front window and the outer edge of Rojalio's Bar. The Blue Ribbon Beer sign up on the pole flashes on and off, and you can see it all the way from McNary in the east and Fort Hancock in the west.

I got to know Doc when he came down to visit his uncle, Shorty Williams, who lives on the big farm down the hill from McNary. Shorty had an old palomino gelding he let Doc ride. Last summer we even rode out to the mountains and camped out for a few days, cooking bacon and eggs in a skillet and pinto beans in a coffee can for ourselves. We slept in blankets we rolled up and tied behind our saddles. We sat by campfires at night with Doc playing the guitar and singing cowboy songs. It was the way I'd always dreamed a real cowboy's life would be.

Ol' Paint didn't like Doc. She said he was a city slicker and a "dude." Once when he climbed up on her for a ride, she balked. She refused to move till I got on her and apologized and promised her I wouldn't let him get on her again without asking her first.

When we were out camping, we got caught in a thunderstorm, and his slick black leather jacket got all wet. Then it got all scratched up when we rode through a catclaw thicket, so he doesn't wear it much anymore. But he has it on tonight because it's kind of cold.

He has come down from El Paso to spend Thanksgiving with me and Mom. With Junior married now and Sis away at school, Mom suggested I invite him. His dad died in the past year too, and when I wrote to invite him, his mom let us know she'd be glad to have him come. It seems she is having enough problems with his two younger brothers and two sisters. It's Saturday after Thanksgiving, and with a lot of begging, I had convinced Mom to let us drive into Fort Hancock to "see what was going on." Since Rojalio's Bar is halfway between, I figure there's nothing wrong if we stop along the way.

Manuel, heading in the opposite direction, drives up and stops beside us. He is driving his dad's old '36 Ford pickup. Willy and Bubba are with him.

"Hey, man. What you guy's doin'?" Bubba asks from the passenger's side of Manuel's pickup.

"Havin' a Lucky Strike. Want a drag?" I say.

"Sure, pass it over."

I reach out the window and hand the half-smoked cigarette to Manuel. "You ever smoked a ready roll before?"

"Naw," he says, and takes a deep drag. "This is great."

We all laugh when Manuel gags and starts coughing.

Bubba gets out from the other side and walks around to stand between the two pickups and lean on the running board of Manuel's pickup.

Reaching over in front of me, Doc shakes a Lucky Strike out of the pack and offers it to Bubba. Bubba tries to look casual as he places it between his teeth, holding his lips open in a broad smile. Doc fishes a book of paper matches out of a shirt pocket, flips the match pack open, bends a still-attached match, closes the pack again, and strikes the match on the strike pad on the bottom of the pack, lighting the cigarette in Bubba's mouth all with one hand. It's a real smooth movement.

"Cool," Bubba says, letting the smoke roll out his nostrils. He doesn't cough the way Manuel did, but Bubba's been rolling his own Bull Durhams for almost a year now. Bubba has changed a lot lately. He doesn't have a ducktail like Doc, but he's started slicking his hair back with Brylcreem.

I can't resist a jab at Bubba, "I'm surprised to see you and Willy out like this since you're such good Christians, bein' baptized and all."

Bubba laughs good-naturedly. "Well, that was a long time ago, Scout, but the way I look at it, once you've been saved, you can afford to sin a little."

A red Buick pulls off the highway and turns into Rojalio's. A tall scarecrow of a figure climbs out.

"It's Lucky Hubert." Willy yells at him, "Hey, Hubert, *que pasa, pendejo?*"

Seeing us, the lanky figure ambles across the highway toward us. I get a funny feeling, like I see trouble walking toward us. Hubert is called Lucky because he's always getting into scrapes without ever getting into trouble, but somebody else always gets in trouble instead. One day in the locker room, the coach heard how he'd shot Mr. Giles in the back of the head with a spitball, and Monte Moseley got the blame. After hearing the story, Coach said he's so lucky, he could "fall in a bucket of shit and come out smelling like a rose." So everyone calls him Lucky Hubert now. But he has a mean streak too. I've seen him tease and pick on younger kids.

He's skinny as a fence rail and has a big head covered with sandy blond hair at the end of a long thin neck. He's kind of bucktoothed so that, with his teeth protruding over his bottom lip, he usually looks like he's smiling. You have to watch the glint in his little beady eyes to know that's not true.

"Well, whatta we got here, Pavo and Pavo Number Two?" He knows I hate it when he refers to me by the Spanish word for turkey because of my red head, and I can feel my face burning and getting red. I don't think Doc knows what *pavo* means. Otherwise, he'd probably make some wisecrack back.

"What you guys doin' out here in the dark? Y'all planning to rob old Rojalio?"

"Aw, we were just smokin' a cigarette," Bubba says, "Want one?"

"Naw, I got a little matter I gotta take care of up on the other side of Fort Hancock," he says and winks. We all laugh like we know what he means. "I just stopped by to pick up a few beers. You know what they say. Candy is dandy, but liquor is quicker."

We all laugh again. Hubert doesn't laugh. He just looks at me with his beady eyes glinting in the moonlight. "What're you laughing at Pavo? You don't even know what I'm talking about."

I don't say anything. I just take another drag off of my Lucky Strike and feel my face flush.

"Whatcha doin' out with these cats anyway, Pavo? I thought all you ever did was practice ropin' calves."

It's like he hit me in the pit of my stomach, and I take still another drag on the now short cigarette to help me repress the anger I feel building. "Aw, I'm not doin' that no more," I say calmly.

"What's the matter, you figure out there ain't no future in them stupid caballos?"

His use of the Spanish word for horses gives an even more derogatory tone to the inflection of his voice. I can feel my face burning redder. It's all I can do to hold back the anger. "Naw, I just quit doin' it." I hope the darkness hides the redness of my face, and I appear as calm as I'm trying to sound. Another drag on the cigarette not only helps hold back the anger and desire to punch Hubert in the nose, but it also dulls the pain and frustration that is in my chest constantly these days. I keep trying to put it out of my mind, to suppress the frustration, to keep from feeling sorry for myself. It's not my fault ol' Paint can't run fast enough to catch those damned fast Brahman calves.

I lash back at Hubert and change the subject. "I bet you can't buy beer, even if you are a senior in high school. You're not twenty-one."

"Well, what you wanna bet, Pavo? It's not so much how old you are, but how you handle yourself. Old Rojalio don't know how old anyone is anyway."

Bubba is impressed. "Will you get us some beer?"

"Sure, you guys shell out enough to buy me one too."

As we all dig in our pockets for money Bubba says, "Armando told me they're havin' a big Thanksgiving dance down there at Fort Quitman where he lives now."

"Gosh, that's over forty miles from here with about thirty-five miles of dirt road after you run off the pavement." Manuel says doubtfully.

"So, what's the big deal? This pickup of Pavo's is almost new. It'll make it all right, won't it, Pavo? It's yours since your old man died, ain't it?" Hubert says.

I shrink in my seat. I hadn't figured on something like this. There's no doubt the '46 Chevy pickup will make it. It's still practically new. Dad bought it just before he died, with money from the sale of some of the milk cows. Mom'll skin me alive if I take it off down there and get in trouble.

Lucky Hubert stuffs our money in his pocket and struts across the highway and into the bar.

"I don't trust him. He'll keep our money," I whisper as he goes in the bar.

"Naw," says Doc. "He'll get the beer just to prove he can."

It seems like Hubert is in the bar a long time. He has to come out to get his car, so I know he hasn't run away with our money. "Maybe he's just gonna sit in there and drink all the beer he bought with our money," I suggest after a while.

Doc is getting nervous and a little angry. I wouldn't want Doc to be mad at me, but Lucky Hubert may be too cocky to worry, figuring he can talk his way out of anything.

Suddenly, the screen door on the bar swings open and Hubert appears carrying a box. "Here it is you guys." He says as he sets the box on the ground and takes out a bottle of beer. "Anybody got a opener?"

Willy pulls out a big Boy Scout pocket knife with an opener on it and slips the cap off Hubert's beer. Doc reaches in the box and pulls bottles out one by one as Willy pops the caps off and passes them around.

I feel the cold wetness as Willy places a beer bottle in my hand. I hesitate. Maybe I shouldn't. Mom has trusted me with the pickup. If she finds out, she'll never trust me again.

"Hey, Scout, drink up," Doc says, as he clinks his bottle against mine. "Here's to champion cowboys." He knows about my dream, but I haven't told him about Paint not being able to catch those fast Brahman calves.

"Yeah, champion cowboys," I say as I tip the bottle to my mouth.

The pickup bounces as the road goes down into an arroyo, and the back wheels chatter in the loose sand as we ease across and come up the other side. All six of us are crammed into the cab, and Hubert is driving. Next to him, I hold my half-full bottle of beer with both hands to keep it from spilling as I try to remember how I got myself in this situation. While Willy was passing out the beer, Hubert had said we better not sit there across from Rojalio's drinking it, so they all climbed in my pickup, and Hubert started driving south. After we had started out, Hubert told us he knows a place down by Fort Quitman where we can cross the Rio Grande into Old Mexico and over there we can buy all the beer and whiskey we want. He had said that if we wanted to go down there to that dance, he'd go with us and show us the way, so long as we paid for the booze. It seems he forgot all about the "little matter" he needed to take care of on the other side of Fort Hancock.

"Slow down, Hubert," I say. "You're gonna kill us."

Hubert laughs as he steps on the gas. I look over at Manuel sitting next to me on the other side. He's sitting on top of Doc, and Willy is squeezed against the door with Bubba sitting on top of him. I wouldn't have agreed to this if Manuel hadn't acted like he thought it'd be okay. He's usually the most level-headed and careful of my friends. But now he's all glassy-eyed and giggling, having finished his beer and dropped the bottle on the floorboard a long time ago. I wonder what I'll tell Mom about where we went.

"Yea ha! Ride 'em, cowboy!" Bubba yells as the pickup bounces over a deep rut, causing him to bounce his head on the ceiling. He laughs and rubs his head. "Can you imagine havin' to ride a school bus over this road twice a day like Armando does?"

In the small settlement of Fort Quitman it is easy to find Armando's house. As we drive into his front yard, we're greeted by a big German Shepherd followed by several smaller dogs all barking a loud and unfriendly greeting. We stop in the yard and wait, afraid to get out. After a while Armando appears, pulling on a shirt as he comes out the door. He can't tell who it is in the dark until Manuel yells at him to call off the dogs.

"What you guys doin' down here?" He's pushing his long black hair back on his head, obviously trying to wake up.

"We came down to go to that dance you told me about. Where is it, aren't you goin'?" I can see Bubba is worried he might have been wrong.

"Aw, I hadn't expected to see you guys. I'd already gone to bed. My mom and dad are over there." He sniffs. "Y'all got beer in there?"

"I think we drank it all, but we're gonna go down and cross the river and get some more," Hubert says.

"You wanna come?" I ask.

"Let me go wash my face and put on some other clothes," Armando says as he heads back to the house.

A lone cricket chirping is the only sound. It seems strange to hear a cricket this time of year, but it's warm down here by the river. I can't see the grass in the dark, but it feels soft and pliable like it's still green. I climb up out of the salt cedar thicket to the top of the levy and look back toward where we parked the pickup. Can't see it from here. No reflection from the moon. The Immigration probably won't see it unless they happen to shine a spotlight on it. That's unlikely unless they suspect something's going on.

Thankful I won't get loose sand and gravel in my high top boots, I slide and run down the other side of the levy toward the river. There's a flat clearing from here to the water, so I run to the river edge where I can drop off the bank to hide if a car comes along. Now I can smell the river and hear the water whispering as it carves out the border between the U.S. and Mexico. Behind me, I can see Willy and Bubba following my trail.

"Jesus Christ, it's cold!" Doc has taken his boots off down by the water's edge and stepped in.

Out in the middle, I can see Manuel making his way to the other side. Hubert and Armando have already made it.

At the water's edge, I sit on a rock and pull off my boots and socks, roll up my Levi's as high as I can, and step into the water. Doc's right—it's cold. I grit my teeth to keep from complaining. As I follow Doc, the water only comes up about half way to my knees. Suddenly, it gets deeper.

"Doc, did you walk into deep water?" I whisper loud enough to be heard for a mile.

"Move to your right a little. It'll be okay."

I'm surprised how soon I come up out of the water. Hubert and Armando are sitting on the ground, putting their boots back on.

"Welcome to Mexico," Hubert says.

The headlights of a car appear on the levy just as Bubba follows Willy out of the water. It's about half a mile away.

"Quick, you guys. Get over here in these bushes, and we'll just sit here till he goes by," Hubert says.

My heart is pounding in my ears as I move down close to Manuel huddled among some cattail reeds. I feel Willy drop down beside me and then Bubba on top of us.

"Be careful! You about broke my ribs," Willy complains.

Bubba falls between me and Willy. I can feel him shivering.

The lights shine above us as an old pickup rattles down the road on top of the levy.

"Just some old Mexican," says Hubert as he stands up, beating the river sand out of his pants.

As I start to do the same, I realize I'm lying in a mud puddle. My whole right leg is wet and muddy. "Shit."

"That's alright. It'll dry." Doc helps me up.

After everyone's got his boots or shoes back on, we run in a group across the clearing from the water's edge to the levy on the Mexico side. The road up on top isn't nearly as well traveled as it is on the American side. In single file, we follow Hubert and Armando to a well-defined trail through the cedar thicket that lays for some distance from the levy away from the river. Suddenly, we're on a well-traveled road.

Even though I'm breathing hard from the rapid pace, I continue to shiver. I can't tell if it's the cold or the excitement.

My heart stops when Hubert stops dead in his tracks. Something white and ghostlike looms before us. We all stand frozen, afraid to breath. Suddenly, the ghost snorts and runs into the thicket beside the road.

"A big ol' steer," someone whispers in a relieved voice.

We continue along silently, ever alert for any danger that may jump out of the dark at us. A dog barks in the distance.

Suddenly, there's a light ahead. "There's a grocery store. We can get some beer there," says Armando in a relaxed normal voice. I can't believe how cool he is.

We enter the little one-room adobe building lit by a lantern hanging from the ceiling. A candle burns on the counter at the back where an old man with a long white beard sits motionless. At first, it doesn't seem he has even seen us, but then he looks at us and stands up slowly.

"*Buenas noches*," the old man says finally.

"Talk to him, Armando," Hubert says. "Tell him what we want."

After a few minutes of conversation in Spanish, Armando turns to us. "Okay, what you guys want?"

"Does he have any tequila?" Doc wants to know.

"Aw, that stuff'll kill us. Let's get beer," Manuel says.

"How about some of both?" the old man suggests in English as he pulls a gunnysack from under the counter, goes to a box in the corner, and starts putting in bottles of Dos Equis one at a time, carefully. Then, reaching up on a nearby shelf, he adds two larger clear bottles, placing them on top for easy access.

Payment is made, and we're on our way, with Bubba and Armando carrying the gunnysack. As soon as we're out of sight of the store, Hubert stops.

"I think I been bit by a snake. Quick! Give me some medicine." He reaches into the gunnysack and pulls out one of the clear bottles and starts to work the cork out with his teeth while we all laugh.

"Wait, let's open a couple of beers for chasers." Willy has his pocket knife with the bottle opener out and working. Hubert takes a pull at the tequila, hands it to Doc, and grabs the open beer bottle from Willy's hand. After a long pull on the beer bottle, he relaxes.

"Whee, that's smooth."

Doc follows suit and passes the bottles to Manuel. It's my turn next. I hesitate. A thought of concern flickers through my mind, concern about Mom finding out, or that I might drink too much and have a wreck on the way home. But I notice for the first time that, ever since I finished that first beer and cigarette, that lump that has been in my chest is smaller than it has been since that miserable failure at trying to rope that fast Brahman last August. Or maybe since Dad died. Or maybe it had been there even longer than that. I don't know, and right now I don't care any more.

"Come on, don't be chicken," Bubba says.

"Yeah," says Doc, as he regains his breath. "Don't be chicken, Scout. It's real smooth." His voice is deep, and he drags the words out. He's lost the imitation of Bugs Bunny.

What the hell, I think to myself. It doesn't make any difference anyway. I'm not gonna be roping calves any more. I take a deep breath, turn the bottle up to my lips, and take two big swallows. Doc has his face close to mine to be sure I don't cheat.

"God! He took two swallows," he says as he hands the beer to me.

I burn from my mouth, down my throat, gullet, to the bottom of my stomach. The bubbles in the beer make the burn worse. I grit my teeth and give thanks for the dark so they can't see the tears in my eyes.

As I watch the others take their turn, I realize they only take a small sip of the tequila and follow it with a large swallow of beer.

It's a happy group that reaches the river's edge. Suddenly, I find myself standing in the middle of the river, water running over the tops of my boots. Beside me Manuel makes a big splash as he falls face down in the water. Giggling and laughing, Armando and I try to help him up, and all three of us end up in a heap in the cold shallow water.

Finally, we splash our way to the river bank on the U.S. side. Doc, Bubba, Willy, and Hubert are already there, sitting on the grass. Lucky Hubert pulls the bottle out of the sack again. He takes another long pull, chases it with beer, and passes it around to all of us. I only take a little this time.

"Oh, man!" says Bubba, falling over on his back. "This is great!"

"Yeah," Hubert says. "The only thing better is a soft, willing woman."

"Yeah!" says Bubba.

Willy laughs, spewing a mouthful of beer all over all of us. "What are you talkin' about Bubba? You never even kissed a girl."

"That's what you think," Bubba says, sitting up.

"Oh yeah? Who?" Willy's really interested now.

"Think I'd tell you?"

"I seen you flirtin' with Jenke Harmon but you never kissed her. I bet you never even held her hand," Willy insists.

In spite of the liquor I'm surprised to feel anger rising in my chest when Bubba says, "I been closer'n anybody else. I bet every guy in high school would like to bird-dog that little bitch. You ever notice how her little ass fills out those tight Levi's she wears sometimes?"

I don't know why it should make any difference to me, but I'm about to object to any indecent talk about Jenke when Hubert interrupts, "Shit! I'm not talking about just kissing," Hubert says. "Haven't you guys ever done it?"

There's a moment of silence. "Sure," Bubba says.

Hubert laughs. "You're lying. I bet none of you guys have ever done it. I bet none of you ever even saw a girl naked. I'll bet you haven't, have you, Pavo?"

Again I can feel my face growing red in the darkness, and I don't know what to say. I'm saved by a rustling sound in the tall grass along the river, though. Doc jumps up and whispers. "Let's get out of here before the Immigration catches us."

We quickly pile in the pickup, and Armando drives to Fort Quitman to the old schoolhouse where we can hear the beat of Spanish guitars, blare of a trumpet, whine of a squeeze-box, and the squeal of a fiddle flowing out over the crowd of parked cars, pickups, and horse buggies in the schoolyard. Here and there small groups stand talking in hushed tones, passing a bottle.

"Come on. Let's go inside and see if we can find some girls." Bubba is anxious.

"Let's have one more round," says Hubert. I'm surprised by Hubert's hesitation. The way he's been talking, I expected him to go right in, grab a pretty girl, and start swinging across the dance floor. But I'm ready for another sip of the tequila. That lump in my chest is almost gone now. I feel better than I've felt in a long time.

After a pull on the tequila bottle, chased by a couple swallows of beer, all the others except Manuel and me head inside to the dance. Holding the tequila bottle in one hand and a half-full beer bottle in the other, I watch them enter the old schoolhouse-turned-dancehall. I can hear and feel the beat of the music, and through the door I see varied-color skirts moving about, shaking, and, occasionally, one will spin out full, exposing smooth bare thighs and a flash of lacy underwear. I wonder how it would feel to hold a girl close and dance with her—to feel her body next to mine, and I can't help thinking about those things Hubert was talking about either. Also I can't help wondering about Willy and Bubba. They are saved Christians, but they have been drinking as much as everybody else, and they sure don't seem to be bothered about charging in there to the dance.

Suddenly, I think I see a blurry vision of Reverend Johnson in the doorway pointing his finger right at me. "It is sinful to enjoy pleasures of the flesh. Dancing women are harlots. A decent man won't succumb to their charms. Theirs are the charms of the devil." I take a long pull at the tequila and slowly wash it down with a swallow of beer, swishing the beer between my teeth so as to get the full taste.

"Where's Doc? I gotta go find Doc. He's pro'l'y in trouble."

"Who?" Manuel is sitting beside me in the back of the pickup. His head rolls on his shoulders as he speaks.

"You're drunk. I gotta go find Doc." As I start to crawl out of the pickup bed, I feel a body lying motionless in my path. I push on it. It moans. Bubba. I crawl over and fall off the tailgate onto the ground.

I hear someone laugh as I walk through the parking lot on my way to the door to the schoolhouse. I don't know what they're laughing about. Seems perfectly natural for me to lean against each car and pickup as I pass.

The band is blaring out "El Rancho Grande" as I reach the door. Every few seconds a dancer gives out with a cowboy's "Yea ha!" I can see the swirling skirts, fast-moving feet, and bare legs up close now. A beautiful black-haired Mexican woman, her dark brown smiling eyes inviting me, swings out close to my face, then before I can move, disappears in the crowd again. I'm assailed by the heavy tobacco smoke and body sweat as I ease myself along the wall, trying to focus on the blurred faces in the crowd, looking for that beautiful face again. I can't find her, and I can't find Doc either.

All the moving bodies and the loud music begin to make me dizzy. I hadn't noticed before how hot it is. How close the bodies feel. How they all seem to be closing in on me. The wall sways. I can feel the wooden floor shake as the dancers stomp the floor in time to the music, and they're all coming toward me, pressing against me, trying to stomp me.

Suddenly, Hubert is holding me by the collar of my shirt. "You okay?"

Doc and Willy are beside him, leaning against the wall.

"Where'sh yer girls? Why aren't y' dancin'?" I say, but it doesn't seem like my voice. It seems to be coming from somewhere outside my body, and I giggle at the funny sound.

"Ain't no girls. Le's go git a drink," Doc says.

As Hubert pushes me toward the door, still holding to my collar, a familiar face appears before me. I'd know that carved bull's head with ivory horns on the curved pipe anywhere. I try to focus my eyes on the face behind the pipe, and then I cringe because I know what's coming.

"Speck! What're you doin' way down here?"

I try to pull myself up straight and push Hubert's hand away from my collar, but he continues to hold on.

"None a' y'r goddamn bizniz," I say, trying hard to focus on the face I know is there.

The old man has to take the pipe out of his mouth as his whole body shakes with laughter.

"Well, when you sober up come see me. I got a proposition for you." The old man walks away, laughing.

"Ol' som' bitch. I oughta kick his ass."

Hubert pulls me hard by the collar and pushes me out the door.

"Whozzat?" Doc asks, following behind us.

"Mean ol' bastard. Don't like 'im." I stumble, almost falling, but Hubert holds me up pushing on toward the pickup.

"Aaauugh! Oooh."

I open my eyes and turn my head in the direction of the moaning. It's Willy over in the barrow ditch throwing up. Hubert is there beside him. I'm lying face down, with my head hanging off the end of the pickup tailgate. The coldness of the metal seems to make me more alert. My head starts spinning again, and I close my eyes. Involuntarily, I turn on my side and draw my knees up to my chest as my stomach retches, and I gag. Long empty of any content, the knot in the middle of my body produces only the bitter taste of bile into my mouth.

As the retching eases, and my body relaxes, I become aware of a faint light blinking on and off. I hear a groan beside me. I roll over on the other side, and I feel the smoothness of Doc's leather jacket. Over Doc's trembling body and the side of the pickup bed I can see the Blue Ribbon Beer sign faithfully flashing its signal to the dark world. The neon lights around the edge of the building of Rojalio's Bar are off now.

"Aaaw! I think I'm gonna die." It's Doc retching again.

Suddenly, a car pulls up and stops behind the pickup with its headlights shining directly on us.

"What's goin' on here?" It's Junior. I can't see him, but I recognize his voice. I rise up and wave my hand.

"Here, Junior."

"Scout! Are you hurt? What happened? Who're you fighting?"

"'S no fight. 'S okay."

"Who's that over there?"

"'S Willy. 'S okay. Don' worry. 'S okay." I close my eyes.

"Beth Ann! Get up. Put on a pot of coffee. I got some drunk boys here we got to sober up."

Junior pushes me into an overstuffed chair and goes back for Doc. Junior and Beth Ann got married shortly before Dad died. Mom had a fit because they were both only eighteen, but she and Dad figured that if they tried to stop it, they'd run off and elope anyway. Now Junior works for Leon Levitt, Beth Ann's uncle, as a foreman on his huge cotton farm.

"I gotta take Hubert back so he can take those other boys home. Be back in just a minute. They both got the dry heaves so I don't think they'll throw up on anything," Junior says, as he lays Doc out in a stuffed chair beside me.

Holding a robe tight around her, my sister-in-law leans over close to my face. The sweetness of her perfume is the first pleasant smell I've known in a long time, but it's so sweet, my stomach becomes queasy again. Her black hair falling around her face accents the whiteness of her skin. Her big smile with those perfectly shaped teeth make her the most beautiful woman I've ever seen.

"What have you been doing, Scout?" She recoils from the smell of my breath.

I just look at her, trying to focus on that beautiful face as Junior comes in.

"Where'd you boys get the booze? I thought you'd been in a fight and got all beat up when I first saw you. It's sure a good thing I had to get up to go change the irrigation water and recognized the pickup when I came by on the way home." He leans over and looks me close in the face. "You better be thankful for Hubert too. He was workin' real hard to take care of y'all. If he hadn't been there and had y'all laid out in the back of the pickup, I might not of noticed anything was wrong. That Manuel was out cold as a cucumber. We never could wake him up. We finally just loaded him into the back of his pickup, and Hubert was goin' to drive them all home. Willy and Bubba were both just as sick as you two are. Y'all better be thankful for good ol' Hubert."

Now Junior is digging in the kitchen cabinet for something. "We'll try some soda water to settle your stomachs. Then let's get some coffee down y'all, and we'll drive you home. If we hurry, we can get you there before daylight. Maybe we can get you into the house without Mom finding out. Boy, you'll really be in for it if she ever does find out."

* * *

"Time to get up, boys. You'll need to hurry so we won't be late for church."

I manage to open one of my eyes, but the effort makes my head hurt. I see Mom smiling down at me. I close my eye again, afraid to let her see me, afraid she'll be able to see what happened last night. Then I open both of them again, just as quick. I don't want to look guilty. I have to try to look normal.

Mom had told us on Thanksgiving Day she wanted us to go to church. Ever since Dad died, she has been going to church nearly every Sunday. Even though she hasn't been making me go to

Sunday School classes, she still likes for me to go sit with her during the preaching. As much as I hate it, I figure I should do it anyway without complaining if it makes her feel better, and I'm sure not going to complain today. No matter how much my head hurts.

The first thing I notice when we get to church is that Willy and Bubba didn't make it.

Reverend Johnson is in his usual high form today. He's pounding the pulpit and shouting his list of things we better do or not do so we won't die and go to hell before next Sunday.

I'm sitting with Doc on one side and Mom on the other. With every single one of those whacks the preacher gives the pulpit, the vice I think I have around my head gets tighter.

Mom hasn't said a word about how peaked I look, or how slow I move, but still I wonder if she suspects anything. Doc and I had been sleeping in an extra room on the ground level of the depot, so she may not have heard us come in. The way she smiles it doesn't look like it, but I think she knows.

I've felt all morning like I was going to die. I know Doc feels the same way. I had to drag him out of bed. When Mom offered breakfast, we both decided we needed to go out to milk the cow and feed the livestock. And as soon as we got the chance, we both stuck our faces in the water trough to get our heads cleared.

But it's warm now here in the church, and I'm feeling queasy again. My head starts slowly spinning.

Reverend Johnson is on his favorite subject of sins of the flesh. He goes on and on, denouncing people who do things that feel good. On account of the way I feel now, I begin to realize that there really is such a thing as a sin of the flesh. But I'm not so sure it's doing things that feel good. It's got to be a sin to do anything that makes you feel as bad as I do right now. I feel like last night I did a lot of sinning. I feel like I really damaged my flesh all over, maybe even permanently.

It feels good to let my head hang down so my chin can rest on my chest while the reverend prays. I wonder for a moment how

Dad will feel about what I did last night, and then I remember I haven't seen him for a long time. I wonder where he is.

I grit my teeth to pull myself together and turn to look at Doc sitting beside me. He has his hand on his stomach and his eyes roll back and slowly close.

I jab him in the ribs with my elbow. "Wake up, you sinner. You better give your soul to Jesus before you die," I whisper.

CHAPTER 15

I finish milking Betsy, our only milk cow now, and start to feed her and Paint when I hear a car door slam. The days are getting longer now, and it's still daylight. Looking across the tracks toward the depot, I'm surprised to see Vernon Delaney coming toward the corral. I stand there inside the pen, not knowing what to do or expect. I can feel the old knot building in my stomach, moving up to my chest.

"Hidey," he says, with a friendly smile.

I nod, but I don't say anything. I'm determined not to make it easy for him.

"How you and that old paint mare doin'?" He puts one foot on the lower fence rail and, with his arms folded, leans over the top rail. It's the first time I've ever seen him when he wasn't puffing on that pipe with the carved bull's head and ivory horns.

"Fine."

"Haven't seen y'all at the ropin' club for a while."

I just look at him without saying anything.

"We got some Spanish goats that make good ropin' practice. I figured y'all would be over there eatin' that up."

"We been busy." I can't continue to meet his cool gaze. I have to look away.

After a long silence, he takes a deep breath. "I'll just state my business, then I'll be on my way." Now I can't keep from looking back at him. What can this old man want from me? "School's gonna be out for the summer pretty soon, and I'm needin' some help out at the ranch. I thought maybe you and your paint mare would like to come out and work for me this summer. You can ride the mare to work cattle, and then I've got several other horses you can ride when she's tired. In fact, I got a few young broncs you could help me break."

I'm stunned. I want to believe this is a dream come true, but my gut pulls tight. I remind myself I can't trust this grizzly old man. I notice ol' Paint is standing close by, ears perked, listening closely.

"In fact," he continues, "a couple of those young broncs can probably run fast enough to catch those fast Brahman calves, and we might be able to make a ropin' horse outta one of 'em."

Now I'm mad. "Ol' Paint's fast enough for me. She's all the horse I'll ever need. Besides, we're not goin' way out there on that ranch where you can make fun of us." I'm almost yelling.

"Now just a minute. You oughta give this some thought. I'll bet that old mare would enjoy bein' out there."

I look at Paint. I can tell she's thinking now she'd love it, but she doesn't know what's good for her. "Aw, I doubt it," I hear myself saying. "She's just like me. She don't like bein' told what to do."

"It sounds to me you're actin' like a spoiled brat. You oughta grow up some and quit feelin' sorry for yourself."

I look at Paint. To my surprise, she's agreeing with him.

"Listen, Speck." Vernon is getting mad. I can see his face getting red. "Just because that old mare can't run good enough to catch those fast calves is no reason for you to give up your dreams of bein' a champion calf roper. If you'll just let me, I can help you."

Hearing him call me Speck is the final straw, and I can't take the insult toward Paint, even if she is still agreeing with him. "I don't need you to tell me what to do." I'm talking through clenched teeth and trying to make sure Paint hears me too. "I don't want any gifts from you. If ol' Paint isn't good enough for me, then I don't need to be a champion roper. Besides, I got other things to do with my time." I pick up the milk bucket, walk out the gate, and start toward the depot. "I gotta go strain this milk before it sours."

When I'm halfway to the tracks, I turn and look back at him still leaning against the fence, still red-faced, and ol' Paint on the other side looking at me. Damn them. They don't know how bad I feel inside. They don't know about the lump in my chest that, except for those few hours at the dance, has been there almost constantly since that day last August. Nobody understands how I feel. Nobody cares how I feel.

"I already got another job for this summer," I lie. I turn on my heel and head inside the depot without looking back.

It rained a light shower this afternoon, leaving a small puddle by the corner of the depot. I'm sitting on the doorstep, smelling the freshness that always fills the desert air after a rain. I'm watching the sun sink slowly below the rim of the distant blue mountains to the west in Old Mexico on the other side of the Rio Grande. It glows bright as it peeks through the space between the low clouds and the mountain rim, giving the bottoms of the clouds a bright purple, red, and yellow glow. It's the beautiful ceremony of changing colors made by the setting of the sun that we see in this part of the county almost every night. But I'm not thinking about that now. I'm thinking about my dream of being a champion cowboy and how it seems to be sinking just like the sun—getting farther and farther out of my reach.

I'm thinking about Dad and how I miss him, and I wonder what he thinks about old Vernon Delaney's offer to help me. It's been such a long time now since I've felt his presence to talk to. I hope he knows, though, that I could never take anything from that old bastard.

"Whatcha doin', cowboy? You look like you lost your last friend." I'm startled by Uncle Jack. He has come to stay with us for a while. I'd heard him coming down the stairs of the depot but expected him to go on by without noticing me.

"Aw, I wasn't doin' nothin' much."

"Whatcha lookin' so sad about? You been mopin' around like somethin's really eatin' at you lately."

"Aw, its nothin'. I don't feel like talkin' about it."

"Hey, somethin' really is eatin' on you. What is it?"

"Leave me alone! It's none of your business." How can I tell anyone how I hurt? How can I tell him about how I want to be a champion roper? How can I tell him that almost everything I've ever dreamed of all my life is suddenly gone, vanished?

I try to look away but Uncle Jack stands on the ground, places one foot on the top step, and leans over, putting his face right in front of mine. He looks me closely in the eye a minute then his expression becomes more understanding. "You're beginnin' to sound a lot like me, tellin' people to leave you alone," he says. "Tell you what. I'm goin' up the valley for a while. Got a few fish to fry up that way. How's about you come along with me, and maybe we can shake loose whatever it is that's botherin' you."

* * *

I've heard a lot about the Red Rooster from the older guys. I used to see it from the highway on the outskirts of El Paso when I'd drive Dad up to the doctor, but I've never been in there. Doc told me he had been there a couple of times, and every time he'd seen some guys get in a fight.

As Uncle Jack pulls his old '37 Chevy into the parking lot, I wonder what Mom would say if she knew Uncle Jack was going in there and taking me with him. She'd protested when he told her I was going "up the valley" with him, but he's smooth and persuasive. He never said what we were going to do or made any promises, but she still agreed to let me go along.

We stop at Rojalio's Bar, and Uncle Jack went in to get a half dozen bottles of beer. He opens one and puts it in my hand. "See if this'll help settle what's goin' on inside you." As I sip on mine and watch him guzzle two bottles fast, I want to ask him why he drinks so much. But I remembered how he'd said it wasn't any of my business the last time I asked, so I decide to keep my mouth shut.

We also stop at a bar in Fabens. This time Uncle Jack lets me go inside with him, since he doesn't think there will be anyone there who knows me. We sit at a table and drink another beer while he makes small talk with the pretty blond waitress. She flashes him a big smile, and I can tell she likes him. That's when I see a faint glimmer of that old sparkle in his eye that used to be there before he went off to war. When other customers come in and the waitress gets busy, he buys three more beers and tells her he'll try to "get back by later."

"I'll be lookin' for you," she'd says.

It's only a short drive from Fabens on up to the Red Rooster. "He's my kid brother," Uncle Jack says, as he winks to the big bouncer when we go through the big double doors.

High Pockets McKinzie and his western band are beating out a rendition of "Hey, Good Lookin'" as the people on the dance floor keep time with a fast two-step. We find a table in the crowded night club, and Uncle Jack orders himself a shot of Old Crow to go with his beer, but before the drinks arrive, a petite dark-headed girl with dark brown eyes appears at his side. "Where you been, stranger?"

"Aw, I been kinda busy," Uncle Jack stammers as though he's caught by surprise. Finally, after a long silence, "This here's my nephew, Scout. Scout say hello to . . ."

I can tell he's forgotten her name, so I jump to my feet. "Pleased to meetcha, ma'am."

"I'm Bobbie Jo," she says sweetly, shaking my hand before she turns back and glares at Uncle Jack. "Aren't you gonna ask me to dance?"

Uncle Jack was right. The lump in my chest feels smaller now, and I begin to relax as I inhale the thick air of the honky-tonk laden with cigarette smoke, whiskey, and the malty smell of beer. I feel the beat of the music and begin to tap my foot as the waitress brings the drinks, and I watch Uncle Jack dancing with the pretty brunette.

As I pour my beer in the frosted glass, I notice the whiskey in the shot glass the waitress has left for Uncle Jack. I take a small sip and wash it down with the bubbly beer.

Suddenly, Uncle Jack is beside the table alone. "Where's Bobbie Jo?" I ask as he sits down and picks up the shot glass.

"Aw, she decided she needed to go talk to some of her friends." He smiles before he throws the full shot down and swishes it in his mouth then swallows slowly so as to get the full taste.

"Don't you like her?"

He sips on the beer bottle, ignoring the frosted glass in front of him. "I like all women. It's just that I like some more than others." Then, after a moment of what appears to be dark thought, he asks, "You got a girl friend?"

"Naw," I say too quickly. "I never paid much attention to them."

I'm lying of course. I notice them all the time. I've especially been noticing Jenke Harmon lately. She sure has changed a lot. Bubba was right. She does fill out her Levi's nicely, and her chest has started to bulge out real nice too. She doesn't bug me the way she used to either. In fact, she doesn't even seem to notice me anymore. It's like I'm invisible. Of course, I'd never get up the nerve to say anything to make her notice me, but she's always got some other guy around her anyway. Usually Bubba Hillis.

It's funny how all those years I've known her I never noticed the way her blue eyes crinkle and sparkle when she laughs. I like the way she walks too—not prissy the way some girls walk, but kind of a long-gaited stride, swinging her arms and holding her head high like she owned the world. The other day, when I was sitting behind her in algebra class, I could smell her hair, and it smelled so good I wanted to reach out and touch it. Then when I heard the sound of her voice as she asked a question about factoring or something, it seemed like I couldn't think about anything else except the way she said her words. I can't tell Uncle Jack any of that, though. He'd think I'd lost my mind.

He looks at me through closely squinted eyes, "You ever been with a woman?"

I look at him blankly. He can tell I don't understand.

"I mean have you ever made love to a woman? You ever fucked a girl?"

In spite of the booze, I can feel my face burning and getting red. "No," I say finally.

My answer seems to put an end to the matter because Uncle Jack waves for the waitress to bring another round, and I begin to relax even more.

As the fresh drinks arrive, and Uncle Jack pours his beer in the frosted glass, he seems to be thinking about something real hard. "So are you gonna tell me what's been eatin' at you?"

I'm stumped for a moment. I want to tell him, and I'm so relaxed, I start to say something. But it sticks in my throat, and I feel like I'll cry. Instead, I take a long drink on my beer. "You wanna tell me what's been eatin' at you?" I ask.

"Whadda you mean?" he looks at me angrily.

"Back a long time ago when I asked you why you drink so much, and if it was because of what happened in the war, you told me it wasn't none of my business."

Slowly the angry look in his eyes mellows, and a slight grin pulls his mouth to the side. He sits silent, thinking, as he plays with the full shot glass between his fingers. Finally, he throws the shot down and follows it with several big gulps of beer then sets the glass down hard. "That's right," he says. "There's just some things that shouldn't be talked about. What I saw happen and the things I did over there should never have happened. All that death and torture and destruction shouldn't be talked about either, lest they might happen again. Besides, if I started talking about all that, I might break down and bawl like a baby, and you know that's not the way a real man handles hisself. But that's my problem, not yours, and it's no reason why you shouldn't tell me what's bothering you. I doubt you've seen anything like what I had to deal with over there."

"It don't matter. It still hurts, and if I started talking about it, I'd probably cry. You just said yourself that's not the way a man should act." With the fortification of the booze, I'm able to keep my voice calm.

Uncle Jack empties his beer glass, then sits twirling it on its edge across the table top for a long while, lost in thought. Finally, "You may be right, but I'm gonna tell you somethin', Scout, that I want you to think about and remember. Then when you figure it out, you can do what you want to about it. A man once told me that the ability to enjoy life is directly in proportion to your ability to be afraid. Used to, before the war started, I really enjoyed and loved life, but I was scared a lot of the time. Scared something bad would happen to me. Since I got back, I haven't been able to find much pleasure in this world. It wasn't till just the other day I realized I'm not scared of nothin' anymore. It really don't matter to me what happens." He had been looking at the beer bottle in his hand, but now he turns his eyes directly at me, and the sadness there makes me bite my lip to keep from crying.

He reaches over and takes my beer bottle that is about half full, drinks it empty, and waves for the waitress to bring another round. "It may be that holdin' all that anger and frustration inside you all the time will make you hard and unable to enjoy life, like me."

"So how do you get it out if you're not allowed to cry?" I ask matter-of-factly.

When the waitress sets the new round on the table and carries the empty bottles away, I reach over, pick up the shot glass from in front of Uncle Jack, drink about half, then chase it with beer as he had been doing.

"Well, I don't know how you get it out, but drinkin' just like that is a good way to drown the pain in your chest." He has that wiry smile again.

We sit silent for a while, and the drinks begin to really hit me. I begin to tap my foot and slap my leg in time with the music.

"You wanna dance with one of them gals?"

"Naw, I don't know how."

"Maybe I oughta get Bobbie Jo over here, and she can teach you how."

"Naw, I don't want to," I say emphatically.

"You're scared of women, aren't you?" he says, showing the surprise in his voice. Then, after a while, as though he's talking more to himself than to me, "Maybe I oughta take you over to Juárez and get you bred."

It's kind of a blur how we got here, but I remember walking down the street and Uncle Jack stopping at a little streetcar without any wheels made into a kitchen that sits by the curb. He ordered some flautas, and then he said, "You need to eat something to keep you from getting sick from all that booze." He stuck two of the hard-cooked rolled corn tortillas in my hand.

We're sitting at the bar, and I can see the neon lights flashing blue and red outside the window. I've heard of El Gato Negro before. Doc said he'd been here with some guys from his school. "It's the most famous whorehouse in Juárez. There's more *putas* in that place than you can imagine," he'd said.

The Dos Equis beer made in Mexico has a flatter, stronger taste than the Blue Ribbon we had been drinking earlier. There are men sitting at a number of tables drinking, and a mariachi band is pounding out a heavy beat and singing, "Ay, Yi, Yi, Yi . . . ." *Laugh and don't cry* is the meaning of the Spanish words they sing.

There are several women around. They all seem to be dressed in tight skirts and low-slung blouses. Now and then one of them will walk up to a man, and after a brief conversation, they will leave the bar area, going through some curtains toward the back of the room. I try to look between the curtains to see what goes on back there.

When the band stops playing, and it becomes quieter in the bar, Uncle Jack points at me and yells in Spanish, "Hey, ladies, I have a cherry here."

Suddenly, I'm surrounded by soft, sweet-smelling feminine bodies, all in tight skirts with boobs swelling over the tops of their blouses. One puts an arm around my neck, kisses me in the ear. I feel myself become aroused, and she asks in Spanish if I want to do something I don't understand. Another giggles and runs her hand inside my shirt massaging my chest, causing me to become even harder, so that my tight Levi's make me hurt. "Wanna come with me, honey?" she asks.

Another takes my hand and places it inside her blouse, making me massage her breast. "You likee this, Cherry Babe?"

I start to try to pull away when the crowd is parted by a large buxom woman with bleached hair. She's older and bigger than most of the others and clearly in charge. "*Usted un* cherry?" she demands.

My mouth is dry, and I can't speak, but I feel myself nodding.

"This one is mine," she declares in Spanish, as she pulls me by the arm out of the crowd, through the curtains, down a long hall into a room with a big bed in the middle. Before I know what's happened, she has undressed me and herself, and we're lying in bed together. I'm aroused and eager. "Take it easy, Cherry Babe," she says.

In what seems like a surprisingly short time, I find myself strolling back through the curtain into the bar as I buckle my belt.

I half expect to encounter all the other women again and prepare to defend myself, but nobody seems to notice as I enter the room and walk bewildered over to find my seat at the bar beside Uncle Jack.

Uncle Jack places a fresh beer in my hand and smiles that crooked smile as he turns to me. "Well, you're not a cherry anymore. The first one's free, but from now on you gotta pay." Then he pokes me in the chest. "I bet it feels better in there too, don't it?"

I quietly sip my beer as I try to gather my feelings and thoughts. I don't know what to say, but he's right. My groin feels pleasantly drained, and the lump in my chest is gone. This, I say to myself, works better than booze.

Fuzz Watson is a big burly man. He has lots of curly blond hair all over his body except on top of his head. He wears small, gold-rimmed glasses that look funny on his huge round face, but the gold rims match his blond hair and set off the redness of his face and the top of his bald head. He talks tough, and he's a hard worker, but when you get to know him, he's really soft-hearted. At first he'd refused, saying I was too young, when I asked him to let me work on his water drilling rig this summer. But he remembered Dad and finally mumbled about being indebted "to that old bastard" for something I couldn't understand and that maybe he could keep an eye on me and return a favor.

"All right, you assholes, listen to me," he yells. He's standing shirtless as usual on the deck of the drilling rig where he can see every man on the crew. Everything comes to a stop, and the big diesel engine that runs the rig is cut back to an idle.

"I just had to send Johnny Rodríguez to the doctor. He's the third one on this crew that's come down with a dose of the claps in the last month. Just the other day Henry had to take off so he could go get treatment for the crabs. If you guys don't be more careful who you screw or take some precaution, I'm gonna have to put a stop to you guys goin' to Juárez altogether. If I have to, I'll start firin' every man that comes on this rig with VD. Now y'all mark my words, I don't want no more of it on this job."

I turn to Henry as we start fitting pipe again. "What's VD?"

"Aw, you damned punkin'-headed kid. Don't you know nothin'? It's like when you get the claps." Henry is about the same age as Uncle Jack, and we've been going to Juárez together nearly every Saturday night since I started working on the rig.

I'm embarrassed, but I ask anyway. "What's claps?"

"Boy, you really don't know nothin', do ya? Claps is what you catch that makes your dong sore from screwin' them *putas* in Juárez." Then he turns to Joe Armijo on the other side of the rig. "Hey, Joe, did you know this dumb kid don't know what claps is? I bet he's had it all summer and hasn't told us about it."

I know Joe is going to start in on me. I hate it when they tease me, but Fuzz told me in the beginning I'd have to be able to take it if I was going to work for him.

"Hey, Scottie, you got the claps?" Joe yells so everyone can hear. Everyone on the crew calls me Scottie instead of Scout. They all know I hate it, but no matter how often I correct them, they just ignore me and make it clear that on this crew my name is Scottie.

"No, I don't have nothin'," I yell back.

"How you know? You been goin' over there every Saturday. Henry tells me you spend nearly all your pay on them *putas* and buying cheap booze. As many of them gals as you've screwed, you gotta catch the claps some time. You know that stuff'll make your dong rot off if you don't take penicillin before it's too late. I bet it's already too late for you."

I know I'm walking into it, but I can't keep from asking. "What's it feel like when you get the claps?" I say as quietly as I can to Henry.

"Well, I never had 'em, but I understand you don't know anything about it until your dong falls off."

"How do you know you don't have them then?"

"Well, I been takin' penicillin all the time to be sure. Haven't you?" My heart sinks to the pit of my stomach as he looks at me with a look of disbelief.

As soon as our shift is over, I borrow the company pickup and head for El Paso as fast as I can. Since the rig is putting in a well on a farm north of Fabens, it shouldn't take me long to get there. Maybe I can get there before Doc Stevenson leaves his office.

As I drive, I curse myself for not knowing if what those guys say is true or not. I curse myself for going to Juárez, for drinking all that booze, for being with those *putas* even though it has only been a few times. But, as I curse, I feel that lump building bigger in my chest than it's been in a long time. All summer it would be gone after I had been to Juárez, but usually by Tuesday or Wednesday, I'd start to get that old desire to feel a horse between my legs and rope a fast calf. I'd feel that dream of winning a championship and the disappointment, anger, and frustration of not being able to ride ol' Paint to a championship after that dream. The dream would dominate my thoughts so much that, by Saturday, the pain in my chest would be almost unbearable again. It's a good thing I've been able to stay in the little trailer house Fuzz keeps at the rig, so I've been free to go where I wanted without having to worry about Mom finding out.

* * *

"No, you don't have anything wrong with you." Doctor Stevenson is smiling behind his thick bushy mustache as I put my pants back on. "Those guys you work with have been pulling your leg. You're a little young to be hanging around with those girls over in Juárez, and you'd be a lot better off if you'd stay away from there and stick to going out with girls you know that are your own age. But if you had the claps, you'd know it right away, and we could treat it with penicillin and everything would probably be okay. On the other hand, there's a lot worse things over there than claps, like syphilis, that we don't have any cure for. You'd be a lot better off to just stay away from there all together."

As I drive away from the doctor's office, I swear to myself I'll never go back to Juárez again no matter how painful that lump in my chest gets. I'll find a way to deal with it. There's got to be a better way than drowning it with booze and lying with whores.

I remember that school will be starting again in about two more weeks, and I'll be quitting this damned job. Then I'll be able to be back with Paint again. Maybe by now she's gotten over being mad at me for not taking the job old Vernon Delaney offered.

After driving a few blocks in the city traffic, I'm forced to stop at a red light. As I sit waiting for the light to change, my attention is pulled up over the top of one of the city's tall buildings and there, in the clear blue sky, I see Dad sitting on Tar Baby. It's the first time I've seen them since that fateful Saturday in August last year when Paint and I tried to catch and rope that fast Brahman calf. I want to talk to him and tell him what's been going on and ask him what I should do, but before I can say anything, Dad winks at me knowingly. "You're heading the right direction now," he says, and Tar Baby lopes off in the direction of home.

CHAPTER 16

I saw Dad again this morning just after I finished milking, and he told me to ride down to the river by the old Harris place about three miles from McNary. I'm not clear why. I haven't got any business down that way. I haven't even been down there in a long time, but there's no question where we should head. Paint has fallen into her easy saddle. She knows where we're going, and we're moving rapidly along the road on top of the irrigation canal that divides the Harris place from the Miller place when we meet a horseman leading four other horses coming toward us. As we come close to the tall, lanky rider, I recognize him as Roger Harris. He pulls up and hails me.

"You're Boots McBride's boy, aren't you?"

"Yes, sir."

"I understand you're pretty good with a horse. Is that right?"

"Aw, I don't know. Haven't done much ridin' lately."

"You know anythin' about race horses?"

"Not really. I guess they're mostly spoilt and sometimes get kinda crazy."

"Yeah. Well, I guess you know a little about them then." He moves his horse a little closer and assumes a friendly tone. He's a little older than Uncle Jack, but not as old as Dad would be. "Tell you what, I've got four horses here I'm takin' over to the county fair in Sierra Blanca next Saturday, and I need some help handling them. I've got a six-horse trailer, so there'd be room for your little mare if you'd like to bring her along."

"What are you gettin' at?" I ask.

"You could be my exercise man. I'd even pay your entry fee if you wanted to enter the ropin'."

"I don't know nothin' about exercisin' racehorses. I've never done that."

"Well, it's no big deal. All you gotta do is lead them around to get them warmed up before they race. In fact, lookin' at you, you're probably light enough I might let you be my jockey in a race or two."

I'm not sure I want to be a jockey, and I'm not sure about the roping, either. Paint's too small. The same thing would happen that happened last time. But Paint snorts, shakes her head, and switches her tail violently like she's fighting a big horsefly. "Take it. Let's go with him," she says when I look for the horsefly that isn't there.

"When you plannin' on goin' over, Mr. Harris?" I ask.

He smiles and starts off with his remuda, "I'll be at your place five o'clock sharp, Saturday mornin'."

The livestock show and other booths for the Hudspeth County Fair are set up just south of the roping arena, and on the west side there is a long cleared strip of land.

"It's a landing strip," says Tom Harris, as we drive past the arena. "There hasn't been an airplane on it in two years, but it makes a hell of a good place for horse racing."

As we unload the horses, I notice there are already several other trailers close by that have brought racehorses. On the landing strip I see several horses with jockey saddles being led at a trot or lope to warm up. On the way over, Mr. Harris had explained they wanted to get started early while it's still cool out and be through before everyone takes a break to go down to the train station to see President Harry Truman, who will be coming through on his campaign train.

"Take this bay mare first," Mr. Harris says as we unload the horses. "Watch her—she's a little skittish. Keep your lead rope wrapped around your saddle horn to be sure she don't jerk away from you. I've got her matched with that sorrel over yonder," Mr. Harris says, pointing to a long thin sorrel being led by another exercise boy toward the strip.

After a trip down the strip and back, Mr. Harris tells me his match is going to be the first race, and his jockey hasn't shown up. "I need you to jockey this mare," he says. When I show my doubt, he says, "You can do it. All you gotta do is gallup up to the line, and when they drop the flag, let her run straight down the track. You're only racin' for two hunerd and twenty yards. You can keep her runnin' straight that far."

At first I agree, but when I see the little jockey saddle he puts on the mare, I object. "I never rode one of those things. I'll fall off for sure."

"Aw, come on. Get up there. You can do it."

I look around, but I don't see Dad anywhere. Is this the reason he wanted me to ride down by the old Harris place?

Mr. Harris has the bay mare snubbed up to the saddle horn of his saddle horse. I use his stirrup to mount his saddle horse behind him. Then I slip over onto the bay mare. She stands quietly until I get both feet in the little short stirrups. I feel strangely precarious with my knees pulled up under my chin. "Take a rein in each hand so you can keep your balance," Mr. Harris says, as he lets out the lead rope, giving the mare her head.

She runs backward against the lead rope. Then, when it tightens, she lunges and bucks forward up against the saddle horse. "Hold on!" But it's too late. I sail over the mare's head, do a complete somersault, and land flat on my back on the other side of the saddle horse.

"You don't got a jockey, you forfeit the race, Harris," I hear a man standing by the long thin sorrel say as I stagger around trying to get my breath. Mounted on the sorrel is a jockey in a shiny silk shirt looking like a real professional.

"Come on, Scout. You can do it," Mr. Harris pleads.

"Take that stupid saddle off, and maybe I can stay on her," I whisper between gasps for breath.

"She'll run out from under you if you ride her bareback."

"Then tie a rope around her neck that I can hold on to."

I can see the desperation in his face as Mr. Harris begins to loosen the cinch strap on the little saddle. I feel guilty, but I know I'll never be able to handle that crazy mare in that saddle. I can feel a knot of fear building in my stomach as I try to think how I might ride her bareback. She's so powerful, I could easily slide off and be run over by the other horse.

"I didn't know you wanted to be a jockey," a voice says, as I feel a hand on my shoulder. Turning, I face a vaguely familiar face in a big straw hat. The man is about my same size. When he sees the blank look on my face, "It's me, Johnny Scott, the guy you and your dad pulled outta that wreck."

Swallowing the anger that immediately swells in my throat, I hear myself saying, "I don't wanna be a jockey, but somebody's gotta ride this crazy bitch."

"I'll ride 'er for you." Seeing the sudden change of my expression and the obvious relief, he turns to Mr. Harris. "You just give me a minute to change clothes. We'll show that jerk a real race."

"I can't afford to pay a professional." Mr. Harris is doubtful.

"This one's on me. You just be sure this kid gets treated fair."

The high school band is playing "Happy Days are Here Again," and L. D. Ward, the county judge, all dressed up in a long-tail black coat, is nervously pacing back and forth as the big steam engine pulls by the crowd, slowing to a stop just as the end of the train pulls even with the depot. I'm standing in the crowd between Roger Harris and Johnny Scott. On the other side of Johnny, beautiful Billy Jean towers over him. She's told me they're married now, and Johnny hasn't had another drink since the accident. We're all happy because Johnny won the horse race and then rode two more for Mr. Harris before we came down with the whole fair crowd to see the president.

A man appears on the Pullman platform at the rear of the train and briefly thanks the crowd for being there and then introduces the person everyone came to see, the president of the United States—a momentous occasion for a remote place like Sierra Blanca, Texas.

The president appears on the platform waving amid all the applause as the band plays "For He's A Jolly Good Fellow."

"There he is," Roger Harris says, "Ol' Give-'Em-Hell-Harry!"

L. D. Ward steps up on the platform and presents the president with a new Stetson hat, welcomes him to Hudspeth County, and launches into a speech about what a great man the president is, how he's going to be re-elected, and what a wonderful job he's going to do for the country. After a while, the crowd starts milling around, so L. D. shuts up and lets the president speak.

Waving his arms and giving us that "Missouri Mule" grin, the president tells us how great America is, how great the Democratic party is, how bad the Republican party is, and how he and our congressmen are going to put this country on the road to economic recovery.

There doesn't seem to be any question in the minds of the crowd who the greatest man in the world is. Many are awed just to be able to say they've seen the president in person. We've all seen his pictures many times, and I hear one woman whisper, "He looks just like his pictures, but I thought he was a lot taller."

Like everyone else in the crowd, I'm proud to be an American and glad to get to see the greatest man in the world. I'm convinced he'll do good things for us.

As the president brings his speech to a close, he surprises everyone. "Ladies and gentlemen, before I say adios to this wonderful town and county and all you fine people, I want to introduce a man that lives right here among you who is a longtime friend of mine. We served with the field artillery in France together during World War I. I thought he had the makin's of a fine politician, but, instead, he chose to return to the beautiful state of Texas to continue his family's ranching business. Can you come on up here, Vernon?" Everyone turns to the back of the crowd to see Vernon Delaney astride a large, slick sorrel gelding with a white blaze down his face. Everyone except me claps wildly, and someone sets off a string of firecrackers over by the depot as Vernon makes his way around the crowd, rides up to the train platform, and shakes hands with the president.

I stand with my mouth open, hands in my pockets, as the president reaches over the railing of the Pullman platform, slaps Vernon

Delaney on the back affectionately, shakes his hand, and then waves to the crowd while the train moves slowly away.

Back at the fair, barbeque is served for lunch. Then a speaker climbs up in the stand over the roping box of the arena and calls for entries in a jackpot roping. I'm sitting astride ol' Paint near the arena fence finishing up the ribs, pinto beans, and potato salad that were served on a flimsy paper plate when Roger Harris comes up and asks, "Aren't you gonna enter the ropin'?"

Paint's ears flick, and I can tell she's unhappy when I say, "Naw, I don't want to."

Just as Mr. Harris starts to walk away, Vernon Delaney rides up on the big sorrel. I'd heard of the sorrel from Sonny Walsh. "Vernon Delaney calls him Popcorn. He's probably the best ropin' horse west of the Pecos River," he'd said.

Vernon reins in, facing me. "I saw you over at the races this morning. I got ol' Popcorn here, and he's a fair one to rope off of. I know you're probably chicken to ride a horse like this, and I kinda doubt you can do it anyway, but if you wanna try, and if you'll enter the ropin', I'll let you ride ol' Popcorn."

Before I can answer him, Paint has a fit, shaking her head like she's been attacked by a big horsefly again. As I try to calm her and find the fly, she says softly, "Go to it, Scout. You can do it, and that's what I want you to do."

"This stupid ol' mare is goin' crazy," I say, as I try to think of an excuse. But Roger Harris is staring at me, so I can't say I can't afford the entry fee. If I refuse now, everyone will think I'm chicken. But I still don't want the bastard to do anything for me.

Before I can do anything, I hear Festus Gibbs from across the fence yell, "Yeah, Vernon. Put that McBride kid on the sorrel. We'll all have a good laugh."

Sonny Walsh had told me Festus Gibbs had tried the sorrel over at the roping club once, and the sorrel stopped so quick, Festus flew over his head. I feel the red rising in my face as I say between my teeth, "I can ride that horse or anything else you got."

I'm the third roper up, but the other two have only fair times of twenty-three and twenty-seven seconds. Paint is tied inside the arena and watches as I ride Popcorn around, getting a feel for the way he moves. He's a lot taller than ol' Paint, and his neck is thick and hard. He moves easy and quick, though, and when I kick him into a lope, the power is like nothing I've ever felt. A small knot of fear builds in the pit of my stomach as I ride him into the box and shake out a loop.

In the box, he whirls on his hind legs and sets easy against the far corner, ears pointed toward the chute gate, ready. There is even more power than I thought when the calf is released. I almost have to grab the saddle horn to keep the big horse from running out from under me.

By the time I can get myself set, Popcorn has placed the calf in perfect position. I take one swing over my head and let the loop sail. As it settles around the calf's neck, I hear Festus Gibbs yell, "Now just raise your leg," which is what I'm doing as he speaks.

The swiftness of this horse's sliding stop is no myth. As I begin to dismount, he stops so quickly, I am thrown forward, and I land running about halfway between the horse and the calf, who has already felt the tight rope pulling him backward. I meet the calf as Popcorn runs backward, and I'm able to grab his front leg. Lifting against the pressure of the rope, the calf lands on his side with me on top. But that's all the help Popcorn can give; from here on it's all up to me. Struggling with the kicking calf, I finally get the pigging string on the front leg, and then it's a struggle to get the two hind legs across the front one before I can wrap them tight with the small rope. Exhausted, I throw my hands in the air, signaling the calf is tied.

I'm wondering what my time is as I remount Popcorn and the horse loosens the pressure on the lariat around the calf's neck. As the flagman steps down to take the loop off the calf, he struggles and kicks loose from the pigging string. As the calf stands up and runs away, I hear the announcer say, "We had a time of thirty-eight-point-nine seconds, but the calf got up so this roper takes 'no time.'"

I ride up by ol' Paint, feeling ashamed and disappointed, but she looks proud even though I got no time. Vernon Delaney is there, loosening the cinch on my saddle so Popcorn can breathe easy. "Well, you roped the calf quick and you were able to dismount in a right stylish fashion. Maybe you can ride this horse and rope a calf off him after all. But you sure as hell need some practice at tying those rank calves. Tell you what, Speck, you come on out to the ranch and work for me next summer, and I'll give you all the practice you need."

I start to react to being called Speck, but Paint snorts. Out over the far end of the arena I see Dad and Tar Baby. Dad waves and I know this is the reason he told me to ride down by the river.

"I'll be there," I hear myself saying.

I'm still feeling embarrassed and down in the mouth about the poor showing I made, and I start to walk away, my head down, leading Paint.

"You did great, Scout. You'll do better next time." The voice startles me, and when I look up, I'm even more startled. There she is in front of me, smiling up at me. When did I get taller than Jenke Harmon? And her eyes are so blue. For a minute I think I've got lockjaw, because I just can't talk. I couldn't think of anything to say even if I could. "That Popcorn's a great horse, and only a few men are good enough to ride him. You rode him good. Now all you gotta do is practice tyin' those calves down." Her voice is as soft as a thistle falling apart on the wind.

"Yeah," I finally manage to say. "All I gotta do is practice."

"If you do, I bet you'll be winnin' the ropin' all the time," she says. She smiles and starts to walk away.

"Jenke!" I call. She turns around and looks at me. "I'll see you around. Okay?"

She smiles, and it lights up her whole face. "Okay," she says, and turns away, walking with that long stride of hers. My heart skips a beat as I watch her long blond ponytail bouncing. I wonder why I never noticed before how beautiful she is.

CHAPTER 17

J uanita sets a cup of coffee in front of me. "You awake?" she asks in Spanish.

I shake my head and rub my eyes, "I'm tryin'."

"You must hurry. El Patrón and Pablo are out saddling the horses now," she says in her broken English.

I go to the sink and work the pump fast, sticking my head under the cold water when it starts to run. I come awake as I dry my face and comb my hair, looking in the mirror that hangs over the sink, hurrying now. We got in so late last night I had forgotten we're riding up into Jack Rabbit Canyon today to look for some missing cattle.

I take a breakfast biscuit, break it apart, stuff two slices of bacon between the halves, roll them in wax paper and stuff them in my shirt pocket, then grab another to eat on the way as Vernon Delaney comes through the back door. He has his chaps on, indicating he thinks we'll be riding in thick mesquite and catclaw. "I'm ridin' Popcorn even if he may be a little tired from yesterday. He needs a little toughenin' up. These Sunday ropin's haven't been enough to keep him in good condition. We put your saddle on the big roan. I want you to bring that little short .30-30 of your dad's just in case we need a gun."

I look up in surprise. "What're we needin' a gun for?" I've been proud of Dad's old .30-30 because it was his, even though I've never shot it. I brought it along to the ranch just because I thought cowboys were supposed to carry a gun. This is the first time there's been any indication of any use for one. I hope he doesn't want me to shoot anything.

"I don't know, I just got a feelin' there's some varmints botherin' those cows up there. We'll just have to wait and see." He grabs himself a biscuit, gives it the bacon treatment, and takes a sip out of a coffee cup he'd left sitting on the table earlier. "Come on now. Let's hurry. Sun's almost up."

It's hard traveling. The trail is rocky, narrow, and mostly uphill, so we ride silently in single file with Vernon and Popcorn leading the way. In spite of the coolness, the big red roan is already sweating, and I can tell he's glad when Vernon pulls up on a level wide spot in the trail to take a breather. The sun has just broken over the top of Blanco Mountain, and I take the moment to enjoy watching light spread out over the draw and headquarters below, bringing the green, red, and blue colors of the rocks and vegetation to life.

Vernon Delaney's ranch lies at the foot of Blanco Mountain, the highest mountain anywhere around these parts. His folks crossed the Pecos River in a covered wagon and set up a homestead in the rocky desert country populated mostly by mesquite, catclaw, and cactus. The ranch headquarters is nestled against a large rock outcropping on the south side of a wide draw that runs from the foot of the big mountain all the way down to the Rio Grande. Since the headquarters is about forty miles from the nearest town and about half of that is dirt road, there aren't many visitors. When Vernon goes to town, he buys supplies to last a long time.

It hasn't taken me long to learn that this real cowboy's life isn't all I had thought it was. I spend more of my time checking and fixing windmills and patching broken fences than anything else. There aren't any outlaws to chase like in the movies, and the only time I get to rope anything is to doctor a sick cow or when we round up and brand calves. The only chance to do any bronc busting is when I take a fresh horse out to ride fence and he has a kink in his back that needs to be worked out before we can get down to business. That's only happened once so far this summer.

I ride ol' Paint every chance I get, but these long rides over rocky trails up and down the foothills of Blanco Mountain and sometimes into deep canyons that go up high are tough on a horse, and they need to rest several days before they do it again.

Every afternoon after the day's work is finished and chores have been done, I try to take out my lariat and practice roping a bale of alfalfa. Sometimes I'll catch one of the rank Brahman calves Vernon is feeding in a big pen west of the ranch house, tie him to a post on a long rope, then I run down the rope like I have just roped him from horseback, and practice wrestling him to the ground and tying him like we do in roping contests. These calves are getting bigger than they usually have in regular roping contests, and Vernon says if I can tie these big calves quick, it'll be easier for me in a real contest.

I have bruises all up and down my legs and even one on my right shoulder where they've kicked me. One broke free of my grip, caught me in the pit of my stomach with his hard hoof, and knocked me on my butt. It made me sick, and I threw up all night. That's when I learned to keep a better grip and to use a different approach by putting my shoulder against the calf's shoulder as I lift his front leg so as to stay away from those flailing hind legs.

Nearly every Sunday we've loaded Paint and Popcorn into the two-horse trailer and driven in to the roping club at Fort Hancock where we practice until dark then make the long trip back to the ranch. I've seen Jenke nearly every Sunday. She always offers me encouragement, and it's got to where I look forward to seeing her and having her there to watch me rope as much as anything.

I ride Popcorn to rope the calves, and then when they take a break, Paint and I will chase a few Mexican goats. Paint enjoys this because they can't run so fast, even though they cut and duck a lot quicker than the calves. In fact, the goats are so tricky they're harder to rope than the calves are. Vernon says it's good practice for me, and if I can catch them with two out of three loops, I should catch a calf with every loop.

We didn't get in from the roping until late last night, and if Juanita, Vernon's cook and housekeeper, hadn't pulled the cover off me and yelled at me to get up, I'd still be sleeping.

"Let's go," Vernon says. "We still got a long ways to go."

"There it is," Vernon says, as he pulls Popcorn up overlooking a ridge and points down into a deep ravine. We've been seeing buzzards circling for about a mile now, and what Vernon is pointing at is a swollen carcass, all four legs sticking straight out stiffly. Several buzzards are sitting on it, pecking at holes that have been torn in the reddish brown cow's hide. Several more buzzards are sitting on the ground around the carcass, waiting for a chance to jump in for a bite.

"Pablo, you circle around to the south and see if you can find any cat or other varmint signs. Speck and I'll go down and see if we can figure what killed it. Keep your eyes out for her calf. It may still be alive, hidin' in the bushes somewhere."

The buzzards don't want to give up their meal, but Vernon dismounts Popcorn and hits one in the side with a big rock so they all slowly take flight. Some just spread their wings and sail to a landing only a short distance away as though they intend to attack if they have a chance. Seeing my wariness, Vernon says, "Don't worry, they're cowards. They'll only try to scare us. But don't ever try to grab one of them suckers. I did that one time when I was about your age, and he 'bout beat me and pecked me to death before I could turn him loose."

I can tell the cow has been dead for some time by the putrid smell, and when Vernon places a boot on the horn so as to turn the head, I can see maggots eating in the flesh on the underside where moisture has accumulated and the sunlight hasn't hit it. There is a big hole torn in the cow's swollen side in the hollow just in front of the hip bone, and inside there is a big hole that has been eaten out by the buzzards. Down deep inside it there are more maggots.

The sound of the blowflies buzzing around is loud while Vernon examines the scene without talking. I have to step away to keep from being sick. I'm able to justify my absence from the carcass by walking around looking at the ground "searching for signs."

"Coyotes. I think coyotes did this," Vernon says finally. "If you look at all the tracks around, you can see that coyotes and cats both been eatin' off her." He points to a big round track in the soft sand of the ravine bottom which shows clear imprints of four huge paws.

"That's a big ol' cougar, but I don't think he did the killin'. If he had, she'd be more torn up, and he would've eaten more than he has."

"I thought coyotes wouldn't kill a cow," I say, as I begin to get control of my stomach.

"Sometimes a pack of coyotes will get after a cow and just keep after her and worry her until she falls down. Then they'll jump on and kill her, but that usually won't happen unless the cow's sick and weak." He studies the carcass again. "It doesn't look like this cow was sick or weak. In fact, it looks like she was in pretty good shape until they got her."

Pablo breaks the silence as he rides into the ravine from above. "You see any varmints?" Vernon asks.

"No, but you can see what killed her, can't you?" Pablo asks.

"Well, I thought it was coyotes, but this cow was in pretty good shape."

"Not coyotes. Dogs," says Pablo.

Vernon looks startled, then he begins to search the tracks in the sand more closely. "By God, you're right. These older tracks are round like a dog instead of pointed like a coyote. I missed 'em because they haven't been around since she died." I'm standing close to Vernon now, looking at the difference in the tracks as he points.

Pablo continues, "I think there's another dead one over in the next ravine, but most of the cows and their calves are up there on that mesa by that old windmill. Looks like they're okay."

"Well, I'll just have to get Johnny Watkins up here to trap them bastards," Vernon says as he mounts Popcorn. "We'll have problems until he kills every last one of 'em."

"You're awful quiet," Vernon says, as he pulls Popcorn alongside the roan. We're taking a different trail down that's smoother and wider but is a lot steeper than the one we came up the mountain on. "Somethin' eatin' on you?"

"I was just thinkin' about those dogs. Wouldn't it be possible to just catch them and take 'em to town instead of killin' 'em?"

Vernon laughs, as he lights and takes a drag on his pipe. "Who'd take them in town? They'd have to keep 'em tied up or in cages. These are wild dogs. If they get loose, they'll be right back out here killin' again. Naw, they'll have to be killed."

"How will he kill them?" I ask, hoping it won't be by poison as I remember the terrible way Tuffy died.

"I don't know. He'll have to be careful, otherwise he'll kill all the coyotes. Probably the best way is to trap them in cages. Then he can shoot 'em."

"Why do you care about the coyotes?" I'm surprised that the old bastard cares about anything.

"Well, we have to try to keep things in balance around here. About twenty years ago, we had a bad drought, and there was hardly any grass. We sold off most of our cattle, but there still wasn't enough for the rabbits or the rats or anything else to eat. Then the rabbits and rats died off and the coyotes and cougars didn't have enough to eat, so they started killin' the brood cows we'd kept. A trapper was sent in here by the government to kill all the coyotes, and they paid a bounty of twenty-five cents a head. Pretty soon, everybody was killin' coyotes, and it got to where there was hardly any left in the whole county."

Vernon ties a knot in his reins so he can drop them on Popcorn's neck and use both hands to light his pipe without having to stop the horse's easy pace. "Then when it started rainin' again," he continues, "we had a couple of good years, and the rabbits and rats got so thick they were eatin' all the grass. That's when I learned seven jack rabbits will eat more than a grown, nursin' mama cow. So we had to start poisonin' rats and rabbits. Then that threw things even more outta balance, because when the buzzards and what coyotes were left ate the poisoned rabbits, it killed them too. Then, since there wasn't no more rats or rabbits, the cougars and what few coyotes survived started killin' cattle again because there wasn't anything else for them to eat."

Vernon is silent for a long time. I can tell he's remembering unpleasant things. "You could ride out across this desert, and there wasn't a thing but one dead carcass after another." He points in a sweeping circle at all the land below us. In my mind I have a vision of a barren desert littered with dead animals as far as the eye can see. "It all happened 'cause we didn't use some restraint in killin' the coyotes during that damned drought in the first place. Now that we got some balance in things, I'm not gonna let anything happen that'll knock it off again."

I can't conceal my frustration. "I thought you said you wanted Johnny Watkins to kill every one of those wild dogs."

"Well, those damned dogs are different. They weren't part of the natural setup in the first place. They're invaders. They been brought in by men. Besides that, a lot of the time they don't kill to eat. They just do it for the fun of it. If you noticed, they didn't bother to stay around to eat that cow they killed back there. After she was dead, they left her to the buzzards and other carrion eaters and went off lookin' for somethin' else to kill. They don't serve any purpose in the natural scheme of things around here."

I kick the roan into a trot to try to get ahead of Vernon and Pablo to be alone, to sort things out in my mind, but Vernon pushes Popcorn to stay up with me. "All this talk of death and killing gets to you, don't it?"

I pull the roan to a stop and look him directly in the eye. "Yes, sir, it does. I don't see why anything has to die."

He has to hold Popcorn, who shakes his head and paws the ground with one hoof now, anxious to get home. "I'd like for you to think about the things I said. If you look at it, you should see that what I've been talkin' about is not the end of life like most people think of when somethin' dies. What I'm talkin' about is the whole process, the continuin' process of life. You're old enough now to see that without death, there'd be no life. If things didn't die, nothin' new could be born."

"But when somethin' dies, doesn't that life come to an end?" I argue. I think about Dad and about the feeling I get that he's guiding me. But I know it's not the same as when he was alive. Dad is dead. It will never be the same.

"I can see you got the same hang-up most other people have. They think when somethin' dies as that bein' the end of that life. Well, it may be in a sense, but it's really only a change of direction of the life process. Now, you just saw that change in direction back there with that cow. Them buzzards and the maggots were tearin' that cow's body apart. It was decayin', but those buzzards grow bigger and fly higher from eatin' her body. The maggots go on to grow into blowflies, and then they fly around and lay their eggs in any place they can find somethin' rotten to eat. That's their life cycle. You see what I'm talkin' about?" There's a touch of frustration in Vernon's gravelly voice as he struggles to make me understand.

Seeing the blank expression on my face, he takes a deep breath and tries again. "When a seed sprouts, the plant grows until it matures and then it stops growin'. It's the same thing with an animal. When it's born, it grows until it get's old. When it stops growin', it's dead. But the life process doesn't stop. It just changes direction from one of growth to one of decay. Then it becomes a process of breaking down the body into its smallest parts so it can enter into a growth process again."

Vernon stops talking and looks up toward the sky. Then he points with his arm in a sweeping arc over our heads, "This whole universe," he says, "is part of this life process, which is one of constant change. Most people don't like change because it's usually painful. The more drastic the change, the more violent and painful it is, and sometimes it's so bad a man just has to sit down and bawl to be able to take it. But as long as he can do that, get the pain out and adjust to the changes, he's still alive and growin'. If he don't adjust, he's dead as a doornail. But if he can survive the changes, he'll usually find the result is beautiful, and that's when it's easy to see that change is really the essence of life itself."

I look at him, but he just keeps his craggy old face turned in profile to me, puffing away on that pipe, and he doesn't look back. I'm shocked at what he just said—that a man may have to *cry* to be able to take all the pain. Dad always said cowboys don't cry. Dad, Uncle Jack, just about every man I know always said men don't cry. What does this old bastard mean?

Vernon seems to have exhausted his supply of words, and we ride along in silence. I keep hearing Manuel's grandmother, old Magdalena Gonzales, telling me I must find the answers to many secrets of life if I'm ever to find peace. I never wanted to learn anything from old Vernon Delaney, though. And then I remember her words: "*You will find them in a place you don't want to look.*"

*   *

I'm sitting on the ranch house porch, feeling full after a big meal of Juanita's beans, tamales, and red chile. I watch a hummingbird flitting about the red blossoms of a large ocotillo plant in the circle of the driveway as the last rays of sunlight begin to fade. I can hear bees buzzing about the blooms on the nearby catclaw bush, and a cricket over by the well begins to tune up for the evening.

Vernon settles beside me, leans against his favorite post, and begins to fill the bull's-head pipe. "Anything I need to know about in that letter?" This is his subtle way of finding out about the rare letter Pablo brought in from town addressed to me today.

"Naw, it's just a letter from Miz Winters, my English teacher. She wrote a letter to all the kids in my class and told us we're gonna study poetry this year. She wants us all to write a poem and bring it to school the first day. She's crazy."

"Why do you say that?"

"I don't know nothin' about poetry. I don't even know what poetry is."

Vernon puffs at the pipe a moment. "Maybe I can help you a little with that." His voice sounds a little hesitant.

"What do you know about poetry?" I challenge.

"Well, I went to school once, but I've learned more about poetry right here on this ranch than I ever learned back East."

Now I feel like I'm the one that's been challenged. "Where do you ever find any poetry around here?"

"Well, you know, when I was back East, them high falutin' folks in their tuxedos and long evening dresses thought it was poetry when them fancy fiddlers played at the symphony and them women dressed up like shorthorn cows and hollered their heads off at the opera. But I tell you, Speck, here in the desert and mountains, we live among more poetry every day than they ever put together in all the symphonies and operas in the world. All you gotta do is watch that hummin'bird buzzin' around them ocotillo blooms, or listen to that cricket over by the well, or when you see a coyote trottin' along, sniffin' a trail tryin' to catch a rabbit, or when you listen to those springs drippin' water in the pool up there in Dead Horse Canyon. If you ever watched a mama cow nursin' a newborn calf, you've seen real poetry. All you gotta do is look, listen, smell, taste, and feel what's around you to find poetry."

Now I'm really confused. "I guess I really don't know what poetry is," I say. "I thought poetry was just a bunch of words that rhymed."

"It takes more than rhymin' words to make poetry, but if it makes your skin crawl or gives you goose bumps, if it makes you feel sorta sick at the pit of your stomach, if it puts a lump in your throat, or if it puts a smile on your face or a tear in your eye, then it's poetry. If you can feel it, then it's real poetry. But if you don't feel it, it's not real."

I start to laugh. "If you're right, then they got a lot of poetry down there at the church, the way they all get up in front and bawl and say how happy they are they been saved."

Vernon laughs too. "Yeah, well, you gotta admit they get a lot of feelin' in their religion."

We sit silent a few minutes, and I find myself enjoying the sunset. I don't want to admit it, but I'm enjoying the old bastard's company too. Then I feel compelled to ask, "Do you believe in God?"

"Why sure." Vernon sounds insulted. "Why do you ask a question like that?"

"Well, the way you was describin' the life process the other day, it sounds like everything is all put in motion, and there ain't any room left for God."

Vernon strikes a match on the wooden floor of the porch, all the time looking at me through squinted eyes. "You sure got a way of puttin' people on the spot." He turns his attention to relighting the bull's-head pipe. Then he sits puffing and thinking. Finally, "They's a lot of things in this universe we don't understand. Just because we can't see it or touch it or smell it don't mean we can't feel it. I bet you there's not a man alive who hasn't felt a presence guidin' 'im at one time or another."

I feel a shiver down my back, and goose pimples on my arms. How could this old bastard know about things like that? What would he think if I told him about me talking to Dad and about me talking to Paint and other animals. Would he understand if I told him a long time ago a snake spoke to me? Would he understand if I told him I knew Uncle Jack was going to come home from the war?

"I think everyone has had an experience when they knew somethin' was goin' to happen before it did," Vernon goes on. "Now some people think that's witchcraft or voodoo or something like that. But, whatever it is, it seems to me to be some supreme power or some bein' actin' through forces of the universe we just don't understand."

He gets up and starts pacing the length of the long open porch that stretches the length of the old adobe ranch house, puffing on the pipe all the while.

"I think it's good for people to go to church and give their attention to the Almighty. But, where I get crosswise with these people is they seem all hung up on the idea that the world is all bad. All they ever talk about is what's wrong with the world. They say it's sinful and corrupt and they talk about a better heaven where there's no sin or pain or suffering or death. When I listen to this stuff, it sounds to me like they think God screwed up when He created the universe and this little old world we live on. If you listen to them, they think He was a real nincompoop. I think over ninety percent of what they put out is an insult to the Almighty Creator of this universe, and it gets me all mad."

The pipe has gone out now, so Vernon Delaney sits down on the edge of the porch beside me again and strikes another match. This time he gets the pipe going like a steam engine; then he starts again.

"If they'd just stop and look at this world we live in, they'd see that it's perfect. They'd see it can't be improved upon. They'd see that the pain, suffering, and death are all an important part of the overall scheme of life, and without those things, there couldn't be any life as we know it. But they don't wanna be satisfied with what the Good Lord give 'em. They want God to give them somethin' they think is better. They want Him to give them a heaven that don't have any pain, suffering, or death. If they ever get around to seein' how important those things are to the overall life process, then they'd quit worryin' about gettin' somethin' better and start trying to protect, hold on to, and appreciate what we already got."

The sun has set now, and dark has settled on us, so I can only see a faint glow over the western mountains. The cricket is singing loud, and a coyote in the distance lets out with his lonesome song. I sit there beside the big old man surrounded by the smell of pipe tobacco, feeling close and strangely peaceful.

Suddenly, Vernon Delaney punches me in the side with his elbow. "It's time for you to get to bed, Speck. You gotta cover five miles of fence on the west end tomorrow."

"Ladies and gentlemen, welcome to the El Paso Rodeo," the announcer is saying. I can hear him over the speaker that has been set up in the horse barn where Popcorn is stabled.

"You've got about another half hour before they get to the ropin'." Vernon is looking at his big gold pocket watch for the twentieth time in the last five minutes.

I can tell he's nervous, but I don't think he's half as nervous as I am, in spite of his telling me to relax every twenty minutes all day long. He, Popcorn, and I came up Thursday, the first night of the rodeo. I was one of the first ropers up in the first go-round. We got in late, so Popcorn and I didn't have time to ride in the arena and check it out. I didn't have a chance to see how the calf chute worked so I'd be able to judge when the calf would be coming out of the gate. And the barrier line is farther out than what we're used to at the roping club arena, so I was afraid that if I let Popcorn start too soon, we'd break the barrier.

But it all went pretty good. Our time of seventeen-point-two seconds wasn't bad, but I thought we could do a lot better. It was good enough for third place in the first go-round. Sid Kennedy from Marfa won first with a time of fifteen-point-two seconds, and Russell Sheppard won second with sixteen-point-eight.

Things went so fast I hadn't had time to look for Jenke. I hoped she would be able to be here to see me rope. Even though she told me she might not be able to make it up for the first night, I was really disappointed when she didn't show up.

Tonight's the last performance, and I'm the last roper. I'm trying not to worry about whether Jenke will be here to see me and concentrate on the roping. Sheppard did twenty-seven-point-five on his second calf during the afternoon performance and is now leading for the championship. Sid Kennedy ropes just before me tonight, so this is the decisive performance for the championship.

The time passes fast, and I hear the announcer call Sid Kennedy as the next roper. I mount Popcorn, start to build my loop, and check my pigging string. I keep thinking Jenke will show up to offer me her usual encouragement, but she never does.

Vernon is walking and leading Popcorn to the back of the roping box where we'll wait for my turn. "I don't want you to even listen to his time. You just go out there and rope your calf the best you can just like you was the very first roper in the show. You hear?"

My mouth is so dry I can't talk, but I nod. Popcorn dances around like a race horse. He feels the tension too.

"The time for Sid Kennedy is twenty-seven-point-six, just one tenth of a second behind Russell Sheppard, who is leading the second go-round. But it puts him in the lead for the average and the roping championship, with just one more roper to go," the announcer is yelling over the speaker.

Vernon smiles at me, and I smile back. "Used to I'd be sayin' somethin' to make you mad about now, but I can't think of anything right off hand."

I find my voice, "I don't think there's anything you could say that would make me mad at you anymore," I say.

"You're up, McBride!" someone from inside the arena yells.

Vernon slaps Popcorn on the neck, "Go make this speckled-faced kid look good." Then to me, "You just don't worry about what that announcer said. You just go out there and make me and your dad proud."

Popcorn sets easy in the box, ears perked, and I nod. The calf is released, the timing is perfect. Popcorn clears the barrier perfectly and falls in behind the calf. With a swish, my loop snakes around the calf's neck. In a blur I don't remember, the calf is down. One wrap and a hooey and I throw both hands in the air, signaling the calf is tied. The crowd is on its feet, cheering. The sudden roar is so loud it scares Popcorn, but he stands steady, flicking his ears back and forth. I run to him as fast as I can to comfort him.

"Ladies and gentlemen!" The announcer is trying to get their attention. "Ladies and gentlemen!" The din begins to lessen. "Ladies and gentlemen! The time is thirteen seconds flat—a new all-time record here at the El Paso Rodeo!"

I reach over and stroke Popcorn on the neck feeling proud as we ride out of the arena leaving the cheering crowd behind. Vernon is there, proud as a Bantam rooster, and then I see her. She's running toward me. I dismount, and before I know it, she throws her arms around my neck.

"You're the champion! I knew you could do it!" she says. Her face is close to mine, and I can see tears in her eyes. "I couldn't come the first night. Daddy said we couldn't afford both nights. But I made him let me drive the pickup in tonight because I knew you could do it, I just knew . . ."

She doesn't finish her sentence because I'm kissing her now. Or she's kissing me. I don't know. I'm all mixed up. When she pulls away, I see that she looks a little embarrassed, and the tears are still in her eyes, but she's smiling. She moves away from me, and I make a movement to reach for her, but she's gone, walking backward, smiling, waving to me. I don't know what to think.

Then there's a crowd of people around me, shaking my hand, giving me their congratulations. I thank all of them and slip away as quickly as I can. I look out over the top of the barns for Dad, expecting to see him there, expecting him to wave congratulations to me, but he's nowhere in sight.

We leave for the ranch as soon as the trophy saddles are presented. Vernon straps mine on the hood of the pickup so everyone can see it as we drive through town.

As we get away from the city lights, I expect again to see Dad. Maybe the city lights kept me from seeing him sooner. I can't understand why he hasn't shown up. Isn't this championship where Dad has always been leading me?

CHAPTER 18

I got permission to miss two days of school so Paint and I could come out and help Vernon with the fall roundup.

Pablo and I are trailing about thirty head of cows with their calves down off Blanco Mountain. We'll take them down over the bluff above Dead Horse Canyon and on into headquarters. The trail leads north straight down a long ridge that ends suddenly where the arroyo that leads into the canyon has washed the hill away, leaving the steep bluff. There the trail turns off to the west, down into the canyon, and on to the ranch house. I feel like a real cowboy riding ol' Paint leading the herd with the Little Wonder between my legs and Dad's rifle in the boot. I just wish I could see Dad. I still can't understand why he hasn't shown up to congratulate me on winning the roping.

My thoughts drift to Jenke. I've seen a lot of her lately. We sit together in class as often as we can, and we usually go to a picture show in Fabens on Saturday night. I asked her to come out for roundup but she refused, saying she would only be in the way, and she didn't want to interfere with my time with Vernon since I probably won't see him again until Christmas or maybe next spring.

I'm brought out of my daydream by Pablo yelling from behind the herd, "Hey, Scout, bring your rifle, quick."

There's just enough room on the ridge for Paint to lope past the herd without disturbing their movement down the trail.

"There's them dogs Johnny Watkins told us about." Pablo is pointing across the narrow draw to the next ridge. Following his pointing arm, I can see two black dogs trotting along the ridge as though they are following and staying even with our herd of cattle. Johnny told us he thought he had killed all the dogs up here on Vernon's ranch except two that he'd never been able to trap, even though he'd seen them several times.

"Can you shoot 'em?" Pablo asks.

"Naw, I never even tried to shoot this gun. Here you try." I pull the short .30–30 from the boot and hand it to him.

Pablo quickly steps off his horse, kneels, with one elbow resting on his knee, takes aim, and fires. The sudden noise scares Paint so bad she almost jumps out from under me. Pablo's horse breaks away and starts down the ridge the same direction the cattle are going. As Paint calms, I see the bullet kick up dust a short distance downhill from the lead dog.

Having gotten the range now, Pablo fires four times in rapid succession. One dog falls, and the other yelps and runs over the ridge on the other side. Paint is shaking, scared of the noise.

I suddenly remember the herd and turn to see Pablo's horse running hard behind them, making the cows believe they are being chased into a fast run.

"Stampede!" I yell and kick Paint to run as fast as she can to try to slow them.

The mama cows are slow, and Paint can outrun them fairly easily, but they're strung out now and running hard. We'll have to pass them all to get them stopped. Then I remember the bluff.

"Hurry, Paint, we gotta turn them before they run off the bluff!"

Paint lays her ears back against her neck and runs as hard as she can. The lead animal is a big yearling running hard. As Paint comes up even, shoulder to shoulder to the big steer, I see the edge of the bluff.

"Turn, Paint!" I yell, as I rein her hard against the racing calf's shoulder, forcing him to turn off the ridge when they come into contact. But Paint loses her footing, and I feel her stumble under me. I think she is going to fall and roll over, but with a valiant effort, she begins to recover her footing. Then it's too late. There is nothing to hold her up. She runs off the edge of the cliff.

I'm flying, separated from ol' Paint. I hit against the steep cliff, bounce, airborne again, then I hit on soft, loose sand. I'm aware of Paint landing close to me then turning a somersault further on down the cliff as I slide and roll until I come to rest on a small caliche outcropping.

I hear a strange noise and look up toward the top of the cliff to see a boulder the size of a small pickup truck airborne just as I was a moment ago, then the boulder is bouncing and rolling. I see Paint struggling to get up, but something's wrong with her hind leg.

"Look out, Paint!" I scream, but it's too late. The boulder strikes Paint in the hips and hind legs, sending her rolling and bouncing farther down the steep slope. When the dust clears, I see Paint lying next to the stream at the bottom of the bluff, motionless.

*   *   *

"We can get a vet down here from El Paso and probably he can keep her alive," Vernon says to me, as I hold Paint's head in my lap. "But you got to know, Son, she'll never walk again. In fact, she'll probably never even be able to stand up."

Vernon is squatting across from me, so it's impossible to hide my face and keep him from seeing the tears that well up in my eyes as I bite my lip. "I know you love this old mare, and I don't blame you for wanting to save her, but you better think about how she'll be from now on."

When I try to turn my face away from him, he gets up and walks over to the stream with his back to me. I can hear the water gurgling over the rocks. A bullbat flitters by, chasing bugs in the evening dusk. I hug Paint and bite back the lump of sadness in my chest.

After a long time, Vernon turns on his heel, "I tell you what. You'll probably want to stay here a while alone with your pony. I think she's as comfortable as we can make her now, but she's still in pain. I'll ride on back to the house and send Pablo back with some blankets and chow and a horse for you to ride if you decide to come in tonight. If you don't come in tonight, I'll check on you in the mornin'."

I'm almost asleep when Paint squeals and starts thrashing about again, tossing her head so as to throw me away from her.

"Don't, babe, don't thrash. It'll just make you hurt more."

I can see the pain in her face as she grits her teeth with every muscle in her neck straining. She has been in so much pain she hasn't been able to talk to me. Unable to take it any longer, I walk up on the hill behind us, looking at the clear sky and quarter moon shining down on us. I look for Dad. Why has he abandoned me? Will I ever see him again? How am I to know what's best for Paint? How am I to hold all this pain and frustration inside me?

I hear Paint groan, and I run back to her. "Take it easy, babe. Tell me what you want. What can I do?" I take her head in my lap again and hug her close to make the pain go away, but she only moans. She still doesn't say anything.

Dawn is breaking when Paint stirs. She is lying with her head facing away from me. I'm sitting on the Little Wonder where we threw it after we pulled it off to make her more comfortable. The .30–30 is leaning against the pommel where Pablo left it. Paint still hasn't talked to me the way she usually does, but somehow what she wants to tell me becomes clear. It is as if I have no choice. It's as if Paint is directing me on what to do. Paint would rather die than live as a useless cripple. Moving quickly now, with knowing determination, I approach from her blind side, talking to her, all the time offering encouragement, telling her it will be all right soon. Still she doesn't say anything. She doesn't move.

I hold Dad's old .30–30 to the back of her head and pull the trigger.

There's no stopping it now. The knot in my chest has broken loose. Tears stream down my face in a steady river. Sometimes I hear myself sob, spilling out years of frustration, rage, and sadness. I work steadily, hauling rocks to place around her body to keep the varmints away.

I see the old snake and the little drowned puppy. "Now you understand," the snake says, and it looks like he has a slight smile. I mourn for Paint, for the pain she felt and for the fact that she isn't here anymore. I mourn that she died at my own hands. Then I mourn the loss of the farm at Acala. I mourn for Tuffy and all the animals that have died and all the people that died in the war. I mourn for all the pain Uncle Jack feels and is still trying to drink away. I mourn that Paint couldn't run fast enough to catch a fast calf, and I mourn that I couldn't see that Vernon Delaney was trying to helpqq me and he was really one of the best friends I have. I look for Dad, but I can't find him, so I cry for him too. Most of all, I mourn that I could never cry before.

I see Vernon Delaney riding up to check on me, and I look around for a way to hide my tears that continue to flow, but then I wonder why I should care. Didn't he say that sometimes a man has to cry to deal with the pain and adjust to the inevitable change?

I perch on a large rock to face Vernon, still crying unashamedly, and look him in the eye as he pulls up Popcorn some distance away. "I can see you got things worked out here," he says. He looks at Paint, but I know he knows I'm working out more things than just putting her out of her misery. "I brought you some more grub. I'll see you at the house whenever you're through here," he says, as he drops a gunnysack on the ground and rides away.

My hands are raw from carrying the rocks for two days, but the tears are dry now, as I place the last big rock in place on the mound I've built over Paint. Sore and exhausted, I sit on the monument, surveying my work. The sun is getting low now, but I can still make it to the ranch before dark. I'll tell Jenke all about this when I get back to school. I know she'll understand.

Suddenly, I feel a presence. Looking up, at the top of the bluff is the vision of Dad sitting on Tar Baby. But this time he's holding his hat in his hand, and there's a tear in his eye. "I knew Vernon would teach you what I couldn't," he says. "I never learned to cry."

He turns the black stallion, and they slowly disappear over the ridge.